Once Upon a Time in Bliss

—

Other Books by Lexi Blake

ROMANTIC SUSPENSE
Masters And Mercenaries
The Dom Who Loved Me
The Men With The Golden Cuffs
A Dom is Forever
On Her Master's Secret Service
Sanctum: A Masters and Mercenaries Novella
Love and Let Die
Unconditional: A Masters and Mercenaries Novella
Dungeon Royale
Dungeon Games: A Masters and Mercenaries Novella
A View to a Thrill
Cherished: A Masters and Mercenaries Novella
You Only Love Twice
Luscious: Masters and Mercenaries~Topped
Adored: A Masters and Mercenaries Novella
Master No
Just One Taste: Masters and Mercenaries~Topped 2
From Sanctum with Love
Devoted: A Masters and Mercenaries Novella
Dominance Never Dies
Submission is Not Enough
Master Bits and Mercenary Bites~The Secret Recipes of Topped
Perfectly Paired: Masters and Mercenaries~Topped 3
For His Eyes Only
Arranged: A Masters and Mercenaries Novella
Love Another Day
At Your Service: Masters and Mercenaries~Topped 4
Master Bits and Mercenary Bites~Girls Night
Nobody Does It Better
Close Cover
Protected: A Masters and Mercenaries Novella
Enchanted: A Masters and Mercenaries Novella
Charmed: A Masters and Mercenaries Novella, Coming June 23, 2020

Masters and Mercenaries: The Forgotten
Lost Hearts (Memento Mori)
Lost and Found
Lost in You

Long Lost
No Love Lost, Coming September 29, 2020

Butterfly Bayou
Butterfly Bayou, Coming May 5, 2020
Bayou Baby, Coming August 25, 2020

Lawless
Ruthless
Satisfaction
Revenge

Courting Justice
Order of Protection
Evidence of Desire

Masters Of Ménage (by Shayla Black and Lexi Blake)
Their Virgin Captive
Their Virgin's Secret
Their Virgin Concubine
Their Virgin Princess
Their Virgin Hostage
Their Virgin Secretary
Their Virgin Mistress

The Perfect Gentlemen (by Shayla Black and Lexi Blake)
Scandal Never Sleeps
Seduction in Session
Big Easy Temptation
Smoke and Sin
At the Pleasure of the President

URBAN FANTASY
Thieves
Steal the Light
Steal the Day
Steal the Moon
Steal the Sun
Steal the Night
Ripper
Addict
Sleeper

Outcast
Stealing Summer, Coming soon

LEXI BLAKE WRITING AS SOPHIE OAK
Texas Sirens
Small Town Siren
Siren in the City
Siren Enslaved
Siren Beloved
Siren in Waiting
Siren in Bloom
Siren Unleashed
Siren Reborn

Nights in Bliss, Colorado
Three to Ride
Two to Love
One to Keep
Lost in Bliss
Found in Bliss
Pure Bliss
Chasing Bliss
Once Upon a Time in Bliss
Back in Bliss
Sirens in Bliss

A Faery Story
Bound
Beast
Beauty

Standalone
Away From Me
Snowed In

Once Upon a Time in Bliss

Nights in Bliss, Colorado Book 8

**Lexi Blake
writing as
Sophie Oak**

Once Upon a Time in Bliss
Nights in Bliss, Colorado Book 8

Published by DLZ Entertainment LLC at Smashwords

Copyright 2019 DLZ Entertainment LLC
Edited by Chloe Vale
ISBN: 978-1-942297-18-5

Sign up for Lexi Blake's newsletter
and be entered to win a $25 gift certificate
to the bookseller of your choice.

Join us for news, fun, and exclusive content
including free short stories.

There's a new contest every month!

Go to www.LexiBlake.net to subscribe.

Dedication

For Kim, who always believes.

Dedication 2019

Flashback to roughly 2000. I meet this woman named Kim. She seems pretty cool. Our older kids are in the same kindergarten class and our younger kids are the same age. So we start a play group. It's nothing more than a few hours a week. We're all housewives and it's good to have some connection to other adults. It's something to pass the long afternoons waiting to pick up the older kids.

We do not know it at the time, but this is the beginning of a friendship that will change my life and alter my future because Lexi Blake does not exist without Kim Guidroz.

Flash forward a few years and our kids are in third grade. We volunteer for the school and we're room moms. We've fallen into a deep friendship. I've finished two books at the time but I'm not looking to actually publish them. They're for fun. Somewhere in the back of my mind maybe one day I'll do it. Kim asks to read one. I let her. She's the first person to read my book and she offers to edit it. She encourages me. I make a crazy offer. Hey, if you help me out I'll give you a percentage. It's a good deal for me since I'm giving her a percentage of nothing. She works her ass off for that percentage and I start thinking…maybe.

2010. It's been years and she's still with me. She's still giving me her time and energy, lending me her inexhaustible strength when I am tired. She is beside me not because she thinks she'll get a payday. She is beside me because we're in this life together. Somehow we've become family in a way that will prove even stronger than blood. And I'm finally ready. We work hard and get a book called *Small Town Siren* in what we hope is good shape. We hit submit and pray.

Ten years after we started, we're an overnight success.

I say "we" because this is truly a collaboration. She is my first editor, my assistant, the one who keeps me in line, often times my inspiration and always, always, always my sister. It's been said that I am good at writing "found" family. It's because she taught me what that means.

So here we are almost ten years after we published our first book – twenty years into the friendship that changed the course of my life, and I'm so happy to put Nell back into the world.

This book is dedicated now and forever to Kim – who always believes in me…

Prologue

Six years before
A classified location in Colombia

The man known as Bishop looked down at his handiwork.

So much fucking blood. Why did the human body have to contain so much blood? The average male body contained six quarts of blood and there were six men on the floor. Thirty-six quarts of blood. That was what he'd spilled today. Thirty-six quarts of evil, drug-running blood, and it wasn't enough and it never would be. The US government would make sure of that.

"You doing okay?" a deep voice asked.

He looked up and Ian Taggart was standing there. Tag was one of the younger operatives he was mentoring. He'd been recruited straight out of the Green Berets, and sometimes Bishop wondered if it would have been better for the man if he'd been left there. The big blond Viking of a man smiled less and less as the months went by. He was becoming a true CIA operative. "I'm fine. Did we lose anyone?"

Bishop took a long breath, the hot Colombian air humid in his lungs. He was so fucking sick of foreign countries. He didn't go to the nice parts. He didn't get to walk around the pretty parts of Cartagena or enjoy the beach. No, he was sent to the pits of the world—the places where humanity and rights were a distant dream. Now he was here in a drug-torn section of Colombia.

"Absolutely not," Tag replied. "They might be soft because they're SEALs and not Green Berets, but they're still US military."

"Fuck you, Tag," one of the aforementioned SEALs shouted, but there was no malice in the words.

The SEAL team he'd gone in with high-fived and smiled as they joked with Taggart. They were heroes. They'd done their job, and they'd done it with precision and the perfect amount of mercy. They didn't play with their targets. They took them out quickly when they could, giving the vicious killers an easier death than they deserved, because they were soldiers, not animals.

Not like Bishop. Bishop did know what it was like to play with his targets. He was well versed in the art of getting what he needed. He knew the fine line between torture and reward and when to walk it. Yes, he knew how to get what he needed.

But a question increasingly plagued him. What did he want?

Lieutenant Wilder walked up, a smile on his face. Wilder was a big man, six foot seven at least. He dwarfed Bishop. He was lean and mean, and Bishop would bet Wilder had nothing on him when it came to brutality. "Hey, Mr. Bishop, are we done here? What more do you need from us? I'd like to call the extraction team and get my boys home."

Home. For SEAL Team 4, home was Little Creek, Virginia. For Bishop, home was a one-bedroom in DC with next to nothing in it. He lived out of a suitcase. He roamed from place to place with little to call his own. Nothing except the next bloody plan.

"Give the boss a minute," Tag said, sounding serious for once. The man could take sarcasm to its limits, but he also knew when to pull it back.

Wilder's brow furrowed as he looked at Bishop. "Come on, man, you gotta be happy about this. We just took down the biggest drug cartel in Colombia. Do you know how much coke we're going to keep out of the States?"

He didn't have the heart to tell Wilder the truth. Even if he had, he was contractually obligated not to. This operation wouldn't keep an ounce of cocaine off the streets. The CIA and the American government had taken down one cartel to give the business to another. A more US-friendly drug dealer. One that would prop up the US-approved local government.

But SEAL Team 4 was just a tool, and they didn't get to make the big decisions.

Fuck, the world would be a better place if they did. "Yes, Lieutenant. We're done here. You can call the extraction unit."

The choppers would come for them all, and he would be taken back to

Langley where he would debrief all the right people and say all the right things, and spend a night or two in that bland apartment that held nothing of his soul before being shipped out to the next hellhole.

Was this what a midlife crisis felt like?

"Awesome," the lieutenant said. "I've got a little girl who's having a birthday party tomorrow and I don't want to miss it."

The lieutenant strode off, calling his men to him.

"I do not get that." Tag shook his head. "Kids. They're stinky and weird, and did I mention they make a lot of poop they expect you to clean up? I'm never having kids."

Having children wasn't a good idea when one worked for the Agency.

He was thirty-five years old, and he had no idea who the hell he was. He was who the Black Ops team had made him. He was who the CIA had molded him into.

"That's probably a good idea. They make such excellent leverage against a man," Bishop commented.

"Dude, you are even more cranky than normal. Let's get on the chopper, head back to the States, and find a club to hit." Taggart spent a lot of his off time in BDSM clubs, a hobby they shared, though Taggart went about it with his normal enthusiasm and Bishop went through the motions these days.

Taggart was something like a son to him, though they weren't so far apart in age. He'd been in the Agency years longer, and sometimes wondered if he'd ever had the younger man's energy. "I think I'll have to pass this time. I've got a couple of leads I need to follow up on while I'm here in Colombia. And you shouldn't party too hard. I heard you're heading to the Middle East with Tennessee."

Another of his protégées. Ten was incredibly smart. He was ruthless in a way Bishop wasn't sure Tag was yet. He would get there.

For some reason the thought made Bishop infinitely sad.

"Yeah," Tag said with a sigh. "I really need to find some bad shit happening in France or Spain. I could use some tapas. Germany, maybe. I'm Ten's backup, and we all know that means I'm stuck in some craphole motel without room service eating MREs and trying to figure out how the TV works."

Unfortunately, he didn't see a lot of work for Tag in the more luxurious parts of the world. "Have you talked to your brother lately? Isn't he in the Middle East?"

Tag's face went completely blank, a sure sign he didn't want to talk about this. "Sean's busy. He just got promoted and he's got a group of friends. He's in good with a couple of guys on his team. Adam and Jake. They seem cool. I don't think he needs his big brother taking up time, if you know what I mean."

Oh, he knew exactly what Tag meant. Talking to his brother would mean lying to his brother, so he simply ignored the situation. All the while he was putting distance between himself and the people he'd cared about before he'd joined the Agency. Yes, Bishop understood that far too well.

"I think you should call him." He put a hand on Tag's broad shoulder. "Make it a part of your routine. Once a month you call your brother. I know it's hard, but it's necessary for you to maintain ties to the outside world. You need to remember that this isn't normal."

Tag's lips quirked up. "Standing around in the middle of dead bodies? It oddly feels normal to me."

And that was the problem. Bishop winced and moved toward the door that led outside. There was a large porch that wrapped around the house that cocaine had built. It looked out over the peaceful grounds. Of course they were only peaceful now because the SEALs had done their jobs, and done them well.

"But I do get you," Tag was saying as he joined him on the porch. "I'll call my brother and I'll reach out to a couple of friends. Alex and Eve. They're throwing themselves an anniversary party soon. I was kind of thinking of skipping it, but I was Alex's best man. I was thinking I could throw him a flashback bachelor party and if I leave it to Sean, it will be all about gourmet food and won't have a stripper in sight."

"You can't have that."

"You know you could come with me. Alex lives right outside DC. He's a cool guy," Tag offered.

He knew everything there was to know about the young FBI agent. Working up dossiers on all the people in Taggart's life had been part of the process of recruiting him. Actually meeting those people in real life would be a breach of his personal protocol.

He could get on that chopper with the SEALs and Tag, but it wouldn't take him anywhere close to home. He didn't have one. He'd given up his search for a home the minute he'd decided to join the CIA and forgo the whole "have a life" thing.

At the time, it had seemed like the right thing to do. Years and experience had proven otherwise. He hadn't truly made a difference. He'd simply made it easier for blood to flow and the power players to get exactly what they wanted.

There was no such thing as good. No such thing as humanity.

He sat down in a chair that had likely been chosen by a dead man. He didn't want to get on that helicopter, but he didn't know where he would go. He had no place. No friends he could be open and honest with.

He liked Taggart, but he was the man's boss. He had to hold himself apart. He had to make decisions that could actively put him in danger. He couldn't be friends with anyone.

"Unfortunately, I have to stay here for a few days." He didn't, but he couldn't work up the will to tell Taggart the truth about why he wasn't going to take him up on the offer. He couldn't tell him that men who called themselves Bishop and ignored their real names didn't get to have friends.

Well, he had one. Bill Hartman, his former CO. Where had that come from? He hadn't thought about Bill in years. Bill had been the one who'd tried to convince him he shouldn't leave the Army to join the CIA. Bill had offered him a job in his business back in Colorado. He'd been like a father, but Bishop hadn't had a father in so long, he'd forgotten to listen.

What if he didn't go back to DC? What if he decided to come in from the cold and find somewhere warm and private? What if he walked away from it all?

His real name was gone. Erased. He had no home. No family. No life.

He was nothing. Nothing at all.

"It's probably for the best." Taggart shook his head as he looked out over the yard where the SEALs were packing up. "They are one lovey-dovey couple. I mean it can get nauseating. I love them. I do, but sometimes Alex looks like he's going to burst into song or something. I'm never getting married."

Tag went on, talking about all the ways he was going to keep his life simple. Bishop found a set of comfortable-looking chairs.

He sat in a dead man's chair, the sun moving over the horizon like a veil closing, beckoning him to choose a side. The comfortable side? The one where he was a ghost and he didn't have to worry about anything but completing his next assignment? Or something new?

Time passed, the sun waning in the background as the blood around him cooled. It was a mess that would be left for someone else to clean up. His brain worked but nothing really congealed. He was stuck. He was lost.

He had no idea how to be found.

"Hey, Bishop, Tag." The lieutenant leading the SEAL team ran up, his pack slung over his back as the *thud thud* of the chopper blades could be heard in the distance. "We need to get to the extraction point. We're green in five minutes. Back home. First beer's on me."

It was a false promise the lieutenant made. He knew damn well that once they hit US soil, Bishop would walk away and they would likely never see each other again. CIA operatives didn't go out for a cold one with the team afterward. CIA operatives didn't get close to the soldiers they might have to sacrifice like chess pieces in a nasty game.

Tag grabbed his own pack. "I will take you up on that, Lieutenant. Where I'm going next, the beer is nonexistent."

Taggart would sit with the men. He would joke around and be one of them for a while. He wasn't so far gone he couldn't still be one of the guys.

How long since he'd sat down for a beer with a human being who knew his real name? Sometimes it seemed so fucking far away.

What if he took a vacation? Would the world really end? What if he took a single week to relax and be someone else? And then he'd go back to this life he'd chosen. Surely he could take one week.

He had passports the CIA didn't even know about. He wasn't stupid. He knew he could be burned at any moment. He had money and IDs stashed. He could say he'd gotten a lead and had to follow on the down low.

One friend. Maybe it was time to visit him. Just for a week to clear his head.

"Go on. I'll make my own way back," he said, rising from the chair, his choice made.

"Must be a hell of a lead." Tag jogged down the steps. "Stay safe."

The lieutenant gave him a thumbs-up. "Good luck, Bishop. Fight the good fight."

The SEALs jogged out in their tight formation, Taggart joining them like he'd done it a million times.

The good fight? He'd thought he was, but now he wasn't sure. Maybe there was no good to be fought for.

He turned his mind to his friend. The last he'd heard, Bill was in a little town in Colorado.

Bliss.

Bliss was a good thing to seek. He hadn't had a whole lot of bliss in his life. And he didn't have a family anymore. He hadn't had a family in a long time. It had just been him and his mother, and after she'd died, he'd been through a long stream of foster parents until he'd made his way into the Army. Bill had been his family for a while.

He didn't have a home to go to. Maybe a friend was the closest thing. If Bill even recognized him now.

Bishop started the long walk to Cartagena. To the airport.

To Bliss.

Chapter One

Two Days Later
Bliss, Colorado

"What should I call you this time?" Bill Hartman asked the question with an uptick of his lips that let Bishop know he was amused.

He was also naked.

Bill Hartman, former commando and wildly successful venture capitalist, now ran a nudist colony called the Mountain and Valley Naturist Community. It had been a shock to walk in and realize everyone was naked. Really, really naked.

It took a lot to shock Bishop.

"Henry Flanders." It was his private ID. He'd bought it off a man in Mexico City years before. It was one of three passports the Agency didn't know about. He was a careful man and knew damn straight that even the best agent could be thrown under the proverbial bus if it suited the needs of the CIA. He didn't intend to get ground under those large wheels. He'd always had an out if the Agency decided to burn him. His preparedness came in handy when he wanted to walk away briefly.

So he was Henry Flanders for now.

Bill looked him over. "You look every inch the college professor. Where did you get the glasses?"

It hadn't been hard to change his appearance. He had one of those blandly attractive faces that people tended to forget. Throw on a pair of glasses and a blazer and everyone assumed he was an academic. "They're not real. The lenses are regular glass. I thought this would be a good cover in a place like Colorado. I considered doing the cowboy thing, but Henry didn't strike me as a common cowboy name."

Bill frowned from his wingback chair. Bishop had seen a lot of odd things in his time, but a naked man behind a power desk was one for the books. "I'm glad you didn't. Our cowboys take their lifestyle quite seriously. If you aren't prepared, they would figure out your ruse fairly quickly."

Bishop doubted it. He was exceptionally good at what he did. If he'd created a cowboy persona, he would have written himself a history that no one could challenge. But he'd decided to go the brainy route. Henry Flanders loved history and shit. Maybe by playing the role of a guy who had all the answers, he could find some for himself.

"Are you all right with me staying here for a couple of days?" He sat, patiently waiting for Bill's judgment. It was an oddly vulnerable moment for him even though Bill was the one without a stitch on. He was waiting for Bill to give him a reasonable excuse why he should find a place in town instead of rooming at his precious resort. It was disconcerting since he hadn't felt vulnerable in a very long time. Not since he'd been a twelve-year-old kid shuttled from home to home, always being packed up because he knew damn well no one really wanted him.

What the hell was he doing?

Bill leaned forward, his face open and concerned. "Of course. You don't need to ask. John, my home is your home, son."

His real name. John. Only a few people knew it. Almost no one ever used it. He'd had so damn many names that he wondered at times if he still existed or if he'd become the ghost the Agency claimed he was. "Thank you, sir."

It was just for a week. That was how long he could give himself. He'd given his boss the same dumbass excuse of chasing down a lead he'd given Taggart and they'd bought it. He'd been intentionally vague. It would buy him some time. He'd earned back enough goodwill since the incident in Chechnya that got him sent to South America. South America was hopping with all kinds of potential threats, so going silent wasn't unheard of. They wouldn't give him hell for a few days.

If they realized he wasn't where he said he was, that was when the trouble would start, but by then he would be back in the game.

He needed a few days of freedom.

"Are you going to be all right with the lifestyle?" Bill leaned back as though trying to show Bishop how relaxed he was with having his dork hanging out.

"I think I'll manage." Running around naked actually freaked him out a bit. Clothes were such a part of his daily ruse that the thought of not being in costume was disturbing. He glanced at the window to his left. Snow was falling lightly, blanketing the ground in a pure white powder. The mountains were beautiful here. Deadly, of course, since all things were, but beautiful. "How do you handle the cold?"

"Well, I wear a coat outside, and I spend a small fortune keeping things toasty warm inside. I wish you had come in the summer. There's nothing like the high valley in summertime. It's beautiful and you haven't lived until you've gone swimming in a mountain lake with nothing but the water and the sun on your back."

Bishop felt himself frowning. There was so much he didn't understand about his former CO. "How do you do it, Bill?"

"Well, I take off my pants first. Some people will tell you to deal with the shirt first, but really it's the pants that chafe." Bill seemed to catch the deeply unamused look Bishop knew he was sending out. "Sorry, I was having some fun with you. Listen, the first few years out of the military were hard. I won't lie to you about that. Some of the missions haunted me, but I found this place. I came up here with a friend who was in the lifestyle. I think I was a little lost during those first days of civilian life, and he seemed to understand that. I came here and in the beginning, I laughed at everyone. I kept my clothes on. They were idiots. But the days went by and I realized they weren't at all stupid people. They'd found something that made them happy, a way to live that spoke to their souls. I decided to give it a try. It was stupidly difficult to take off my clothes. Sounds simple, huh?"

No. It didn't sound simple at all. It sounded slightly terrifying, and now Bishop was wondering if he'd made a mistake, but he nodded and allowed Bill to continue.

"It's not simple at all. It's hard. Clothes hide so much of who we are. They're an armor of a sort. The first time I took off my clothes and joined the group, I actually worried that they could see through me, that they would know the things I'd done." Bill sighed, obviously lost in the memory. "I was sure they would tell me to leave their paradise. I stood at the edge of the party like some blushing kid. And then this woman, this lovely, amazing woman, walked over and took my hand, and suddenly I didn't see a dumb hippie. I saw kindness and beauty. When the older couple who founded this place retired, I bought it and now I run this place not just for me, but because I want to make this mountain a place of peace. It's everything I fought for, got my hands bloody over. This mountain is my reward for serving my country. I thought I had given up pieces of my soul, but this place and that woman gave them back to me."

Bishop nodded, not entirely understanding, but happy for his friend. If this place brought Bill any measure of peace, then he would never say a thing against it. But he was sure his problems couldn't be solved by walking around with his junk swinging.

Maybe this had all been a big mistake. Bill seemed to have reintegrated into the world, albeit an abnormal version of it. Bishop doubted he could ever do the same.

There was a brisk knock at the door and then it swung open, a lovely woman with dark hair striding through, followed by three other women. One was roughly the first's age and the other two were young, possibly in their mid-twenties. Both younger women were brunettes, one with a sweet face and glasses, and the other caught Bishop's eye.

Rich chocolate brown hair, startling brown eyes, and a mouth created to suck a cock. She didn't seem to move the way the others did. She was so graceful and light on her feet. Even though she wore a heavy coat, he would bet she had curves and hips and breasts.

That was what he'd been looking for. He'd wanted a distraction from all the crap in his life, and it had just walked in the door.

"Pam." Bill stood immediately, every bit of his attention focused on the woman who had opened the door. Bill practically fucking glowed looking at her. "Callie. This is a nice surprise. Moira and Nell. Please come in and meet my friend."

Bishop stood, straightening his jacket. He hoped Bill remembered the cover. This place seemed to have made him soft. His eyes went straight to the girl with the big doe eyes, though she seemed to not even notice he was in the room. She took off her coat. Unfortunately, she wasn't wearing her birthday suit. She was dressed in a perfectly respectable sweater and jeans, but he'd been right. She was petite but built for sex. He'd bet her breasts were a small C. She had a tiny waist that curved into luscious hips.

"Hello, I'm Pam Sheppard. This is my daughter Callie." Pam was a pretty woman in her early fifties, he would guess. She didn't have the gorgeous girl's problem with clothes. She'd shed her coat and stood wearing nothing but her boots.

Callie smiled at him and her glasses fogged over. She took them off

23

but had nothing to wipe them on because she was also wearing what her momma had given her. "Sorry. There are some drawbacks to the lifestyle, especially this time of year. My glasses rarely fog over in the summertime."

Bishop tried to keep his eyes on her face. It was increasingly hard with all the boobs and stuff on display.

"I've got it." Gorgeous Girl plucked the glasses from Callie's hand and quickly wiped them down using the hem of her sweater. She passed them back and looked around the room. "Should I take off my clothes?"

Yes. Yes. Yes. Bishop felt his heart rate accelerate at the thought. It was a bit alarming. He was ice cold. He didn't run hot, but she was making him warm all over. He was damn happy he had *his* clothes on. He was getting a woody right here. It proved how perverse he was that the erection was for the girl who didn't have her clothes off.

"Nell, dear, don't worry about your clothing. We have much bigger things to worry about." Moira. She looked rather regal in her turtleneck sweater and tailored slacks. She turned to Bill. "Our cabin was broken into. I'm afraid my past has caught up to my daughter and me. I should never have stayed on this plane. I should have kept moving. I can't remember if time is faster here or slower. I think it's both sometimes."

And the older lady was insane. Good to know Bill took in all types.

Nell flushed, a gorgeous pinkening of her skin. "Mother, please. Let me handle this. We agreed I'm the best person to deal with this situation. And you're being perfectly impolite. We haven't even been introduced to the guest, yet." She finally turned those chocolate eyes on him. She was half a foot shorter, barely coming to his shoulders, and that did something for him. Standing over her gave him the oddest feeling of protectiveness. "I apologize for my mother. She's a bit odd and not very interested in the social niceties. I'm Eleanor Finn, but everyone calls me Nell. I live down in the valley with my mother, Moira Finn. It's nice to meet you."

So polite. She held out her hand. Social niceties. He didn't have much use for them either, but he was good at them. He took her hand in his, a spark lighting up his skin. He dismissed it as nothing more than static electricity. "I'm Professor Henry Flanders."

Her eyes held his for the barest of moments before she found a place on his chest to stare at. Nice. Submissive. Perhaps not everywhere, but she would be in bed, and that was all he really cared about. Bill might like the whole nude thing, but Bishop had games he liked to play, too. And he was seriously thinking about playing them with Nell Finn.

Yes, he'd needed a distraction for a few days, and she would do quite nicely.

* * * *

Nell Finn looked up at the most beautiful man she'd ever seen. *Destiny*. She'd wondered about the word, thought at times that it was a silly thing to believe in, but here he was standing right in front of her.

She'd even felt a spark of lightning when he'd touched her for the first time. All the faery tales her mother had told her were true. There really was one person out there for her. Of course because her mother was slightly insane, she'd claimed that the one person out there was likely on another plane of existence and trapped by an evil relative, but she was wrong. He was standing right in front of her and she couldn't quite breathe.

Henry Flanders. It was a perfectly lovely name.

Why couldn't he have met her at a better time? Maybe destiny was a cruel goddess. Or maybe she could still save this first meeting. Her mother hadn't talked too much yet. If she could get Henry out of the room, it might take him a few days to figure out her mom was crazy and thought that faeries were real and god, please don't let her go into her spiel about corporate vampires. Yes, Henry had to leave because she really did have a problem, and Bill was the best person to deal with it.

She turned to Bill, forcing her attention away from Henry's chest. He was still dressed, and that was likely a good thing. She was well used to the men of Mountain and Valley and their chosen belief system. She would honor it as she honored all people's philosophical beliefs, but it would have been difficult to not stare at the handsome professor, and staring at a nudist's privates was considered quite rude.

"Bill, could we please schedule a time to talk to you about our security problem?" They could go and have lunch in the cafeteria. Mountain and Valley always offered a vegan option for every meal. She could settle her mother down and then come back this afternoon when Henry was off doing activities or relaxing, and then what? How would she see him again? Her mind went in a hundred different directions. She had no idea how to pursue a man. She'd spent her college years learning how to protest. If Henry was a corporation violating EPA standards, she would totally know what to do with him.

Bill sat back down behind his massive, very important-looking desk.

25

Nell loved the desk but worried about how many trees had died to create it. Still, it was well crafted and not some throwaway furniture. It was the kind of desk that could last several generations, thereby making the loss of the trees worthwhile. Someday she would find a desk like that.

She wondered if Henry had a desk like that.

"Nell, dear, if this is a security problem that has your mom upset, why don't we talk this out now? There is nothing I enjoy more than helping out Pam's friends," Bill said.

"It's okay. I don't want to bother you when you're talking to your guest." The last thing she wanted was for hot Henry to hear her tale of woe. She didn't have a lot of experience with men. She'd only had a couple of boyfriends, and they'd all been run off either by her dedication to causes or her mother's firm belief in a reality that didn't exist. She was pretty sure that most men also preferred women who weren't high maintenance. They liked independent women who knew their own minds and solved their own problems.

"We were just catching up. Nothing serious." Henry offered her his chair. Everyone else had found a place. "Please, sit."

She didn't want a seat simply because she was female. "Oh, no. You were here first. I'm perfectly healthy. I can stand."

"Please sit down, Nell." His eyes had narrowed slightly and though his voice was perfectly polite, there was something about the tone that told her it was better to not argue.

She found herself settling into the chair.

Why had she done that? She loved arguing. She was quite good at arguing. She'd taken whole semesters of it. Arguing 101. She'd been given an A+ and told she was the most annoying woman the professor had ever met. In her world, it was a compliment. "If you insist, but you should know that I don't think women are any different from men, so there's no need for the whole gentlemanly act."

"It isn't an act," Henry replied. "And we'll discuss exactly how different men and women are at a later date."

He'd whispered the words her way, leaning over the chair she'd just sat down in. She'd been able to feel the warmth of his breath. It shimmered along her skin.

Wow. Nelson Milford, her debate team boyfriend, had never once made her heart pound like that. And what the heck had happened to her nipples?

"Go on, Moira. Tell Bill what you told us," Callie said in an encouraging tone.

Callie had been the first friend Nell had made when she'd followed her mother to Bliss after she'd graduated from college. The minute she'd walked into town, she'd known this was her home.

Nell turned, praying that Henry had left the room. Nope. He was standing there, his arms crossed over his chest. She wondered what he taught. He looked like a professor. Sharp intelligence sparked from his dark eyes. He obviously had no plans to leave, and his eyes were squarely on her. She forced herself to turn back to the others and held off the urge to ask him to leave. He would say no. She knew it deep down. He would say no, and rather forcefully.

So much for destiny. After Henry heard her mother's story, he would stay as far away from her as possible.

She loved her mother, but sometimes she was a burden. *Damn*. She couldn't think that way. Her mother was a lovely woman. Her mother took care of her. Her mother had said all the right things when she'd needed to. She'd held on to reality in order to save Nell. She couldn't ever repay her mom for that. And Henry Flanders had been a fleeting dream. She was lonely, and he was interesting.

The destiny thing was nothing more than a flight of fancy.

She would start dating. She could ask men out. Maybe she would ask Rye Harper if he would like to have dinner some time. He was attractive and charming and ate far too much animal flesh. And came with a brother. She couldn't handle those two even if they'd showed any interest in her at all.

Henry Flanders was the most interesting man to walk into Bliss in forever. That was all.

"Our cabin was broken into by my cousin's forces," Moira explained calmly. "He's finally found us after all these years."

Bill's left eyebrow arched. "You're on the run from your cousin?"

Nell held a hand out, all hope for getting through this with dignity gone. "Mother is talking about her Fae relatives. According to Mom, she's royalty from another plane of existence. She was forced to flee when I was a baby because we're apparently some sort of faerie princesses, and her cousin wanted to kill anyone who could possibly claim the throne. But seriously, our cabin was broken into."

Bill looked to Pam, who shrugged as though to say, *Live and let live*.

Nell felt herself flush. Her mom lived in her own world. It was

27

seemingly harmless. When she was younger she'd loved the stories her mother had told her, but as she grew she realized how much her mom's disconnect could cost them.

"Well, Moira, then we need to look into this." Bill gave Moira a smile. "Don't worry about a thing. Perhaps for the time being you would feel more comfortable here in the community. We're gated and have lots of security. You and your daughter are more than welcome."

Her mother breathed an enormous sigh of relief. "Thank you, Bill. You are such a gentleman. I would feel safer staying here."

Yes, her mother's differences had cost them much, but not in Bliss. Tears sprang to Nell's eyes. She loved it here. No one tried to throw her mom in a home. They let her work and sell her gorgeous pottery in the galleries in town. They let her be part of the community.

Nell blessed the day her mother had met Pamela Sheppard in radiation therapy. Pam had convinced Moira to come home to Bliss with her. Pam had gone into remission. Her mother had not. Nell took a long breath. Nothing was more important than her mom. "Thanks, Bill. I appreciate it. Mom has been worried. Whoever broke in didn't actually take anything. They just destroyed a bunch of furniture."

Furniture she would find hard to replace. Her mom had used every last bit of their money to buy their cabin by the river. Nell thought seriously about finding a job. Her writing career was going to have to get put on hold. It wouldn't be hard. Idealistic, environmentally sound romances did not seem to be selling right now.

"Are you sure it wasn't a bear, hon?" Pam asked. "Sometimes they get in, and they can make a real mess."

"It wasn't a bear. It was Torin, I tell you. He's found me." Moira shook her head as though she'd known it would happen all along.

Torin was apparently their tormentor. Yes, she'd heard many stories about the evil faery. "I don't think it was a bear."

"It wasn't a bear, Mom," Callie agreed. "Bears don't spell as well as this person."

Callie was right. Everything on the message the man had left behind had been properly spelled, if slightly vulgar. Bears rarely left behind personal messages. It was one of the things she liked about them. "He wrote a message on the wall."

"What did he write?" Bill asked, his brow furrowing in consternation.

Nell frowned. She hated this part because she was pretty sure that message hadn't been left for her mom. "Die, bitch. That's what he wrote."

"Did he?" Henry's voice was ice cold.

Nell had to turn around to answer. "Well, yes. Why would I lie about that? It's not exactly something I want to talk about around town."

"Why are you here and not at the sheriff's office?" Henry leaned negligently against the wall, but there was nothing casual about the look on his face. "This sounds like a criminal act. You should involve the authorities."

"Sheriff Bryant was fishing," Nell explained. "And his deputy was on a call."

"Rye is working a traffic accident," Callie said. "He's the deputy. I would really rather Rye look into it than the sheriff. Sheriff Bryant is real close to retirement, and he doesn't expend a whole lot of energy, if you know what I mean."

"I don't," Henry replied. "If the sheriff isn't doing his job, he should be replaced by someone who will."

"That's a very narrow-minded view." Nell was a little surprised at his judgmental attitude. Maybe he wasn't the man of her dreams. The man of her dreams would be a bit more tolerant.

"On what planet, sweetheart?" Henry shot back.

"Uhm, Henry, you'll find things work a bit differently here than the rest of the world," Bill explained. "The sheriff was voted in, and he can't be voted out until the end of next year. I'll put it to you in a way you should be able to understand. Think of it as Sheriff Bryant having tenure. He can't be let go because he takes the odd day off to go fishing. We take fishing damn seriously here in Bliss."

She chose to ignore Henry's glare at that statement. She'd allowed her hormones to rule her very excellent brain. He was obviously like other outsiders. He was judging them, and she wouldn't tolerate that. No matter how nice he looked. Or how pretty his eyes were. Or how broad and masculine his shoulders happened to be. She wasn't going to fall for a Neanderthal.

She turned back to Bill and the problem at hand. "So, do you think you can help us? I know you can't find this guy, but maybe you could help us make the cabin safer for when we go home."

"I'll find him."

Nell was forced to turn again because Henry had said the words, and he'd sounded so very, very sure of himself.

"You want to handle this? I thought you were on vacation," Bill said, a silent moment passing between the men. "I wouldn't like for Nell or her mother to be hurt."

"I'll take care of them."

Those five words from Henry Flanders seemed to settle something in Bill Hartman's mind. He reached over and gripped Pam's hand, bringing it to his lips. "Then it's settled. What do you say we go and get some lunch, dear? Henry will take care of the problem. Moira, why don't you join us? Nell can show Henry the cabin."

That hadn't gone the way she'd planned.

Her mother stood up. "I don't think that's a good idea. They could still be out there waiting for my Nell. I should go with her. I can trade my life for hers if need be."

And that was her mom in a nutshell. Nell sighed and walked across the room to hug her. "I'll be fine. It's only an hour or so and then I'll be back here. I'll bring back your books for you, and then we'll settle in for a while. It can be like a vacation."

A vacation where she found a job because her mom's pottery sales wouldn't cover fixing up the cabin. She would have to see what she could get for her laptop and pray someone was hiring around town.

"I don't know." Her mom looked Bill's way.

"Henry can take care of her," Bill said.

"Nell, grab your coat, and we can be on our way," Henry said. Well, ordered really. He seemed to be a very bossy sort of man. Likely because he was a teacher. Teachers often had to take control, though Nell's favorite teachers had always been the freethinking ones. Her favorite teacher of all time had been Mrs. Joyce, her eighth grade English teacher, who brought a net to class so she could catch dangling participles. Of course, she'd also taught grammar through interpretive dance.

Maybe she could find a teaching job.

"Nell?" Henry was staring at her.

Yes, he was far too bossy for her tastes. She would simply have to survive the afternoon. She would take him to see the cabin and then head into town to talk to Teeny about where she might be able to pawn her computer. And her necklace. It was a silly thing, a little silver snowflake with the words "You're One of a Kind" engraved on it. It had been a gift from a friend. She always touched the necklace when she felt down, a way of reminding herself of the words. Now she would have to pawn it. She sniffled as she walked to where she'd hung up her coat.

Henry stood talking to her mom. He'd leaned in, whispering something to her. Her mother stopped, her pretty face settling in a confused mask.

"Will you really?" she asked.

Henry's face was the same polite blank it had been the whole time. She wondered what it would take for the man to smile. "I promise I will."

A bright, sunny smile replaced her mother's previous gloom. "Excellent. I like you, Henry. Take care of my girl. She's very important to the world, you know."

She could feel her skin flush with embarrassment. "Mom, please."

"I can see that." Henry grabbed his own coat and held the door open for her. "Shall we?"

It was too bad he was so bossy and obviously believed in a patriarchal society worldview because he was quite handsome. She walked out the door wondering what he would look like if he would just smile.

Chapter Two

"What did you say to my mom?"

He didn't look back, merely expected Nell to follow. It was time to start her training, and part of her training was to follow him when he decided to lead. During most of the brief time of their relationship, Bishop would be perfectly fine with trailing after her and allowing her to make most of the unimportant decisions. She could choose where they ate and what they did for fun. He couldn't care less about what movies they might see. All of those daily things would be left to her.

But when it counted, when the chips were down and things got dangerous, he would be in charge.

"I told her I would take care of you." What he'd told her had actually been more about taking care of anyone who thought they could hurt Nell while he was on watch. He'd actually said something more like he would rip the testicles off the fucker and ram them down his throat if he thought to touch her. Moira Finn had seemed suitably impressed.

Somehow he didn't think Nell would be. He rather thought she would give him a lecture on proper masculine behavior in the modern age and how it didn't involve deballing his foes. It was obvious that Nell was one of those bleeding-heart types who would let the whole world go to hell because she didn't want to get her hands dirty. He couldn't stand the type.

And he still wanted her. His cock had been hard as a damn rock since she'd walked in and looked up at him with those innocent eyes. All he'd been able to think about since that minute was getting her under him. The women in his world were typically cold and just as ruthless as he was.

Nell Finn was soft and seemingly innocent. Oh, he was pretty sure she wasn't a virgin. No one was that innocent, but her lack of a hymen didn't mean she was worldly.

"I don't actually require taking care of, but thank you for putting my mother at ease," she said primly as they walked out into the snow. It had blanketed the mountain in white. Nell pulled her knit cap down, covering her ears.

"Tell me something, sweetheart," Bishop started as he moved toward his SUV, a rental that had luckily come complete with snow tires. "Which *bitch* do you think he was referring to? You or your mother?"

It took him a moment to realize she wasn't following him now. He turned, the snow covering his boots. He'd been working in South America for too long. The cold was foreign, alien. He was used to almost junglelike heat.

Nell didn't seem to have the same problem. She stood in her galoshes, that lovely body swallowed up by her parka. The cap on her head practically devoured her as well, covering most of her hair and ending in two knit balls hanging to her shoulders. It wasn't sexy. It wasn't attractive. So why did his heart do a weird shaky thing? She was adorable.

He didn't do adorable.

"That was rude, Henry. I'm not a bitch, and it's mean of you to say it." Her words were quiet, not a real hint of anger in them, but he could feel her hurt.

Damn it. He didn't need this. He needed to completely rethink his position. She was one of those heart-on-her-sleeve, fall-in-love kind of women, and all he was looking for was a nice long fuck. So he should back off. He would solve her problem and then she could go her way and he would go his. Surely there were women in this town who just wanted an orgasm.

"I'm sorry. I wasn't actually calling you a bitch. I was making a bad joke about what was written on your wall."

She stared for a moment as though trying to decide if he was being truthful. "Okay. I'm being touchy. I didn't like you calling me that."

She started to walk again, crossing the distance between them. Fuck, she was pretty.

"You shouldn't like anyone calling you that."

She shrugged. "You get used to it."

"You get used to it? Who the hell routinely calls you vulgar names?" The thought pissed him off. He'd been told this was a nice town, not a town where young women were routinely verbally assaulted.

"Oh, lots of people. Mostly at the places where I protest," she replied.

"Protest?"

"Yes. Protesting is an important part of our political process. In the last week, I've organized or attended five different protests, though one probably shouldn't count because it was completely spontaneous. Max Harper killed a wolf. I protested him. Vigorously."

Bishop had to work to keep up with her. "Why did he kill a wolf? Is he a hunter?"

She shook her head. "No. Although I've heard he hunts, too. He's a rancher, and apparently this poor wolf was very hungry."

Bishop stopped, his hands going to his hips. "Nell, he has the right to protect his property."

Nell turned back to him, a standoff. "And I have the right to protect the earth. He didn't even try to save the wolf. And he wasn't apologetic. He was all tough guy 'I killed one of nature's blessings and that makes me a man.' He used a telescopic rifle. The wolf didn't have a chance. If he wants to prove his big bad manhood, he should take the wolf on without weaponry. Then maybe I will be impressed, though likely not, since I don't think wolves should have been taken off the endangered species list. I protested that, too."

Wow. She could talk a mile a minute. "I think if the wolves want to survive, they should evolve and start creating weapons of their own."

She rolled her eyes. "Oh, you just wait, Mister. When all the predators are gone, fluffy adorable bunnies will overrun the earth. When they eat every vegetable known to man, you're going to be hungry."

She strode past him. Yeah, he didn't need to get involved with a crazy idealist even for a few brief days. She would turn his vacation into a hell of lectures and dumb ideas about kindness saving humanity. There wasn't any actual humanity in most humans. They all paid lip service to the idea, but when the chips were down that's when the claws came out. Sheltered Nell thought she could save the world? Well, he'd done a hell of a lot more than she had to protect her ability to protest.

He stared at her as she walked by, wishing he could see the sway of her hips under all that likely cruelty-free fabric. His brain might understand that she was a bad idea, but his dick wasn't as evolved as his brain.

His dick simply wanted her.

She walked right up to the big-ass SUV he'd rented, and she stood by the passenger door, obviously waiting.

"How did you know that was my car?" There were at least fifteen cars in the small parking lot.

She patted the hood. "Oh, this is absolutely the vilest, most gas-guzzling, earth-killing car out here. It was a good bet it was yours."

That ass was begging for a spanking. He could picture her over his knee, that round ass in the air, muscles clenching because she was so damn nervous. He would wait, hold off because the anticipation of pain was a part of the process. And then he would give it to her. Hard. Fast. Unrelenting. She might cry a little because at first the shock of the sting seemed like real pain, but he knew how to turn that sting into an ache. He would start fast, but end slow, his palm resting with every sharp slap so the heat would sink into her muscles and make its way to her pussy. Wet. She'd be wet within moments. Her pussy would swell, praying for some attention, but he would focus on her ass.

God, he wanted to fuck her. He wanted to use his cock on her pussy as much as he wanted to smack her ass and let her know who the boss was. What was wrong with him? He liked sex, craved it at times, especially when he was coming off a bloody op, but it was the sex he craved, not a particular woman.

"Are you okay?" Nell stood staring at him like she was the tiniest bit worried he was going to go crazy.

Of course, she'd likely run if she knew exactly what he was thinking. The question was—would he catch her? He wasn't sure. He made the safe play and held up his keys. "Found them."

He opened her door.

"I can open my own door."

He felt his eyes narrow. "You know, I would like you a lot more if you would stop pushing this modern ideal that simply because a woman can open her door or stand instead of sit, that a man shouldn't be polite and open it for her or give up his seat. It's a politeness. It makes me feel good, and you're ruining it for me."

She stopped, biting into her bottom lip. "I hadn't thought of it that way."

Yeah, that had been a good way to play her. Oddly enough, it had also been the truth. "Some men enjoy being courteous to the women they meet. Women aren't incapable. They're just far more beautiful inside and out, and I want to honor that."

"You think I'm beautiful?" She flushed and covered her mouth. "I

35

can't believe I said that out loud. You were talking about all women."

"I was talking about you." Whether or not he gave in, she should know she was beautiful. "Now get in and let me take a look at this problem of yours."

She allowed him to open the door and settled into the passenger seat. "Okay, but I should warn you, it's pretty violent. It might be upsetting. You're a college professor. I can't imagine you've seen much violence. This is the nasty side of the world."

He walked around the car shaking his head as he got into the driver's seat.

When he closed his eyes at night, he saw all of the bad things of the world in his dreams. Lately he'd begun wondering if he wasn't one of them. He'd stared into the abyss so fucking long, he'd become a part of it, slowly sliding inside until he didn't remember what he'd been before. He could tell her stories that would shake her faith in humanity. "Oh, I think I'll find a way to handle it. I'm sure if it frightens me that you'll take care of me."

It was a laughable thought. Though not, it seemed, for Nell. She gave him a bright smile and reached over to touch his arm. "I will. I've been in the activist world long enough to know how bad it can be out there, but it's worth it. We have to fight for the world we want."

He stopped, his hands in the middle of turning the ignition. *Fight for the world we want*. It was a child's ideal—that the world could be changed. The world was the same shit hole it had always been, and he was responsible for making sure idealists like Nell didn't realize that truth. If she was forced to face reality, all those ideals would crumble and she would be just like the rest of them—selfish, needy, and willing to trample over anyone to save her own neck.

It was his job to make sure she never knew that truth about herself.

He turned the engine to his earth-killing vehicle over and eased it into reverse, snow crunching under the tires. He had to be careful. The mountains were beautiful, but like everything else in the world, they were deadly as well if not handled with caution.

"So what do you teach, Henry?"

Assassination 101. South American Coups. How to Change Your Identity in Five Easy Steps. "I teach history."

Nell's smile lit up the cab. "Wow. That's exciting. I love history. What type do you teach? British? I love British history. I can't decide which age I would rather have lived in. The Dark Ages were full of things to protest. I mean it. What a time to be an activist. Except they kind of burned all of them at the stake. The Victorian Age was better, except if you marched for women's rights, you often got labeled a whore. I guess this really is the best time to be an activist. Everyone still hates us and thinks we're annoying, but we no longer get lynched or drawn, hanged, and quartered. Wow. History is kind of bloody now that I think about it."

He turned slightly and gave her a grin of his own. He actually kind of liked the way her brain worked. He was used to careful conversations where each word was a pointed gun, but Nell rambled on, giving voice to her every thought. "I specialize in the history of war."

Her smile disappeared. "I bet you eat meat, too. Don't you?"

"I can be persuaded to try a salad every now and then." He wasn't willing to completely scare her off yet. Being this close to her, he could smell the shampoo she'd used on her hair. Nell Finn smelled like sunshine, and he was so used to the gloom. It was a bad idea, and he rarely had bad ideas. She was going to get hurt.

He was still going to have her. Maybe even today.

It was his vacation, after all.

"You'll need to take a left at the stop sign when you're down the mountain," she explained. "Our cabin is near the river. We're a little isolated."

Everything was isolated in Bliss, though the valley he'd passed seemed to have plenty of cabins. "Are you sure it's a good idea to be so far from other people?"

She shrugged. "I like the peace and quiet. It's nice after the city and all those hospitals."

"Why were you in the hospital?"

"I wasn't. Mom was. She has leukemia. We met Pam Sheppard in Denver where she was being treated, and she convinced us to give Bliss a try. I think my mom was hoping she could find a family for me." She was getting emotional, her nose flushing. She wouldn't be able to tell a lie to save her life.

"Your mom is your only family?" He understood what it meant to be alone.

She turned slightly, a grin forming. "Unless you count the vampires on another plane of existence. Sorry. I can joke about it now. My mom has certain quirks in her personality, but she's perfectly harmless."

Her mom was certifiable. "Is she schizophrenic?"

"No." Nell huffed. "Delusional, perhaps, but she doesn't hear voices, and she's never been violent. She's a loving mother and a very kind friend. I blame her artistic temperament, but CPS in Atlanta didn't see it that way."

He made the left turn and the land became flat, moving toward the valley. "You went into foster care."

He didn't like that idea. She was too soft to handle it. A woman like Nell would need someone strong to protect her. Foster parents were a crapshoot. He'd had a couple who cared, but several who had seen him as nothing more than a paycheck. A vision of a young Nell being forced into that life assaulted him.

"Not for too long. My mom complied with everything they asked her to. She immediately went into counseling and started saying all the right things. I remember when she was finally able to pick me up. She smiled and was so calm until we were two blocks away and then she broke down. She hugged me and begged me to forgive her. I was eight. She didn't talk about her family again around anyone until we got here." Nell stared out the window at the trees passing by. "It's funny. In some ways I feel like I got my mother back when we came here. She and this guy named Mel argue all the time about who's worse. Evil faeries versus aliens. They tried to call a town hall meeting and take a vote to see which one would win, but the mayor is too afraid that he'd then be forced to enact a safety plan, and that could get expensive."

The town sounded a little off, too, but that didn't bother him. He would likely find the place wildly entertaining—like reading a comedic book or watching a movie. He would sit back and let them entertain him.

And he would let Nell entertain him, too.

She chattered on as though silence was something to be ruthlessly beaten back. Bishop preferred silence, but he found her voice rather pleasant, soothing even as she talked about how she'd left her place in Denver to come to this remote small town and how she was trying to be a writer.

He didn't have to talk. It was refreshing in a way. He could sit back, and she would take care of that part. Every now and then she would ask him a question about himself and he would sidestep it, turning the conversation back to her.

All he had to do to keep her talking was point out some terrible thing that was happening in the world. Nell had a plan. She had letters to write to dictators and corporations to protest.

Would she protest him if he didn't give her a proper orgasm? He wasn't particularly worried. He intended to make sure she was perfectly satisfied, right down to her Birkenstocks.

"That's the cabin." She pointed through the windshield to a small cabin by the river. It was a real, actual log cabin with a postage stamp of a front porch and a neatly kept yard. He pulled into the gravel drive. She was right. It was isolated. The drive wasn't even paved.

"Where does the road go?" There was a dirt road that led away from her cabin toward another mountain.

"It leads up to Elk Creek Pass. There's not much up that way. There's a ski lodge and a bar called Hell on Wheels, but I've never been to either one. I know the gentlemen who run the bar. They're very nice." She opened her door and slid out.

He needed to train her. It was his job to open her door and hers to wait until he could help her out, his hands sliding over her curves and keeping her balanced. He was a little disgruntled as he followed her, but he held his tongue.

The cabin was old, the chinking in need of work. About the only thing that he'd seen that looked new on the place was the mailbox. It had been painted with gold and green, the name "Finn" done up in pretty flourishes. It was also not where it was supposed to be. Someone had forcibly removed the cheery mailbox, and it had ended up on the porch. He picked it up as Nell pushed the ruined door open.

"I think he must have kicked it in." Nell seemed good at stating the obvious.

He examined the door. Cheap. Thin. Possibly built in the fifties when he would guess the cabin had been built. He stepped inside. The whole place was complete chaos.

The couch had been slashed, the small coffee table broken. Broken dishes littered the tiny kitchen floor.

This was an act of pure hate. Someone hated one of the Finn women. The question was which one. He studied the place, trying to keep a cool professional distance, but it was hard. He'd seen violence over and over again, but something about the thought of Nell having to face it with nothing and no one but her mother at her side sparked a certain anger in him. They were two women, one of whom he suspected was very ill, alone in the world.

He turned and someone had used spray paint to ruin the paneled fireplace.

Die Bitch

Not grammatically correct and a bit rude in his opinion. Inelegant. The paint was a wretched purple. He'd probably gotten it on sale. There wouldn't be many places that sold paint out here. Yes. He could figure this out.

"Do you have any violent ex-boyfriends?" He sifted through the pile of magazines that had spilled from the broken coffee table. Mostly news magazines, with some arts and crafts manuals sprinkled in. The Finn women were serious-minded. No tabloid rags for them.

Nell frowned, reaching down to pick up a legal pad. "Callie thought I should keep things the way they are until Rye gets a chance to look at it. I can't stand the mess."

"He'll need to take some pictures, but you don't have to be here for that. Could you answer my question?"

She looked up at him, her eyes wide. "About the boyfriends? No. I don't have any boyfriends I would imagine could do this. There haven't been that many, but they were all selected for their beliefs in nonviolence."

So she'd dated wimps. It didn't surprise him, but it made him wonder if she'd ever had really good sex. Probably not. She probably wore shapeless dresses that she'd chosen for the cruelty-free nature of their fabric. He would be shocked if she'd ever had a real orgasm. She'd selected her lovers based on their political beliefs and not on whether or not they could make her come. He was damn straight sure he could make her come. "How about your mother?"

Nell shook her head. "My mother hasn't had a boyfriend. She claims my father was the only man she could ever love, and he died when I was very young. I don't remember him at all. I often wonder if losing my dad is what caused her to drift into her fantasy world."

He wasn't about to go into all the ways her mother was insane. "Do you have any idea who could have done this? Who have you pissed off lately?"

She had to have pissed off someone. She'd pissed him off in the very short time he'd known her. Of course, she'd also gotten his cock hard, and that meant something to him.

Her gorgeous lips turned down. "Any number of people. Look, I protest a lot of things. I believe in standing up for what's right."

She was a cute idiot granola girl. Yeah, he got that. "Do you have a list of the companies or people you've protested in the last year or so?"

If he had a list, he could figure out if her protests had actually cost someone money. The loss of money could make a person hate pretty damn quick. The faster he figured out who was after her, the faster she could have perfectly worry-free sex.

Nell nodded. "I can print out my schedule for the last year. I'm very organized. I've been thinking about using the Internet to bring activists together."

"You should do that. I'll take the printout, please," Bishop said as he walked around.

The cabin couldn't be more than seven hundred square feet. He counted two whole bedrooms and poked his head into a bathroom that wouldn't hold more than one person at a time. In the smaller of the two bedrooms, there was a single bed with a pretty pink-and-white quilt that had been slashed to pieces. He could see the room as it had been, pulling back the chaos and forming a picture in his mind of the way Nell's room should be laid out. There was no question the room was Nell's. She would never take the larger room. She would have given that up to anyone she was living with.

She needed a keeper.

It was easy to see what she valued. Books. They were torn and damaged, but she'd lined her walls with books, and not just nonfiction. He caught sight of some racy covers in the midst of the chaos. Romances. So she wasn't only interested in intellectual pursuits. She had a romantic side. He could use that.

Underneath a pile of shredded clothes, he saw a hint of pink fur. He reached down and pulled out a teddy bear. Worn and old, it was a sad-looking little thing. Its middle had been torn open.

"Mr. Snugglebunny. I know. It's a bear, but I was into bunnies back then." A sad smile lit her face as she took the pathetic-looking stuffed animal from his hands. "As far as I know it's the only thing I have left of my father."

He studied the toy. It was an odd thing. It wasn't fashioned from mass-marketed materials. Someone had sewn the thing by hand. The bear had buttons for eyes and a black yarn nose. It was a piece of her childhood, and it meant something to her.

He couldn't miss the tears that pooled in her eyes. "I think you can find someone to fix it."

Her eyes were bright as she looked up. "Yes. Yes, I can. And I can fix the cabin, too. I was thinking I can probably get a new door in town, and I have a book on home repairs. I think it's best if my mom stays with Pam for a while until I get the cabin back into shape. Is there any way you could drop me off in town?"

He felt his eyes narrow because she had plans. That was obvious. He was fairly sure that he wouldn't like her plans. "Why?"

"Because I need to start scheduling the repairs."

That wasn't all she was planning on doing. She was hiding something. It was right there in the way she wouldn't look him in the eyes. And why had she talked about her mom staying with Pam Sheppard and not herself? It was time to start herding Nell in the proper direction. He crowded her. It wasn't hard in the small bedroom.

The minute she realized how close he was, she backed up, ceding the space until her back hit the door. "Henry?"

"How do you intend to pay for those repairs?" This cabin would require extensive repairs. Everything would have to be replaced. The door alone would cost hundreds of dollars, not to mention fixing the windows. He would bet a lot that Nell didn't have that money.

Her face flushed the closer he got. Yes, she was aware of him, finally. That was what he wanted. "I don't know that's your business."

"So it's my business to take care of this for you, but not to know how you'll take care of yourself? Is that how you work when you help someone out? You do one piece of the job and send them on their way?" He was playing on her sympathetic soul. And her body. He leaned in. She smelled sweet, like milk and honey. Damn, but he could eat her up. And there was no way to miss the way her nipples peaked under her sweater because she wasn't wearing a bra.

Her voice was slightly breathless. "I think it's nice that you want to help, but I don't need it. I can fix everything."

He loomed over her, well aware that he was using his height to intimidate her. "How, Nell? Do you have a job you haven't told me about?"

"I have a computer I can pawn," she said quietly.

He'd wondered what she'd intended to do, and still his freaking cold-as-fuck heart softened a fraction. All she'd talked about on the way over here was her writing. "I thought you wrote books."

Her back was against the wall. She had nowhere to go, and that was just what he wanted. Her eyes had dilated. They roamed from his face to his neck to his chest, taking him in even as she spoke. "I do, but I have to admit, I don't think I'm very good at it. I keep getting rejected, so I might as well get rid of the computer. Do you have to stand so close?"

There wasn't a trace of irritation in that question. It had been asked with a delicious breathiness that let him know she was interested.

"If you didn't want me to stand so close, you should have gotten a bigger bedroom," he said, well aware his voice had gone low. He stared down at her, unwilling to let her off the hook for a second. Now that he was close to her, he was damn sure he couldn't let her go. Oh, eventually he would. He would go back to his life and she would move on with hers, but for a week or so, he was going to be in her bed. He was going to be in her body. And he was going to solve a few of her problems. "You can't pawn your computer. How will you keep up with your protests? How will you know what to protest in the first place?"

It didn't make any sense, but he couldn't stand the thought of her walking into some crummy shop and giving up her computer for half of what it was worth.

"I'll figure it out," she replied, her eyes round.

And selling the thing wouldn't do any good. It would be a drop in the bucket of what she would need. "It won't work, Nell." He backed her against the wall. "Let someone help you. I can loan you the money."

It wouldn't be a loan, but she didn't have to know that until he was long gone and she couldn't find him.

"That's not a good idea." Her head tilted up. "None of this is a good idea."

But her lips, those fuck-me, take-me lips, were trembling. Her hands were moving to his waist like she couldn't help herself, and he didn't even want to try to help himself. Everything about his life was plotted and planned and decided on for the best of whatever fucking mission he happened to be on.

He didn't want to think. He wanted her. That was all that mattered.

"It's the best idea I've had in a long time." He moved his head just a bit because despite her words, she'd already gone up on her tiptoes to bring her mouth closer to his. It was the simplest thing in the world to lean over and touch his lips to hers.

So simple and so shattering. The minute he touched her, he lost control. She sighed against him, and the need to dominate her roared through his system. He pushed her against the wall, pulling her up so the only thing supporting her was his strength. She held on to him, clinging like she needed him in order to breathe.

He rubbed his body against hers, wishing they weren't someplace cold. Too many clothes. There was way too much between them. He wanted to be skin to skin, his chest nestling against her breasts. He wanted to feel the hard press of her nipples poking at him. But for now, he simply inhaled her.

He'd been right. She tasted sweet, so fucking sweet. He wound his arms around her waist and felt her breasts crush against his chest as he licked her lower lip. "Open your mouth. Let me in, baby."

He felt the hot rush of her breath along his lips.

"Oh, Henry."

He hated the fact that she was saying his goddamn fake name, but then he didn't give a shit because her mouth opened under his and he invaded, taking the space she'd ceded. His tongue surged in, finding hers and playing in a silky dance. So soft. She was ridiculously soft, and there was a natural submission inside Nell that made his cock long to dominate. She was hesitant at first, but then her tongue touched against his and she picked up the rhythm.

His cock ached. She was too short. He couldn't get her in the right position. He needed to lay her down and spread her out like a feast. Not this first time. He was too hot for that. This first time would be hard and quick, but later he would eat her pussy for hours. He would tie her up and have her begging for his cock.

But for now, her tiny bed would have to do. He gripped her ass. Oh, yeah, he was going to fuck her there, too. He was going to work his cock into her little asshole and enjoy her squirms and the breathy pants she would make. Fuck yeah. "Hold on."

She gasped as he moved her. He was lifting her, carrying her with him. He didn't give her a second to think. He didn't need his mouth in order to turn and fall onto the bed with her. He kept her perfectly occupied, tangling their tongues together. Her hands found his hair, and he felt her fingers running across his scalp, holding him to her as though he would leave. She was seriously underestimating her own appeal. He wasn't leaving until he'd had her a hundred times. He might need more than a week. They wouldn't miss him. Two weeks. That was all it would take. Two weeks and he would surely have fucked her out of his system.

He could fuck her a lot in two weeks.

He buried his face in her neck as his hand found her breast. Definitely a C-cup.

"Henry, that feels so nice."

Nice? He wasn't nice. He was nasty, and he was going to get her nasty, too. He finally managed to get his cock where it needed to be, right against her pussy. He rubbed against her, letting her feel every inch of his erection. "It's not going to be nice, baby. It's going to be hot and fast and hard. I'm going to have you screaming for me before I'm done. Do you understand?"

It was such a small thing. A tiny squeak, but Bishop was too well trained. His cock protested, but his instincts took over. One minute he was promising Nell a violent orgasm, and the next he was off the bed and had his hands wrapped around some kid's throat.

Tall, gangly. The skinny fucker couldn't be more than twenty. His blue eyes went wide with fear. Even at the kid's impressive height, Bishop managed to hold him off the ground with a single hand. The kid's sneakers kicked, trying to find something solid. He dropped the baseball bat he had in his hand.

"Now, see, I told him to leave you two be," a laconic voice said. A man in a khaki uniform and a cowboy hat sat in the living room. From the open door, Bishop could see the man was relaxing, his feet up on the TV stand. "Seth wasn't listening. Logan wasn't either, but he didn't happen to find a piece of sporting good equipment fast enough."

"I'm here." Another equally gangly kid ran into the cabin. "Did Seth save Nell?"

"Uhm, this really hurts," the kid named Seth said. "Could I go now?"

"Henry, you put Seth down this instant." Nell was on her feet, straightening her clothes. She was right back to the buttoned-up, slightly prudish woman she'd been before he'd gotten in between her legs.

He thought about going ahead and killing the little fucker. He could do it. He could decapitate a man without ever breaking the skin. It was one of his many talents.

"Don't, man," the deputy said. He had to be the deputy. This was a man and not a boy, but he wasn't anywhere close to retirement. "I understand the inclination to kill him, but he really did think you were assaulting poor Nell. The kid can't tell the difference between a good moan and a bad one. I think we need to get them both laid, but Logan there has a momma who likes to shoot a man's balls off for target practice."

"She doesn't have to know, Rye." The kid named Logan was carrying a Ping-Pong paddle.

"Oh, Marie would know. Marie knows everything. And what did you think you were going to do with that thing? Were you going to paddle him to death?" Rye got up, a notepad in his hand. "Uh, Mr. whatever your

45

name is, Seth's turning blue. Now, if you're really intent on killing him, I'm going to have to file a report, and I hate reports. The name's Harper by the way. Rye Harper."

"Henry Flanders." Bishop dropped the kid.

Seth hit his knees, gasping for breath.

Nell was right there beside him, offering comfort. To the kid who'd interrupted them, of course. No fucking comfort for him. She stared up at him as she smoothed a hand down the kid's back. "That was horrible of you, Henry. What were you thinking?"

He'd been thinking that the asshole who'd tossed the cabin was back, and he could take the criminal out and then go right back to fucking Nell.

Hell, he hadn't been thinking at all. And obviously the deputy had walked in at some point and had a look around, and Bishop hadn't even noticed. He'd been too busy planning to sink his cock into Nell.

Not once had he suspected they weren't alone until the kid had actually walked into the room with them. He didn't like the feeling. She made him vulnerable. He wasn't vulnerable.

"I apologize, of course." He stood back, watching her. "Next time, I'll let whoever walks into your cabin kill us both."

She looked up, frowning. "All I'm saying is you should have asked him what he was doing. This is Seth Stark. He's the grandson of one of our locals. He's here on his winter break. There was no cause to hurt him. I'm very surprised at you, Henry."

"And I thought you were hurting her. Nell doesn't like men," Seth choked out.

"Yes, I do." She turned that frown on the kid.

Bishop stepped out, entering the living room. Logan was trying to explain to the deputy that his momma would never know if Rye found him a girl and hey, he was willing to share with Seth.

What the hell was up with these people? The deputy seemed more interested in talking to the boys than he did in figuring out who was trying to hurt Nell. And Nell didn't seem the least bit upset by any of it. She was on her feet, walking around and making sure all the other men were taken care of.

She carefully avoided him.

She didn't look to him to handle the deputy. She didn't ask him to help. She ignored him for the most part, like they hadn't kissed.

Maybe she did this sort of thing a lot. Maybe she was used to throwing down with random guys. Yeah, he didn't like this feeling either.

He wasn't a possessive man. He'd learned long ago not to get attached to anything because it would be gone the next day. But watching Nell with the other men made his fists clench, his gut churn.

She hadn't accepted his courtesies, but she allowed the deputy, Rye Harper, to find a seat for her. She allowed him to dust it off and she sat while he stood, taking down her information. Even the dumbass kids were allowed to go and find her some cups since all of her glassware was broken.

But she didn't ask him for a damn thing.

What the hell was he around for?

He stepped out on the porch, the cold still a shock to his system.

"Who are you?"

Seth had walked out behind him. He had on a coat, cashmere by the looks of it. Seth Stark had cash, or rather his parents did. His best friend, the kid with the Ping-Pong paddle, didn't. He was dressed in a sweater that looked hand knitted and well-worn jeans.

"I'm Henry Flanders. I teach military history at a small liberal arts college in the northwest."

The Stark kid stared at him with intelligent eyes. "I doubt it. I've never seen any teacher move the way you do."

Bishop shrugged. He'd pegged the kid's accent the minute he'd started talking. Pure Manhattan. Upper East Side. "You haven't been out of New York enough, kid."

Stark kept his distance. "I'm not stupid. I'm actually quite smart. What do you want with Nell? She's a nice girl."

Stark had a thing for her. He could understand that. "She's not a girl. She's a woman, and I'm trying to help her."

Though he was starting to think she didn't really need his help. Didn't want it.

Stark nodded. "Okay. I heard someone was trying to hurt Nell. It looks like it's true. It probably has something to do with her work. She's shut down some businesses for violating codes. That can make people mad. I can start trying to look on the web. I'm really good with a computer."

That could be helpful. "Check her e-mails. I would be surprised if he hadn't written her before this. This feels like an escalation. You'll need her password."

The kid snorted, an arrogant sound. Bishop appreciated a proper amount of arrogance. "I think I can handle it. I haven't met an account yet that I couldn't hack."

Yeah, sure. "All right."

The kid flushed, his cheeks reddening slightly. "I just mean, I'm pretty good. I can do it. Uhm, I'll ask for her password. You're right. That would be way easier."

And now Bishop was interested in Seth Stark because he was hiding something. It was right there in the pink of his skin and the way his eyes suddenly found the floor. Maybe he was wrong. "Who caught you?"

Those lanky shoulders moved up and down. "No one."

"I can strangle you again. This time Nell isn't around." Killing the kid might release some stress.

His hands came up in defeat. "Fine. I might have been a curious kid. I thought I was a hacker. I got into the tiniest bit of trouble with some suits."

Fuck. Suits? More like feds. Feds were the ones who showed up on a dude's doorstep when he got handsy with someone else's accounts. Yeah, if the FBI was interested in the kid, then maybe he really could help. "Did someone come see you?"

He shrugged again. "I do a little work for the government from time to time."

Then he was really fucking good, and Bishop needed to look into him. "Sure, kid. Just check her e-mail. Find out what you can. I'm staying out at the Mountain and Valley. Get in touch and let me know what you find."

He'd promised Bill he would solve her problem. He glanced back in the room, and she was smiling up at the deputy.

"I will," Stark said.

"And give her a ride back up the mountain, will you?" Bishop asked. He could do this from a distance. "She doesn't need me."

Bishop stepped off the porch and got into the SUV. He needed a place to go so he turned toward that bar she'd mentioned. Hell on Wheels. Sounded like his speed.

He could use a drink.

Chapter Three

Nell picked up her broom, eager to get something done now that Rye had completed the obligatory report. She glanced around. No Henry. He was probably getting some fresh air on the porch.

She still couldn't breathe thinking about how he'd kissed her. She'd been kissed before, but those tiny pecks and awkward fumblings seemed in another universe compared to what Henry Flanders had done. She could still feel his lips on hers. They hadn't been tentative and waiting for her to take the lead. Nope. Not Henry. He'd taken what he wanted, and she had been very surprised to discover that did something for her.

She couldn't allow her female hormones to turn her into a crazed sex addict. But wouldn't it be okay to just be a little bit crazy? What was one step down from addict? Enthusiast. Yes. She could be a crazed sex enthusiast.

Of course she had to actually manage to have sex first.

"Nell, what do you know about that Henry fellow?" Rye Harper asked, his eyebrows arched as though it wasn't the first time he'd asked her.

She could get lost in her own head. "I met him at Mountain and Valley an hour ago. He's friends with Bill."

"An hour ago?" If Rye's eyebrow moved another inch, it would climb right off his forehead.

She felt herself flush but tried to hide it by crossing her arms over her chest and sending him her sternest look. "Are you judging me, Ryan Harper? Do you think I haven't heard the story about the new hostess at the golf course in Del Norte? How long had you known her before you…well, escorted her into the bushes and got to know her in a biblical sense?"

A slow smile spread across Rye's face. "I get your point, darlin'. I really do, but Beer Bringing Becky is a little less lethal than the man you were playing around with." He frowned. "Though she could cut me off from beers. I hadn't thought about that. Oh, well. We didn't talk much. The next time I see her I'll pretend I don't know her, and she'll think it was Max who didn't call."

She knew she should lecture him on the whole turnabout twin thing, but her ears had caught on something else. "He's not lethal. He's a college professor."

And a cranky one at that, but she was rapidly coming to the conclusion that his demeanor was likely brought on by a negative environment. She'd heard many professors complain about how rough it was to get tenure. Publish or perish. The ivory tower could crumble right beneath Henry's feet if he didn't have tenure. Yes, that was likely what was making him so crabby. And she suspected he ate too much red meat.

But she wasn't sure how much that mattered since she could still feel her lips tingling and it had been a good forty-five minutes since he'd touched her and kissed her and thrown her on her bed.

She wasn't a dumb girl, merely a cautious one. She knew what would have happened if Seth hadn't interrupted them. She would have lost her virginity to a man she barely knew, and Rye Harper would have been sitting in her devastated living room listening to the whole thing. She knew how embarrassing that would have been.

And yet she was still the tiniest bit mad at Seth.

"All I know is I haven't seen a man move quite as fast as that one did," Rye said, closing up his notebook.

She frowned. "You were watching?"

Rye Harper was completely immune to her sternest look. "I wasn't watching the sex stuff, but I damn straight wanted to see if Seth could save you."

She sighed. "Do people really think I don't like men?"

Maybe Bliss was less tolerant than she thought.

Rye winked at her. "Honey, Seth is just a kid. He believes anyone who isn't interested in him is likely a lesbian. Well, he hopes that. I happen to notice the way you look at a man when he takes his shirt off. You're not disinterested, you're picky, and that's a good thing to be."

50

She wasn't so sure about that. Her pickiness meant she was a twenty-five-year-old virgin. It wasn't that she placed a special value on her hymen. She didn't. She simply hadn't been moved to get rid of it. Maybe she did place a special value on sex, though. She'd heard one too many faery tales. She wanted to be in love.

It was stupid, but she thought she might be able to love Henry Flanders. There was no intellectual reason to believe in the idea of love, but her heart had softened the minute she'd looked at him. She couldn't take her eyes off him when they were in the same room.

Why wouldn't he come back? She didn't like not being able to see him.

Would he find her obnoxious? Lots of people did.

"I like him." Why did it take such courage to admit that?

Rye gave her a brilliant smile. That was what she loved about Bliss. She could talk to almost anyone and they were open and happy to be engaged. This was a family. She'd spent years with only her mother for company, but everywhere she turned in Bliss she found a brother or a sister. Sure, it meant she had no private life, but privacy was overrated. "I'm glad. You deserve a great guy. And I stand perfectly ready to beat the shit out of him if he isn't worthy of you."

"Ryan!" She was a nonviolent person.

He shook his head, putting his hands on her shoulders. "Nope. I'm not going to feel bad. Every woman needs a couple of men who are willing to kick some ass for her. You don't have any men. So me and Max will step up. Stef, too. You're a nice girl. You need brothers. Unless you're willing to give up your stance on nonviolence and let me teach you how to use a shotgun."

Tears filled her eyes. She should completely disavow the whole violence angle, but she had to admit the idea of having a few men who cared enough to look out for her made her want to cry. "I think I'll keep my deeply held beliefs, but thanks, Rye. I do like him. I'm a little scared though."

Rye reached up, smoothing her hair back in a perfectly nice brotherly gesture. "You have to try. Nothing in this life worth anything comes without some risk. One day some sweet thing is going to come through this town and she's going to be perfect. She's going to love me and she's going to love Max and I believe that. I have to. I can't stand the thought of not having a family. I worry deep down that it won't happen. I think maybe I'm too weird. Not many women want to put up with two men, you know."

She hugged him without reservation, throwing her whole body into it because Rye Harper was a wonderful man and he should know it every second of the day. "You're not weird. You're wonderful and Max is wonderful." Max was a crabby man, but one day some amazing woman would fix that. "You're going to get married and be so happy. It can happen, Rye. I believe it."

Because the universe was what a person made it. Positive thoughts brought about a positive outcome.

"I hope so, sweetheart. I sincerely do." Rye returned the hug and then pulled away. "Now, I'm going to look into this, but I think it would be best if you stayed up at the commune."

"I need to clean this place up." She couldn't leave. The cabin wasn't secure. Without a door, any number of threats would have access to her house, and she wasn't merely thinking about the human ones. There were any number of animals who would view the open entry as an invitation. While she welcomed all of the planet's creatures, she maybe didn't want them in her house. She needed to be here. "I have to watch our cabin. Mom and I sank everything we had into this place, and our insurance isn't the best. I doubt it will cover any of the repairs we need to make."

He frowned. "I don't think staying here alone is a good idea. I'll ask around and see if someone can stay with you."

She didn't want someone. She wanted Henry. "I think I can manage that on my own."

A single brow rose over Rye's eyes that let her know he understood quite well who she wasn't talking about. "Okay, but if he isn't interested in protecting you, you let me know and we'll handle it. We can take turns until this guy is caught. I think Seth and Logan can take first watch. They're prepared to take out whoever comes your way with a Ping-Pong paddle and a couple of rolled-up comic books."

She laughed and let Rye leave as Logan and Seth walked back in the house. They were sweet kids. Seth was a little older, but he was Logan's best friend. He'd spent every summer of his life in Bliss since he was five. Nell envied him finding this place at such a young age.

"Rye said we needed to stay here tonight," Seth said with a smile. "I think we should grab some burgers and watch *Star Trek*. They didn't get your DVD player. It still works. I rewired it so we're good. Do you want fries?"

Logan looked out the window. "We should hurry. Dark thirty comes early this time of year. I'll have to call my moms."

Seth rolled his eyes as Logan walked away. His lips curled up. "I'll take care of you, Nell. My granddad won't mind. He expects me to stay out all night. I'm in college, you know. I'm working on a software system that will change the way we use operating systems, so my parents don't fight me too much on staying out."

How did she put this? "I appreciate it, but I think Henry can take care of me."

She walked to the window, trying to figure out where he'd gone.

Seth frowned. "He left. He went to Hell on Wheels and told me to take care of you. Don't worry. Logan and I can handle it. I promise I won't let him come at some stalker with a Ping-Pong paddle."

Henry had left? His car wasn't in the drive anymore. "When did he go?"

"A while back. He kind of shrugged and said you didn't need him and left. It's cool because Logan and I can totally take care of you. I'll get you some free cable, and we can hang out."

He'd left. He'd walked away, and he hadn't said good-bye. He'd kissed her like there was no tomorrow and she was the only woman in the whole world, and then he'd decided a shot of liquor was more important than saying good-bye to her? He'd put his hands on her breasts and taken her to completely different places and he'd promised to take care of her, and this was how he did it? He went to a nasty bar with a bad reputation?

Did he think that would scare her off? He didn't know her at all. Tears threatened and that made her mad. She wasn't the kind of woman who sat back and accepted the unfairness of the world. She protested. She let people know when they were being douchebags of the highest order because some of them didn't understand.

Henry was about to understand.

She grabbed her coat and then opened the closet and found a knit hat. She had several but selected blue because it would go with Henry's eyes and he didn't have a hat. All he'd had was a leather jacket, and that wasn't the warmest thing in the world. She picked some gloves, too. Even if he was a complete ass, she wasn't going to let him go cold.

Logan walked back in the cabin. "I talked to my moms. I can stay but I have to call in, and I can't have sex with Nell."

"Ewww." Nell sent him her patented look, and it had the proper effect on Logan, who shrank back.

"They kind of laughed when I said I wouldn't sleep with you and then

I got that whole sympathetic tone," Logan admitted, his hands up in a defensive position.

She sighed. "It's okay, guys. I'm going to be fine. Y'all go on back home."

Seth frowned. He was so young, but there was a deeply defined sense of responsibility about him. "That's not going to happen. I talked to both Rye and Henry. I promised them both I wouldn't leave you alone here. I can take you up to Mountain and Valley, but I won't leave you here."

She looked to Logan. He would be the voice of reason.

"Rye said he'd kick my ass if I left you alone." Logan grimaced. "I kind of believe him."

"We're not leaving her alone." Seth sent his best friend a nasty look. "Come on, man. We're over eighteen. It's time we manned up. We have to protect our woman."

"I'm not your woman." Even as she said the words, she winced inwardly. She apparently wasn't Henry's woman either. He'd walked out. He'd walked out after he'd kissed her like she was the air he needed to breathe. He'd walked out after he'd promised to take care of her.

They had two completely different versions of taking care of her.

A slow anger started. She should let it go. He didn't like her. She got that. So why had he touched her? Why had he put his lips on hers and shoved her on a bed? Why had she felt that hard part of him when he rubbed against her pelvis?

He should have thought about all of that before he'd done it. He should have thought about that before he'd made her think he'd liked her. It wasn't fair to pretend.

He should know that. How could he change his behavior and ever become a better person if she didn't point out his flaws?

Nell took a deep breath. She was naïve when it came to men. She knew that. She was kind of a dork. She spent too much time on intellectual things, but she'd learned long ago that it cost her more to fit in than it did to be herself. She sniffled, willing herself not to cry. She was weird. But she was a good person and she didn't lie down and let people walk all over her. She was deserving. She had a lot to give. She wasn't willing to just sit back. Not for him.

He was going to get her speech. He was going to understand exactly what he was missing, and then she would move on knowing she'd spoken her mind.

"I'm going to Hell on Wheels."

Seth frowned. "Why? He left, Nell. He walked out."

Nell shrugged. "I'm going. I need to talk to him."

Seth took a long breath. "All right. I have fake IDs for me and Logan."

"Dude, my moms will kill us both." Logan had turned a nice shade of white. "Seriously, they consider you their second son, so death will come swiftly."

Seth rolled his perfect blue eyes. He was skinny, but it was easy to see he would be a lovely man someday. "What they don't know won't hurt them."

"They know everything," Logan whispered.

"Ignore him," Seth said. "I'll take you up there if that's what you want, but this Henry guy seems like an asshole if you ask me."

She didn't care. He'd made her feel more in a few hours than she'd ever felt before. "I'm going."

Seth opened the door, and she followed him out trying not to think about the fact she was seriously contributing to the delinquency of minors.

* * * *

Bishop looked across the bar at the pretty redhead and knew he'd made a big mistake. She was lovely. She was soft and feminine. She was obviously needy.

She was wrong because she wasn't Nell.

The woman across the bar stared down into her Seven and Seven, ignoring everyone around her, but they weren't ignoring her. He counted at least four men who were eyeing the redhead, and they weren't planning on being her friend.

"Hey, what can I get for you?" The bartender was an enormous man of obvious Native American descent. He looked to be in his mid-twenties and wore a leather vest. MC. Motorcycle Club, and not the Harley-Davidson-riding weekend-warrior type. Nope. Damn. Even small-town Colorado had criminal problems. The man in front of him didn't wear the three-piece patch that would proclaim him a one percenter. He had only one piece, the lower rocker. The word PROSPECT emblazoned on his left side. One day, if he was a very good boy and did all kinds of nasty things, he would trade in his PROSPECT patch for the other two pieces of the three patch and then he would be a fully adult criminal. When he turned, Bishop noticed the prospective club's name. The Colorado Horde. If he moved from prospect to member, that symbol would be inked on his back.

"Scotch, neat. At least fifteen-year."

The bartender rolled his eyes. "Really? Where do you think you are, man?"

"I don't know. A bar." He'd been in plenty of shit-ass places, but he'd hoped for some civilization here in the States.

"This is my grandfather's bar. He's still living in the Wild West. I can get you whiskey or tequila or crap-ass vodka or beer. We have two wines. Red or white, and they both suck ass. Those are your choices," the bartender said.

Bishop sighed. It didn't matter. He needed liquor. A lot of it. If he drank enough, maybe he would forget how hard his cock was. He could still feel Nell's arms around him. He could still feel her breasts pressed against his chest, her hips moving against his. *Damn it.* "Vodka. Double on the rocks."

James Bond didn't have these problems. Everywhere the fucker went there was a good bar, but that wasn't Bishop's life. He was stuck with shit-ass bars. He should have been born British. American operatives got shit. The least he should get for his trouble was a decent drink.

The least he should get as his reward was a soft, sweet, innocent woman to take his cock any way he chose.

The redhead across from him looked up. She had a pretty face, and he could see a nice rack, and it didn't do a thing for him because she wasn't Nell. That freaking woman had wrecked his goddamn vacation.

"Here you go." The bartender slid a glass his way. At least it seemed clean. His head gestured toward the back of the bar. "She's a nice lady, you know."

Bishop shrugged and took a sip. Yep. It was low-grade, cheap vodka. "She's pretty."

"She got divorced a while back. Apparently it was a nasty thing. She's still trying to find her footing. She doesn't need some asshole tourist using her."

Bishop stared at the bartender. "What's your name?"

He frowned. "Sawyer. My granddad owns the place, so if you think you can get my ass fired, think again. I work for free, and I don't like assholes using nice women. Holly's a nice woman. She needs someone to look out for her."

Bishop felt a smile cross his face. "Good for you. As it happens, I'm not terribly interested. I have my eye on someone else in town."

Sawyer crossed his arms over his big chest and leaned back. "I'm trying to figure out who the hell that could be. Harper's sister is too young. Stella's a little too old for you. Red back there's just about right."

Bishop had no idea who any of those women were. "I haven't met many people. I just got in today. I've only been out to Mountain and Valley."

Sawyer's eyes went wide. He snorted. "You a nudist?"

"Nah. I have a friend out there."

"Okay. I can buy that. Look, I have some friends around Bliss. It's a nice town. The women are cool."

He couldn't help himself. He had to ask. "What do you know about Nell Finn?"

The temperature in the room seemed to drop by ten degrees. Sawyer's face hardened and his eyes seemed darker than before. "I know she's a sweet lady, and I wouldn't like to see her hurt by some tourist who blew through town and used her. She's a believer, you know?"

He frowned. "No. What do you mean?"

Sawyer sighed. "She believes in all that good shit. She really thinks she can change the world. Look, I've met plenty of people who say they can change things, but Nell believes. She's one of those people who gives it her all and it matters to her. She's the kind of chick who might actually manage it."

Bishop huffed. Had the guy been drinking his own product? "Seriously? You're wearing an outlaw MC cut. You believe in that shit?"

Sawyer shrugged. "I live in a different world and I don't need to explain myself to you. Nell is an idealist."

"She's a dreamer." And his life was so often a nightmare.

"Dreamers can change the world. Look, man, I'm not that guy, but I also know the world. A hundred years ago women couldn't vote. Today women get elected to some of our highest offices. It was people like Nell who did that, so don't underestimate her. And don't you dare fucking use her. She sounds naïve, but what she says is important."

Sawyer was serious. And maybe he should be serious, too. He still had a job to do. Just because he'd bailed on her physically didn't mean he wouldn't find out who wanted to hurt her. "Has she dated much?"

Sawyer stopped. "No. I kind of thought she wasn't all that interested in men."

Oh, she was interested. She simply needed the right man. "So there's no man in her life."

She'd been flustered. It was easier to pay attention to men who didn't matter. She was a submissive who hadn't been trained to please her Dom. She didn't have a Dom. She'd likely never had a Dom, so she didn't understand that a Dom could take care of her and accept all that sweet love she had to give.

He'd gotten pissed off and walked out too soon. Why had he done that? He was patient. It was his greatest strength. He was known for making careful decisions and then plotting out his next move. But he'd taken one look at Nell with that goddamn deputy and he'd walked out because he'd gotten his freaking feelings hurt.

He'd made a mistake.

"Look, I only know Nell because she comes out to the rez and helps out," Sawyer explained. "We have a lot of poverty and need out there, and she puts in a bunch of time. She's kind of made herself a part of the family. I wouldn't like it if she got hurt. She doesn't have a man looking out for her."

That didn't seem to be her problem. The deputy seemed to care, and those two boys had been all over her. But she wasn't sleeping with any of them. Sex was important. Sex could be the glue that bound people together. A woman would listen to a lover when she wouldn't listen to a friend or family member. No matter how many well-meaning friends she had, Nell couldn't truly count on a man unless he was in her bed and taking responsibility.

What the hell was he thinking? He wasn't someone she should rely on. He wasn't going to be here in a few weeks. He was exactly the kind of lover she should avoid.

The redhead across from him took another long drink. She looked over as though trying to gather her courage.

"That one is going to be so much trouble." Sawyer's jaw firmed. "I wish I hadn't come in tonight. I'm trying to stay out of jail."

"Then you shouldn't be prospecting for an MC." Bishop watched the woman. She was definitely going to be trouble. She was a lovely woman and she was obviously emotional. The sharks were already starting to circle. A nasty-looking asshole with a mean tat on his arm began making his way over, a leer on his face. "You going to take care of this?"

Sawyer sighed. "If I have to. My granddad is going to have my ass if I start a fight. You don't understand how mean an old Ute can be when his shit gets trashed. He always threatens to go old school with the honey and the ants. My childhood bedtime stories were really horrible."

Bishop couldn't help but smile. He could imagine. The redhead pushed off the bar, obviously making a decision. She was on the move before her insanely large and muscular and very likely criminal suitor made his way over. She rounded the bar and made a beeline for someone in particular.

Fuck. She was coming his way.

"Nice. Holly made her choice." Sawyer looked more chipper than he had before. "Now she's your problem."

Motherfucker.

"That's Holly for you." A cowboy slid into the seat beside him, a Stetson on his head. "She goes for the man who looks like he has a college education every time. It's why she usually isn't in real trouble here. I'm going to need a whiskey shot with a beer chaser."

"See, that I can do." Sawyer slapped a hand on the bar. "This guy wanted to know how old my Scotch was."

The cowboy snorted. "Tourist." He nodded the redhead's way, and Bishop stared for a minute. He'd already met this guy. "Holly Lang. She moved here a couple of years back. Nice lady, but every now and then her ex-husband gets to her and she comes to the conclusion that she should have revenge sex. It's a real bad idea, so we take turns hauling her butt back to Bliss. It was Rye's turn, but he's working, so I got called in when Stella saw her buying that new dress. Apparently a woman in a V-neck means business."

Bishop frowned. Holly seemed to have changed her mind and headed for the ladies' room. She turned right on her heels and walked away.

The cowboy next to him sighed. "See. She always changes her mind, but by then she's got some jerk who doesn't want to take no for an answer."

Yep, there were several sets of eyes on her as she walked away.

"You're the deputy's twin." They were physically identical, but this guy had a deep frown where Rye Harper had been fairly sunny.

"Max Harper. I run the Harper Stables on the other side of town," the cowboy offered. "And you're?"

"Henry Flanders. I'm a professor of history. Just here on vacation."

Max nodded his way and then shot the whiskey Sawyer put in front of him down in one quick swallow. "That's got some bite. Where the hell did your granddaddy find that? I think that might strip my insides clean."

"Hey, be grateful," Sawyer shot back, handing him a beer. "Granddad likely would have given you Mel's shit. He and Mel went to a sweat lodge and Mel convinced him to buy a case of his tonic. God, the thought of sitting in that fucking thing with twelve naked dudes in the heat does nothing for me. If they want me to get all spiritual and shit, they should put a couple of ladies inside."

"Damn it. Here comes more trouble." Max rolled his eyes. "I don't know that girl, but she's going to cause a ruckus."

A semi had pulled up in the parking lot, and a blonde woman jumped out. She turned, and though Bishop couldn't hear her, he was pretty sure there was nothing but bile coming out of her mouth. That was one pissed off female. She had a backpack in her hand and as she walked away, she flipped the trucker the finger.

Sawyer grimaced. "I don't need this. Where's the gun? I'm just going to shoot myself and get it over with."

"Hi." Holly was back, and she slid into the chair beside him. "Look, I'm going to admit something horrifically embarrassing to you. I was going to come over here and try to pick you up, but then I realized that I would only be having sex with you because my ex-husband is an asshole, and that's no reason to potentially risk a venereal disease." She flushed. "Not that I think you have one. I kind of picked you because you looked perfectly disease-free."

The door slammed open and the blonde walked in. She wore jeans and a sweater but no coat. And she had on some seriously high heels. She'd also been crying. Like Holly.

He was surrounded by emotional females. He'd been surrounded by hardened killers many times before, but this was far worse. He had no idea how to handle emotional females.

"No need to give him the whole story, darlin'. You don't have to hit on tourists. Your escort is here." Max Harper nodded Holly's way. "Let me finish my beer, and I'll get you back into town."

Holly sighed, a look of deep relief covering her face. "Oh, Max, thanks so much. You know it's really nice that whenever I do something dumb there's always someone around to help me out. This is the best town ever. My ex thought it would be a punishment, but I'm happy here."

The blonde sat down at the bar, a devastated look on her face.

Holly's eyes widened as she looked toward the newcomer. "Do you need a phone, hon?"

The woman turned, frowning. "I don't have anyone to call."

"Hey, I want to talk to you." One of the muscle-bound idiots who had been stalking Holly had a hand on her arm, turning her to face him.

"What?" Holly asked, her eyes flaring with a proper amount of fear.

Max grinned, looking at the redhead and the asshole. "Thank god. I need a good fight. Stef's been twelve kinds of mopey lately. He won't even punch me. Artists. I don't understand them."

"Are you kidding me?" Sawyer's hand slapped on the table as the door opened again. "What the fuck is going on?"

And Bishop felt a bit of righteous indignation course through his veins. Nell walked in, pretty as she pleased, with her two puppy dogs trailing behind her. Seth Stark looked around the bar, taking it in as though it was all just a fun experience and not the site of his potential murder.

Logan, on the other hand, looked scared shitless. He had a Superman T-shirt on, his hands in his pockets.

But Nell walked in like she owned the place. "Sawyer, it's so nice to see you. This is a lovely establishment you have here."

Sawyer frowned, his eyes moving around the room as though assessing all the ways his day was about to go to shit. "No, it's not. It's a dive bar and a nest of criminal activity, so you should leave and take the underagers with you."

"Uhm, you should take your hand off my arm," Holly said politely to the brutish man whose tattoos just might be a roadmap of all his murders. "I'm going home. I don't have time for a dance."

"I do," Max Harper said, putting his hat on the bar. He had a wide grin on his face as he rolled up the sleeves to his Western shirt.

"You were teasing me." The muscular asshole didn't look at Max. His eyes were on Holly. "I saw the way you looked at me."

"Harper, don't break shit," Sawyer said before swinging back to Nell.

"I wasn't looking at you," Holly argued. "Not any more than I look at anyone. If you come into my field of vision, I will be forced to look at you, but that doesn't mean anything."

"You were looking at me like a woman looks at a man she wants to screw hard," Holly's assailant said.

"I think she was looking at me that way, too." A second potential mass murderer stepped up.

"Oh, no. I wasn't looking at anyone that way," Holly insisted. "If I was looking at anyone, it was this guy, and I wasn't thinking about anything like screwing him in a hard fashion. I thought maybe we would start with a foot massage."

He was going to have to kill someone and then Nell would get all pissy about nonviolence and she would probably give him a long lecture on why it was wrong to shove a barstool up someone's rectum.

Bishop took a sip of his horrifying vodka. He didn't need a lecture from her. And he didn't need to shove a piece of furniture up some criminal's asshole. Now, hers, yeah he could do that, although it wouldn't be a piece of furniture and he wouldn't shove. No way. He would be smooth and slow. He would take his time getting that perky, tight asshole ready to take his dick. She would fight him at first, the muscles clenching to keep him out, but he would have his way. Sooner or later, his cock would slide in and then she would fight to keep him inside. That was what he needed.

"Are you going to help me with this, professor?" Max's bark brought him out of his lovely daydream. No one seemed content to leave him be in this place. First, the kids broke up what should have been a nice long fuck, and now the violence was pulling him from thinking about a nice long fuck. The whole town of Bliss seemed intent on cockblocking him.

Holly was now surrounded by five large men who had started to use the term gangbang.

The blonde had jumped off her barstool and she got to Holly before Max could. She swung her backpack like it was a weapon. "You get your hands off of her, you filthy piece of crap. All of you better back away from her."

Chaos. Wow. It was taking over. One minute everything was fairly peaceful, and now it looked like they were on the verge of Armageddon. One of the assholes screamed as the blonde's backpack hit him in the head. She moved well. She was trained, and not in a cardio-at-the-gym way. He would bet she was some form of law enforcement. Or she had been before she'd decided to backpack across America.

"I'm not underage," Seth said with a confident grin. He stood at the bar talking to Sawyer. "I have the ID to prove it."

"It's a fake," Sawyer shot back.

"Prove it." Seth held out his ID.

Sawyer rolled his eyes. "I don't have to. That's Logan Green. He's barely nineteen. He graduated from high school last year."

Seth held up a second ID. "You're wrong. His name is Orion Buchwald. He's twenty-two. We don't know this Logan Green you speak of."

Logan sighed. "Please don't call my moms."

Nell's eyes met Bishop's and then quickly slid away, refocusing on the bartender. "Do you have any organic liquor?"

A rough shout pulled him back to the Holly issue. "Look, bitch, I can take you, too."

He was going to have to deal with the muscular assholes. The whole bar was watching the scene play out.

"You better find some cover." Max got off his barstool. "These things can get nasty."

"Don't you try anything." The blonde reached into her bag as Max stepped up. It was obvious she didn't know he was trying to play savior. "I have pepper spray."

"Why would you pepper spray me? I'm trying to help. Damn. I get sprayed too much as it is." Max took a step back.

"I don't think violence is the answer." Nell had inserted herself into the situation, her hands out in a placating gesture. "We should sit down and have a sharing circle."

Why did he want her? Oh, yeah. Her boobs were really nice. And she had those freaking lips. "Don't get closer."

She was about to get into the middle of this, and that meant he would be forced to take over.

"I'd like a beer." Seth bellied up to the bar like he didn't have a care in the world. Little bastard.

Bishop slid off his barstool. Fuck all. He should pick Nell up and leave, but she would likely protest that action, too. "Nell. Get back here, now."

She frowned his way. "Why should I listen to you? You left me."

She'd come after him. No doubt about it. So the sweet thing was really interested. Now the only problem was the way the world was falling apart around him. "I was thirsty. Get behind me."

"You didn't say good-bye." Nell crossed her arms over her breasts. He could remember the way her nipples had pressed into his chest before the Stark kid had interrupted him.

"I'm not giving you a beer." Sawyer rolled his eyes at Seth.

"Hey, you should get your hands off her." Logan seemed to have stopped worrying about his moms once he finally caught sight of what was happening with Holly.

"Hey!" Seth followed his friend's eyes and stopped bitching about his lack of a beer. He came off his stool and started making his way toward men who outweighed his skinny ass by a hundred pounds of muscle. "I don't think she wants you touching her."

"You two kids better step the fuck back, and blondie there can come with us, too." He numbered the combatants one through five since he preferred a neat order when it came to killing. The biggest of the mean assholes managed to get a hand in the blonde's hair. He tugged her head back.

"My name is Laura, bastard. I'm the blondie who's going to kick your ass." She struggled, trying to get those killer heels to sink into his foot.

Max took a punch to his gut, but it oddly seemed to make him happy. He threw himself at his opponent, his fists flying.

Everyone got in on the action. Almost faster than his eyes could track, the entire bar erupted in pure chaos. Bishop sighed and eyed the door, hoping for a clear path out. The truth was none of this was his problem. Holly had come to the wrong place looking to get laid. The blonde chick was obviously in some sort of trouble, likely on the run from something she'd done. The two kids were obnoxious, and a near-death experience would toughen them up. Max Harper seemed to have found his nirvana, and the dude behind the bar was a baby criminal with the patch to prove it.

Not his problem.

Nell, on the other hand, was. He took her hand and started to lead her out.

"Henry, what are you doing?" Nell asked, her cruelty-free shoes scooting across the floor.

Bishop kept walking. "Getting you out of here. They don't want to join in a sharing circle, Nell. You're going to get hurt."

"My friends are already getting hurt." She tried to pull away from him. "What's wrong with you? We can't leave them."

He heard a crash and someone screaming. He totally could leave them. If he stayed much longer, he would get a headache. "They'll be fine."

She pulled at his arm, finally dropping to the floor, her dead weight causing him to turn. He was surprised to see tears streaming down her face. He was amazed at how much the sight kicked him firmly in the gut. "You go on. I have to help my friends."

She weighed maybe a hundred and fifteen pounds. She'd almost surely never been in a fight in her life. She claimed she abhorred violence, and he believed her.

"They're fighting, Nell. What are you going to do?" Bishop asked.

"I don't know, but I can't leave them." She got to her feet.

"You're going to get hurt."

"Then I get hurt. I'll hurt worse if I know I didn't try. Let me go."

She would do it, he suddenly understood. She would walk into that chaos and try to talk reason to people who would kill her before they would listen to a word she said. She was stupid, and Bishop sort of admired her. He finally got what Sawyer had been trying to tell him. Nell believed, but even more than that, Nell was willing to put herself on the line for her beliefs. They weren't empty words to her. They were who she was.

He pulled her back. "I will take care of it on one condition."

"Take care of it?" She was shouting over the chaos. "How?"

He wasn't about to tell her the how of it. "I'll take care of it but you have to go out with me tonight and you can't blame me for what I'm about to do."

She nodded. "Don't kill anyone, Henry. That kind of karma is hard to shake."

He had so much of that karma he was up to his ears in it, but he gave her a nod. "And don't watch. Just trust me. Can you trust me?"

She put a hand on his chest and closed her eyes. "Don't get hurt, Henry."

It was five against one, like that could hurt him. The main problem he had was saving the civilians, though Max Harper was doing a fine job on his own. He was gleefully taking apart his guy, and Sawyer had another in a headlock. Asshole Number One was trying to pull both Holly and Laura around the bar, likely to get them to the parking lot. Assholes Three and Five were dealing with the kids. Three had Seth Stark's lanky body dangling from his hand, the kid's sneakers kicking for the second time that day. Logan was faring better, surprisingly. He was taking a chair to his asshole's back.

Bishop started with the girls. He walked straight up to Asshole One, no hesitation.

"Get back or I'll have to kill…" Asshole One started in a gruff voice, but Bishop was already close enough. He let his booted foot come back and kicked the fucker's balls so hard he was pretty sure they now resided somewhere next to his large intestine.

The big guy dropped his hold on the women and went down with a low groan. This was the moment when he would normally give his opponent a nice adjustment to vertebrae C1 and C2, and then no one ever had to worry about him again, but he'd made a promise so he merely picked up the nearest bottle. Vodka. No great loss. One little tap and the glass was broken and the asshole was out for a while.

"Thanks." The blonde, Laura, put a hand on her lower abdomen. She'd gone pale, the blood draining from her face. "I think I might have popped a few stitches."

"Go sit with Nell and we'll make sure you get to a hospital." Bishop turned and assessed his next victim. Though he thought the Stark kid was obnoxious, he was also turning a nice shade of blue. If Bishop had his way, he'd get this guy with one punch to the solar plexus. He would break the man's xiphoid process, neatly shoving it into his diaphragm and causing an almost instant death. Instead, he took the boring route and wrapped his arm around the man's neck, cutting off the blood flow to his brain and causing a very quick trip to nighty-nightville.

Seth Stark hit the ground, his chest heaving. "Thanks."

"Go protect the girls." He didn't truly intend for Seth to protect anyone, but he needed to give the kid something to do.

"Logan," he started, looking back to his best friend.

"Is doing just fine." Logan was a mean shit in a fight. His form sucked ass, but he made up for it with pure bile and rage. It was a beautiful thing. And he had to stop it because Nell would be upset by the blood.

He decided to take this shithead out long range. He grabbed Max Harper's empty beer bottle and aimed for the dude's meaty head. One nice *thunk* and Logan was left with a completely defeated opponent.

Logan looked down at the man, scratching his head. "Did I do that?"

"Sawyer, Max, finish them off or I'll do it for you." Those two were perfectly capable of handling it.

Max punched out one last time, blood coming off his fist as he broke his opponent's nose. He got to his feet with a frown on his face. "Spoilsport. I was having fun."

Sawyer finally seemed to find the right angle to cut off his guy's circulation. His opponent went limp, and he slid to the floor.

"That took you long enough. You need to practice more," Bishop said. It had been a sloppy takedown.

"Who the hell are you? Where did you learn that shit?" Sawyer asked, new respect in his eyes.

He learned that shit in Delta Force and later refined it in the CIA. Yeah, he wasn't telling anyone that.

"Krav Maga classes." He stretched his hands out, popping every knuckle, and gave them his best professorial smile. "I take it with the other history professors at my college. You have to keep the body limber, too, you know."

"Henry, can I open my eyes now?" Nell's voice carried across the room.

"Yes, sweetheart. It's over and everyone is alive." He hoped. The beer bottle to the head had been a little stronger than he would have liked. Nope. The asshole was still breathing. Excellent. The asshole would only be brain damaged, but he hadn't seemed that smart before.

"Idiot youngsters, come on. The first and only beer is on me. You did good, boys." Sawyer popped the tops on two cold ones.

Nell flew across the room. One minute Bishop was standing alone and the next his arms were full of Nell.

He wrapped her up and hugged her close. Something settled inside him when she was in his arms. He didn't even try to pretend like he wasn't smelling her hair.

"You did it. Thank you, Henry. Thank you." Nell squeezed him tight.

"Guys, can y'all take it from here?" Holly asked. "I'm going to take Laura into Del Norte and get her looked at. She had surgery a week ago. I'm really sorry. I'm going to stop going to bars looking for my soul mate. It gets me in trouble. If my luck holds, my soul mate is in Russia or Africa or someplace. He's definitely not here."

"I'll drive you," Max said. "Rye would have my head if I didn't."

Sawyer looked up from the bar. "How about you, professor? Want a drink? It's on the house."

"No," he said, unable to stop staring at Nell, who was looking at him like he was a goddamn hero. "I can't. I have a date."

Chapter Four

Henry glanced around the small diner he found himself in and wondered if he'd managed to fall into a time machine. Stella's Café proclaimed itself to have been established in 1970, but if he'd been forced to guess, he would place it all back in the fifties from the vibe coming off of it. Oh, the occupants of the place looked modern enough. They had cell phones and such, but every time the café doors opened, each patron looked up and waved at whoever happened to be walking through the doors.

It was weird. It was disconcerting.

It was kind of cool. It was absolutely the last place a spy should be. Everyone knew everyone else, and any new person would likely be vetted and ruthlessly pursued in order to force them to fit in. Though fitting in here seemed fairly easy, if the bald dude with the weird rat was any indication.

"Princess has been so calm all week. She's been real regular, if you know what I mean. I think it's going to be a nice winter. You know she can tell the weather," the man was saying as he held what looked like a furless rodent but was probably some sort of chihuahua. And if this was what the "dog" looked like calm, he would hate to see her agitated. Her whole body shook and she had the weirdest bug eyes. Yet the man in coveralls held her close and petted her scraggly head. "She loves the sweater you knitted for her, Miss Nell."

Nell beamed under the praise. She seemed to thrive on it. As every good sub did. "She looks adorable in it."

Sure enough the dog/rodent/weather clairvoyant was wearing a tiny sweater. It was purple and probably organic cotton.

"Who's your fellow here?" The bald guy turned his way and held out his free hand.

"Henry Flanders." He shook the man's hand. It was getting easier and easier to say that name. If he wasn't careful, he could fall into Henry Flanders's life and not want to come back out.

He hadn't meant to see Nell again. He'd realized the danger she posed and yet the first chance he'd gotten, he'd taken it. He should have driven her right back to the resort and passed her off to her mother, but no, he was sitting in a diner that served burgers and fries, cream pies and sundaes, and something called elk risotto ala Hal. Yeah, he wasn't trying that.

"Long-Haired Roger," the man replied. "And obviously this is Princess. Hey, I need to talk to Nell for a second. Would you mind holding Princess?"

Yes, he minded. He didn't hold lapdogs. On occasion he set carefully trained attack dogs on the bad guys, but he didn't give Fido a cuddle after he'd taken out some assassin's throat.

He should tell the weirdo to hold his own dog, but Nell was looking at him expectantly. She slid out of the booth and stood next to the poorly named Long-Haired Roger, staring at him like what he did next would help form her opinion of him.

So he found himself holding that shaking thing in his hands as they walked away. Roger drew Nell over to the counter where he leaned over and started talking to her.

He was not comfortable with pets, didn't understand them at all. He held the dog in both hands because Nell would likely protest him if he dropped the thing.

He hadn't ever had a pet. He vaguely remembered a cat from his childhood. An orange tabby who would curl up in his mother's lap as she read at night. It would purr, and the sound soothed him.

Be gentle, Johnny. We have to take care of her.

God, he hadn't thought about that cat in years.

He shook his head and the dog was staring right at him, big bug eyes looking into his soul. The dog didn't care that he'd killed before, that he wasn't a good man. The dog only cared that someone fed it, took care of it. It didn't care about anything else.

It was only a trick of nature that made those eyes look kind, like the dog gave a damn. It was shaking, but it didn't bark or whimper. It simply

69

was. It accepted itself.

He pulled the dog in close, tucking her against his chest. It was only so she would stop the shaking thing. And his arms would get tired if he held her like that for too long. It wasn't because she looked so pathetic. It wasn't because she needed comfort.

The dog lifted her head and then he was getting doggie kisses.

He glanced down and it was another biologic trick that the dog looked grateful and happy. There wasn't any true emotion in the animal. Dogs were like any other creature. They were looking out for themselves.

Except he was almost sure that dumb cat had mourned when his mother died. She'd wandered through the house searching for her just like he had.

"Oh, look at that." Roger was standing by the booth as Nell slid back in across from Henry. "She's really taken to you. You must be good people, Henry Flanders. Princess is an excellent judge of character."

She was a terrible judge of character, but he found himself a bit reluctant as he gave the dog back. "That's good to know. I'll put that on my CV."

Nell beamed at him before looking back at Roger. "That's his curriculum vitae. He's a college professor."

She said it like she was proud of who he was.

He didn't know who he was. What would she say if she knew his real résumé? If she read his true bio.

John Bishop is excellent at manipulating situations to get what he wants. He's made a career out of finding his enemies and making them pay. Strengths: internal decapitation, ability to get excellent young men to leave their futures behind in order to follow him into questionable service. Weaknesses: None until he met an overly idealistic brunette and her weird-ass town.

"That's impressive, but then we always knew you would end up with a smart guy," Roger said, settling Princess against his chest. "Well, I better skedaddle. We've got to meet this one's momma. Liz Two gets upset when we're not on time. 'Night, Nell."

He started to leave, but Henry noted he stopped at every table to say something to the patron sitting there. "Long-Haired Roger?"

Nell simply smiled in that "take his breath away, goddess of all things" beautiful way of hers. "He used to have long, flowing hair back in the sixties. It was lovely until it fell out. Some people say it was due to genetics, but I worry about being around all those chemicals. He owns a mechanic shop in town. He's been around a lot of chemicals in his time. It could have affected him on many physical levels."

"And the dog, too."

"Oh, Princess is a rescue dog," Nell explained. "She's got several ailments. The shaking is her way of trying to regulate her body heat. She's also been diagnosed with anxiety. Roger is always trying to make sure she feels safe and secure. And I'm not sure she's a good indicator of our weather. She pretty much shakes all the time. He wanted to talk to me about her birthday. It's coming up. He wants another sweater and some booties for her paws. He didn't want to spoil the surprise by asking in front of her."

He ignored the obvious problems with that scenario because he had other questions. "Is there a Liz One?"

She nodded. "Yes. But we don't talk about her around Roger because she's Liz Two's sister and they're currently feuding and have been for over three years. Liz One wanted to name her daughter Princess and feels like Liz Two should have respected that and not named her dog Princess."

"What did she name the daughter?" He wasn't sure why, but he was curious. Bliss was a mystery to him, more so with every single person he met.

Nell shook her head. "Oh, she doesn't have one. But she might one day. I mean she's forty-nine, but it's been known to happen. Also, her husband had a vasectomy, so I think it's more like a wish, but she takes that name seriously. I've been trying to orchestrate a peace summit between them, but I can't get either sister to agree to a place. Do you know what you want? Or did you eat something at Hell on Wheels? I didn't think about that when I suggested having dinner."

He wouldn't have eaten anything at that rattrap bar. "I didn't eat anything. I'll probably have a steak or a burger if it won't bother you."

It shouldn't matter if his eating meat would bother her or not. He should eat whatever he wanted to. He didn't ask permission. And yet he found himself wanting to please this one petite woman.

He was in trouble with her.

She seemed startled that he'd asked the question. "Uhm, I'm not going to tell anyone else how to live. You should eat whatever fills your soul, and if that's another soul, then…uhm live and let…I've heard the burger's good."

"Then why do you protest me every Thursday?" A woman with a battle helmet of bleach blonde hair stood at the head of their table, a notepad in her hand. She wore skintight jeans, embroidered cowboy boots, and a Western shirt that had to contain most of a craft store's rhinestone section. The woman, who he guessed was likely in her mid-forties, frowned down at him. "Don't you let her lie to you. She tells everyone how to live."

"But I also eat lunch here every Thursday," Nell argued.

"You eat where you protest?" He didn't understand her.

She had flushed a pretty pink. "Protesting makes me hungry, and Stella's always has a vegan option. And that was all due to my protesting, might I point out. Change has happened right here. I changed Stella's heart and her mind."

The woman named Stella shrugged. "She did change my menu. I can only listen to "We Shall Overcome" so many times. It was easier to offer a daily vegan special. And honestly, it's not so bad. We've got tourists who come here specifically because we have a vegan menu. The only other café close by with vegetarian options is the Sunshine Café."

Nell shuddered. "It's in Del Norte, right next to the big game processing store."

Stella waved that off. "Now I can force the mayor to eat a meal that won't send him immediately into a heart attack, though he complains something fierce about it. And Mel's happier because at least once a week I serve something with beets."

"Is this Mel person a beet farmer?" Henry asked.

"Aliens are afraid of beets," Stella explained.

"And I would protest that we're being very unwelcoming of our alien friends except I really don't think we have a large population showing up here in Bliss." Nell handed Stella her menu. "I support Mel in his beliefs, though. Also, beets are one of nature's superfoods."

"Yes, they make my teeth super pink," Stella pointed out. "And Mel firmly believes Bliss is the potential epicenter of a coming invasion. The mountains attract them or something. Now I know what this one is having for dinner. Hal made you quinoa and black bean delight. Your favorite."

He didn't get it. Despite the fact that the blonde was obviously annoyed by Nell, she was smiling at her and offering her exactly what she wanted. He lived in a world where that would be seen as weakness.

Nell practically glowed as she blew a kiss back toward the kitchen where a rough-looking older man stood, a big spatula in his hand. "You're the best, Hal. Thank you. I love it so much."

The gruff-looking dude who had likely seen combat at some point gave her a wink and a nod. "Always for you, sweetheart. Does your friend want some, too? He looks like he can eat. Luckily I made extra for you to take back up the mountain. Despite what Princess's bowel movements might indicate, the weatherman says we're in for a bad storm. Lots of snow. I hate the thought of you stuck up there eating nothing but granola."

Stella looked expectantly at him. "You want a helping, professor? I heard you teach history somewhere along the West Coast."

So the rumor mill was strong in this town. He shouldn't be surprised. Nell seemed to be firmly planted in the small town. They would look out for their own. He should remember that.

Nell was staring at him. "Like I said, I've heard the burger's pretty good."

He handed the menu back to Stella. "Sure, I'll have two and some fries."

Nell was suddenly looking any way but his and he almost told Stella he'd changed his mind. But he didn't because he wasn't about to change his life for some woman he'd recently met. He wouldn't do it because he wanted so badly to be the one to make her smile. That was ridiculous.

Stella nodded and strode back toward the kitchen to put their order in.

"So tell me all about this place." It was better if she talked. It would definitely be more truthful if she talked since everything that came out of his mouth would be a lie.

For the briefest moment, he thought about talking about Buttons with her. That had been the cat's name. He considered telling her about how Princess had made him think about his mom's cat and how he wished he knew what had happened to her after his mother passed. He could remember vividly the social worker putting the cat in a cage and telling him no one would take them both in. She'd promised to find them both a home, but it wouldn't be together.

It had been that final piece of his mother carted out and carried away in a cage to a future no one thought he had a right to.

"Bliss is the best," Nell said with a sigh. "I bless the day we met Pam Sheppard. We would never have come here without her. We would still be in a tiny apartment in Denver. Don't get me wrong. Denver is beautiful, but it's still a large city."

She went on and he shoved down the impulse to tell her something real about himself.

He couldn't tell her anything real because he was leaving. Henry Flanders was going to disappear, and John Bishop needed to never have existed in her mind.

But he wanted to tell her.

He sat back and let her talk, his mind whirling with the idea that she really could be his weakness.

Two hours later, he walked behind her as she stopped at the door to her room. He'd spent the whole dinner utterly fascinated by her.

And that was a problem.

He'd thought he could fuck her and enjoy her and walk away. He'd planned on her being nothing more than a fun vacation fling. Hell, part of the whole vacation was getting to be someone else for a few days. He did it all the time. His job was about sinking into another persona and fooling everyone around him.

He'd wanted to be John Bishop. Not the operative. No, it was far worse than that. He'd wanted to be the John he'd been before the Agency had gotten hold of him, to tell her about his childhood and find some comfort in her empathy.

Nell Finn was a dangerous woman.

"This is me." Nell stopped in front of the door and her sweet face was turned up to him, an air of expectation making her blush.

She thought he would insist on coming inside with her, make his play to spend the night.

Who the hell would he be in the morning if he spent a whole night in Nell Finn's bed?

He wasn't sure he could afford to find out. He stood there, completely at a loss for once in his adult life.

Nell tucked her hair behind her ear and shifted from one foot to the other, a nervous energy surrounding her now. "Uhm, would you like to come in for some tea?"

If he walked into her room, he wouldn't come out until morning. Hours before it was everything he'd wanted to do—the only thing he'd wanted. Now, after spending real time with her, he was unsure.

She was a mystery, and he wasn't sure he could untangle her. She might always be a mystery to him because she might just be his polar opposite. She believed in so many things.

He wasn't sure he believed in anything.

"I should get to bed." He took a step back, well aware this rejection was going to hurt her. He didn't like the fact that the idea made him queasy.

Her eyes widened and he saw the moment it sank in that he was leaving, that things weren't going to go the way she wanted them to. "Oh. Of course. It's getting late. Well, uhm, good-bye then."

She didn't move to open the door. It was obvious she was waiting for him to make any kind of move. She was offering herself up and he was a fool to not take her.

But she was a trap, a pretty, sweet and comfortable trap, and he couldn't afford to get caught.

He nodded and forced himself to turn away.

He heard the door close between them and the snicking of the lock.

It was better this way. He could go back to his room and think about heading back out in the field. He wasn't cut out for vacationing, it turned out. He would call up Taggart or Tennessee and see if they needed any aid. Once he was back in his world, things would normalize again.

Yet when he got to his room he didn't pick up his phone. He sat on the edge of his lonely bed and stared at the TV for a while. He thought about trying to sleep, but he knew it wouldn't work. Hours after he'd dropped Nell at her door, he was still thinking about her and knew he wouldn't sleep that night. Suddenly the small room that had been cozy before now seemed too tight and he needed to get out.

He walked down the quiet hallway, not really considering where he was going, and found himself in a courtyard, the chill of the air penetrating through his coat.

Yes, he would make that call soon.

He sat down on one of the picnic tables as the snow began to fall and looked up.

The stars twinkled above him, a carpet of diamonds shining down. He never looked at the sky unless he was trying to figure out how someone could send a bullet his way.

It was beautiful.

He laid back and stared and wondered what Nell would think.

Chapter Five

Nell walked out of her room and wondered if she was doomed to always be stuck in the friend zone. She moved down the hallway toward the door that led to the courtyard, a restless energy taking over. Was she one of those women who fell firmly into that class for all men? Like she was perpetually placed in "you're like a sister to me" mode.

It was precisely what she'd been thinking for two hours since Henry had dropped her off at the door of her room at Mountain and Valley without so much as a hug. It wasn't how she'd expected to spend her evening. He'd been so passionate in her cabin. He'd held her and she'd felt the hard ridge of his erection nudging her and she'd thought, "Finally."

And then nothing.

Their date hadn't gone the way she'd thought it would. They'd sat in a booth at Stella's for three hours and not once had he touched her. He'd been a perfectly pleasant companion. He'd let her do most of the talking, urging her to give him her thoughts on topics that ranged from politics to TV shows, but he hadn't reached out and brushed his hand along hers or let his knees rest against hers.

She opened the door to the courtyard and breathed in the chill of the night air. It was time to face a few logical facts. She wasn't a great beauty. Sure, she wasn't an ogre or anything, but she didn't have Holly Lang's figure-eight body or the model good looks of the blonde they had rescued at the bar. Even Callie had a nice set of breasts and sweet good looks. Nell wasn't going to lie to herself. She was sort of plain and earthy and, beyond that, she could be obnoxious when it came to her beliefs. Not an appealing combination for many men. Lots of times men walked away the minute she opened her mouth.

She buttoned up her coat and strode out into the courtyard. He hadn't even kissed her good night. He'd made a big deal about asking her out, and then he'd dropped her off at her doorstep and walked away. It didn't take an idiot to know he'd changed his mind about wanting her. Maybe because he'd gotten a look at Holly and realized there were much better prospects in Bliss.

Nell growled a little. She wasn't going to think that way. She liked Holly. Holly had been through a lot, and just because Nell wanted a man who likely thought Holly was more attractive didn't mean that she would be unkind to Holly. Holly couldn't help the fact that she had great boobs and Nell didn't. Women should stick together, not allow a man to come between them. Holly was her friend, and if she started dating Henry, then Nell would stand by her and support her.

Perhaps she was meant to be alone like her mother had been for her whole life.

Snow covered the courtyard, the world blanketed in white. She walked across, leaving small imprints where her feet touched the earth. This was what she needed. If she stayed in her borrowed room, she would end up crying and feeling sorry for herself. She'd wanted to go back to the cabin, but apparently Henry had called Rye and he was going to close the place up for the night, so now she was stuck here. She wasn't going to let one man who didn't want her wreck her night. It was beautiful in a way only Bliss was. The air was fine, and the stars made a map of the heavens.

Nell turned her face up. A billion stars shone down on her, every single one a miracle. This was what she needed. She needed to be alone and to find her peace. She would sit out here for a few minutes and soak in the beauty of this particular night. There would never be another one like this one. It was like a snowflake—perfectly unique.

"What do you see?"

She gasped and turned. Henry was sitting on the tabletop of one of the picnic benches. So much for being alone and finding peace. "What?"

His face was serious in the moonlight. Naturally he had to be here, sitting there with his graceful body and handsome face. "What do you see when you look up at the sky?"

She shook her head, trying to figure out why he was here. He didn't seem like the kind of man who looked up at the sky as his evening's entertainment. "Why do you care?"

His head turned up, and she could see the way he squinted as he looked at the stars. "Because I see a bunch of stars that died a long time ago, but I don't think that's what you see."

"No," she replied. She glanced up. The night sky was so beautiful. Velvet and diamonds. "That's not what I see, but I'm not dumb. I took science classes. I know the light we see is old."

His face turned back down, staring at her. "Light travels at a speed of one hundred and eighty-six thousand, two hundred and eighty-two miles a second. Given that speed and the relative vastness of the universe, it isn't hard to deduce that some of those stars we look at every night are already gone, turned supernova and blasted from existence, but hey, it's pretty, right?"

Maybe Henry was as cold as the snow under her feet. She was starting to shiver. She had on galoshes and they weren't doing a lot to keep the chill away. She should have put on a fourth pair of socks. "You want to bring science into something that should be emotional. Should we not find a flower in bloom lovely?"

"A flower in bloom is dying." He pointed a finger at her like she'd just stepped into a trap he'd set.

Was she back in debate club? "Yeah, well, a baby just born is dying."

"My point exactly."

She shook her head. Why was he killing her perfectly pleasant alone time? She was supposed to be able to come out here and let him go, not argue against his nihilistic views of the universe. "If I listened to your argument and gave it an ounce of credence, I would just kill myself because nothing matters."

He shrugged as though that was a foregone conclusion. "Hence my question. What do you see?"

She sighed. She should leave, but there was something deep inside her that just couldn't shy away from a fight. "I see light and life. Yes, it might be from a long time ago, but I'm alive in this moment and that's all that matters right now. I see a blanket of life. I see the cradle of creation."

He snorted. "You're going to tell me *you* believe in God?"

"Why wouldn't I?"

He simply stared at her as though the answer was obvious.

She took a long breath. All in one day she'd been called a lesbian and an atheist. Neither one was a bad thing to be, but getting labeled hurt. "You're really more small-minded than I thought you would be. I believe that love exists at the heart of the universe. I don't know how or why we exist, but I know deep down that it's to serve that love and to learn from it. It might not be God as you know it, but it's real and valuable to me."

"How do you know?" He whispered the question, but there was an odd desperation behind it.

"What do you mean?"

He jumped off the table, his feet hitting the snow. His face was a perfect, gorgeous blank. "How do you know there's some pocket of love at the center of the universe? How do you know we're not fucking random and we live and we die and that's the end and nothing matters? What's your empirical evidence?"

Henry seemed to be a professor right down to his soul. She tried to find a way to explain it that he would understand. She went back to her college physics class. "All right, the first law of thermodynamics teaches us that nothing is lost."

He shook his head and gave her a grunt. "That describes energy in closed systems, Nell. Do better."

She crossed her arms over her chest, standing her ground. "No. You think bigger. Energy converts. It changes form. It isn't lost. Why would our souls be lost?"

There was a brisk laugh that came out of his mouth. "You're running on the very sketchy theory that we humans have souls in the first place."

She sighed. He wasn't the one for her if he didn't even believe in souls. "I have a soul, Henry. You do, too. Nothing in the universe is wasted. Everything evolves for a reason. There's no biological reason for the ability to love, for the human need to sacrifice for others. Tout Darwinism all you like. I believe in the theory, too, but only to a point. It isn't present when one human being sacrifices his life for another. It isn't there when a man runs into a burning building on the off chance that he can save the people inside. It isn't there when a thousand soldiers run onto a beach they know they will die on because they want their children to be free. Darwinism isn't there when people risk their lives to stand up for what they believe in when they know they're going to die for it."

He was silent, simply standing there, his big body stiff and unmoving. There was a flat line to his mouth that told her she hadn't gotten through to him. He'd been perfectly polite during dinner, but at some point he'd changed his mind about her because he thought she was a flake.

79

The funny thing was she still would have gone to bed with him. All she'd required from him was that he be polite and somewhat kind. She was ready to understand sex. She felt something deep for him. It didn't necessarily matter that he didn't love her. She couldn't control that, and he was only here for a little while, so she'd been okay with it. But he didn't even like her. He was like a million other people. He thought she was a naïve idiot. She couldn't sleep with a man who didn't even like her. She was too picky. She'd finally found a man who called to her and he was like so many. Closed-minded. Unwilling to listen or to think even for a moment that she had something important to say.

She couldn't sell herself so cheaply.

Perhaps the time had come to ask Holly about a vibrator. Holly talked about sex toys sometimes. She could name it and have a relationship with it. When she wasn't in the mood, maybe she could watch the news with it sitting on the pillow beside her.

God, even her potential sex life with an inanimate object was boring. Henry was still standing there staring, and it was time to cut her losses.

"Uhm, I guess I'll go back inside. Thanks again for dinner." He'd been a gentleman, insisting on paying. She turned to go. She would read until she fell asleep, if she could fall asleep. But she had to get out of here. She couldn't stand how cold her feet had gotten.

Nell had moved exactly two steps before he was in front of her, his big chest a wall blocking her progress.

"I don't understand you," Henry said, his face a complete blank.

"You don't have to."

He was close. So close. She could feel the heat of his body. "I should leave you alone."

Then why wasn't he? Tears threatened. God, she hated that. She couldn't be calm. She always had to get emotional. No matter how many times she got kicked, her heart still got involved. Her brain was willing to let go, but her heart still wanted, and she couldn't seem to make it stop. "Then go away. I didn't come out here looking for you. I'm not going to follow you around. I promise I'm not going to bug you. It was a bad date. We can both walk away."

He frowned, his face setting in hard lines. "It wasn't a bad date. It was nice. I liked talking to you."

She rolled her eyes. "I'm not stupid. You didn't have a good time. You got rid of me as fast as you could."

"No, I didn't. The cook said there was a storm coming in. I wanted to get up the mountain before it hit. I'm not used to driving in the snow."

He'd driven with complete competence. "That's dumb. You're an excellent driver. You wanted to get back so you could get away from me."

His eyes seemed to find the ground. "Maybe."

Her heart sank. "Well, don't let me intrude. I'll try to avoid you from now on."

She would do exactly that. She wasn't going to force herself on the man. It hurt too much. Why? She'd only known him for a day, and she didn't truly know him at all. So why was her heart breaking? Why did she think she was missing out on something good? Why did she think she would regret not being with him for the rest of her life?

"Damn it, Nell." His hand shot out, grabbing her elbow and stopping her from walking away. "I'm not good for you."

Yeah, she got that. "Fine. Then let me go."

His fingers tightened. "I tried. Do you have any fucking idea how hard it was to let you go in the first place?"

"I think it was pretty easy since you did it without batting an eyelash. Let me go. My feet are getting so cold." It was sinking into her skin. She was going to embarrass herself by shaking and chattering.

He leaned over and shoved one muscular arm under her knees, hauling her up before she could protest.

"What are you doing?" She'd never been picked up before. She couldn't think of a time she'd been cradled in another human's arms. She'd been a baby, most likely. This was what it felt like to be adored and cuddled and beloved. And she had to make it stop.

He didn't let her go. He started walking toward the doors, his long legs making quick work of the distance. "I'm taking you inside where you'll be warm."

"I can walk on my own."

"But you don't have to. See. This is the problem. You want to be a completely independent female, and I want to carry you around and protect you and do all the dumb crap you shouldn't have to do."

What game was he playing? He was saying one thing and doing another. "Let me down. You made your choice when you dropped me off, and I'm going to do us both a favor and make you keep to it."

"Then you shouldn't have walked outside. You shouldn't have let me get another shot."

He was so frustrating. "I wasn't giving you another shot, you Neanderthal. I was trying to forget you."

He kicked open the door and started walking down the hallway. At this time of night, it was deserted. "And I was trying to forget you, and you made that utterly impossible by walking out into that courtyard. Did you know there are three separate courtyards in this compound? This one is the furthest one from your room."

She kept her voice down. The community was very tolerant, but they did enjoy a bit of gossip. "If you're trying to say I came looking for you, I didn't. I don't even know where your room is."

"It's two doors away from yours." He wasn't even winded. He seemed to support her like she didn't weigh anything at all. "We both walked the furthest destination we could and at roughly the same time. I'd been sitting there for five minutes and wondering if I shouldn't go inside. Either one of us could have taken a simple left or right and we wouldn't have met tonight, but that didn't happen. You walked all the way here and I walked all the way here and we met."

"And we can unmeet."

His head shook. "No, I thought we could, but now I'm wondering."

"You said you were bad for me." She kept arguing, but a bit of hope was starting to light inside her.

"I am, but I'm starting to wonder if you might be good for me." His arms tightened slightly, cradling her closer.

She loved how small she felt in his arms, but she didn't love what he was saying. "That's not fair."

"The world isn't fair. That's why you do half the shit you do."

"It's not shit, and the fact that you can call it that is precisely why you should put me down."

He stopped in the middle of the hall, setting her on her feet. "Fine. If that's what you want."

He pushed every single button she had. Nell started to turn to go, but she just couldn't. Not without giving him a piece of her mind. He'd shoved his mean-spirited beliefs at her and made her feel dumb. She should walk away. It was what she did, but she couldn't. Not when he was standing there looking secure and blasé, like he didn't care at all. "You think what I do is shit?"

"I think it's naïve," he corrected. "It's braver to accept the world as it is. Smarter, too."

An ember of anger settled in her gut. "You know what I think?"

Henry seemed to steel himself. "I think you're probably going to tell me."

"I think you're the coward. I think everyone who accepts that the world is unfair and doesn't do a thing about it, they're the cowards. Doctors push every day to find new medical breakthroughs. Scientists push to invent new technology. And I push every day so this planet is a better place for everyone, and you can look down on me and call me a kook, but people like me are the reason we have a democracy. We're the reason women can vote. We're the reason we have words in our vocabulary like human rights. Philosophers, thinkers, activists are the reason for every breakthrough humanity has made in becoming a more fair place. You think we're not fair now, buddy? Go back a hundred and fifty years and try being a slave in the South. Activists changed that. And they were considered naïve and foolish, too. The things we accept as normal and fair today were once fought for and won by people like me, so I will keep my naïveté and you can keep your cynicism. I hope you two are very happy together."

She turned to go. She wouldn't think about him again. She'd said what she needed to say. Now she could forget him and move on.

Except his hand reached out, grabbing her elbow and spinning her around.

Nell gasped, her body off-balance. She started to stumble, but Henry's arms went around her, hauling her back up. She was right where she'd been before, cradled against his big, strong chest. "What are you doing?"

"Something dumb."

"You put me down."

"I can't. I tried, but you keep talking, Nell." He walked across the smaller courtyard, the one she should have gone to but didn't. It took him about five long strides to get inside the wing where their respective rooms were. "I was going to leave you alone. I was going to play it smart."

What had changed his mind? "Henry, stop."

"I tried to stop. I tried to be the gentleman, but I've decided that the universe doesn't want that."

"You don't believe in a higher power."

"No, but I'm starting to believe in you." He looked down at her, those deep brown eyes of his hot on her face. He'd said the exact right thing to make her melt. She knew she should call him a liar, but she didn't want to. She wanted him. She wanted to know what it was like to be in Henry Flanders's strong arms. He would leave, but she would know what it meant to be held by him, loved by him.

"Oh, Henry, are you going to make love to me?"

He managed to get his door open without ever putting her down. He was in the room in two strides, placing her on the bed. Like all the single rooms at the Mountain and Valley, it was a small double bed.

He looked down at her, one hand finding her hair. "Make love to you? Yes, I think I am. It's going to be a change of pace for me."

She had no idea what he meant by that, but her head was whirling and she wasn't sure she was capable of making a decent decision, and that was kind of cool. Mistakes. She rarely made them, and life was made of brilliantly beautiful mistakes. Her heart might break later, but she would know what it meant to feel this passion.

She wanted. She wanted in a greedy way, and it was lovely. So much of her life was about giving that this moment seemed perfect because it was shared by two people who wanted the same thing. Pleasure. Connection. Love. She wasn't foolish enough to think that making love meant being together forever, but in a way it did. She would remember it forever. He could forget her all he liked. She didn't control that, but this experience would remain in her heart for as long as she drew breath.

Henry unzipped his coat and tossed it to the side. "Give me your coat, and then I want you to take off your shirt very slowly."

He pulled at his own clothes. He wore the same thing he'd worn to dinner. A plain black cashmere sweater over a black T-shirt. He pulled them both over his head and they went the way of the coat, slung to the corner of the room in a random pile. She couldn't help but stare. His chest was a work of art. It was rather shocking. When he was wearing clothes, there was a blandness to his features that belied the hard state of his body. He was quite cute. She wouldn't deny that. He was handsome but in a professorial way, not a superpredatory, athletic way, yet his chest told a different tale. Perfectly sculpted and defined, Henry liked to work out. No doubt about it.

She wasn't close to his level of fitness. She was a little out of shape. She walked a lot, but there was a curve to her belly that never went away no matter how healthy she ate. What would he think when she got her clothes off?

"When I said slow, I didn't mean a snail's pace." He held out his hand.

She took a long breath.

"What's wrong?"

She hated it but she couldn't be less than honest with him. "I'm not as pretty as you."

His dark eyes rolled. "Uhm, I call bullshit on that. You're far prettier, and I want to see you naked. Are you going to give me hell about it?"

He wanted to see her naked, and she kind of wanted to be naked with him. Totally wanted to be naked with him. She could be a coward or she could try to get what she wanted. If he laughed and walked away, she would rethink her stance on nonviolence. She unbuttoned her coat, passing it to him. Unlike his own clothes, he hung her coat up and held out his hand for her shirt.

She shivered in the still chilly air.

"Damn it, you're freezing." His hands went to her feet, pulling her galoshes off and then her socks. His big hands encased her. He put them to his belly, covering them with his palms. Her freezing feet were enveloped in heat, his skin covering her.

It was the sweetest gesture. She was surrounded by his warmth. Her feet. They weren't sexy. There was nothing even vaguely sexual about her feet. His hands rubbed on her skin. After a moment, he pulled one into his hand and started a long, slow rub that nearly made her purr.

"What do you like, Nell?"

She liked him. Oh, she really liked him. "I like social justice."

Sexy. That was so sexy. Well, it was sexy to her. Probably not so much with him.

"I was talking about sex. What do you like sexually?" He kept up the press of his thumb against her foot. Her eyes rolled back, the sensation relaxing her like nothing else could have. She wasn't worried about how she looked. All she could think about was how good Henry was making her feel, and all by simply touching her.

"I have no idea, but I really like the foot rub. It's making me reconsider pedicures. I've heard the technicians at Polly's Cut and Curl always give a foot rub, but I've stayed away because they also use toxic chemicals. Do you think I could get the rub without the chemicals?"

"Nell, are you trying to tell me you're a virgin?" Henry had stopped his slow rub and stood there staring down at her.

Maybe she shouldn't admit to that. He didn't look like he wanted to hear a "yes" to that particular question. "I was trying to tell you about the foot rub."

His eyes hardened. "Are you a virgin?"

She was going to give lying a really good try. "No."

He flipped her over, and she nearly screamed when his hand came down on her backside in a short, sharp arc. "Don't lie to me."

"You spanked me." She felt her eyes widen as she turned and looked back at him.

A slow, infinitely sexy smile crossed his face. "And I'll do it again if you don't answer me honestly. It's not like you can hide it, baby. I'll know the minute I shove my cock inside, so you should tell me now."

"You spanked me, Henry, and you didn't even set up limits before you disciplined me. We don't have a contract." She wasn't dumb. She knew how things worked. She'd read an enormous amount of erotic fiction. Not that she mentioned it to any of her protesting friends. They could be strangely judgmental about reading material.

He flipped her back over. He needed to stop treating her like she was a toy he was playing with. She was about to mention that fact to him when he looked down at her with the darkest eyes. "Who's your Dom?"

"I don't have a Dom." She shook her head. "You were right. I'm a virgin. But you should know I have done some kissing in my time. And some heavy petting."

The truth was she'd led a fairly isolated life when it came to boyfriends. Friends at all. After what had happened to her when she was a kid, she'd kept to herself for fear that saying anything wrong could get her shoved into foster care again.

He didn't laugh, merely loomed over her, holding her wrists in his hands. "What do you know about contracts and discipline?"

"I read books," she admitted. He would laugh at her like everyone else.

"You read books?" He chuckled, a deeply amused sound. "Books about BDSM? You read BDSM romances. You read silly romances, don't you?"

"They aren't silly. I like them." He was going to make her cry again. Damn it. Sometimes those stupid books were all that got her through the day. They were her comfort food.

"Hey, I'm sorry. Don't take it like that. I think it's sweet." He kissed the tip of her nose. "You read erotica. I wouldn't have expected that. I like it, Nell. You can read it to me. We can get hot together and we'll make love."

"They're about love you know." She felt a need to defend her chosen reading.

"Of course they are. You wouldn't read them otherwise." Henry's lips brushed hers, and she started to sink into that nice, drugged feeling she got whenever he was close. "And it makes it easier to explain what I want from you. I want submission."

"I don't know that I'm very submissive." The words came out in a breathy puff that had Henry laughing.

"Not in your normal life, baby, but here you will be. You've reacted beautifully any time I've taken control. Tell me you're not getting wet right now."

"Henry, that's very forward of you." And yes, her panties were in a state from attempting to soak up her arousal. She hoped that one hundred percent organically grown cotton would do the job, but she was getting quite damp.

He pushed off the bed and stood over her. "I'm going to get a lot more forward. You need to make a decision. I want to fuck you tonight. I want to be your man for as long as I'm here, and while I'm your man, I'll be in charge of this part of our lives. I'll let you take control of everything else."

She hated that phrase "for as long as I'm here," but she understood. He was trying to be honest with her. He couldn't stay here forever. He had a job and a life. This was a brief moment in time. This present moment was all anyone could count on. "All right, Henry. For as long as you're here."

"Take off your clothes. I know this is new to you, but you can stop me at any time. No safewords tonight. A 'no' will suffice." He pulled out the chair that accompanied the small desk every single room had. He curled his lean body into it and sat back. "I want to see you naked. I want to see what my little submissive has to offer me."

His little submissive. She wasn't all that small, but the way he said it made her feel sexy. "You really want to see me?"

It seemed too good to be true.

"Baby, I can't fake this." He scooted his hips out, allowing her to see the way his erection tented his pants.

Wow. That wasn't some teeny tiny thing. That was a big thing. A really big penis.

"Nell, take your clothes off or we will start the discipline. I'll start with twenty smacks, and I promise you'll still be naked at the end of it."

Well, put that way, she should do it. She could see plainly that he wasn't going to make this easy on her, and she was okay with that. She could have had any number of men or boys who would have simply taken her because she was available, but she'd wanted someone who wanted *her*. Henry's dark eyes held hers. He wanted her. Nell Finn.

With shaking hands, she pulled the cotton shirt over her head and was left in her plain white cotton bra.

"That's what I want," he whispered. "I'll take care of you. Do you understand what I mean? Do your books cover that?"

Tears filled her eyes. Yes, her books covered that. If she did as he asked, they were entering a kind of contract where he would offer her affection and comfort and protection in return for trust and acceptance. All in all, it was a sweet trade and far more honest than anything she'd been offered before. "Yes, Henry."

"Oh, I like to hear that. No *Sirs* or *Masters*. Just 'yes, Henry.'" He winked at her as his hand found the fly of his pants and started to work the zipper. "Show me your breasts. I've been thinking about them since the minute I saw you in Bill's office. You walked in and I've been hard ever since. I'm going to be gentle, but don't think for a second that I haven't been hot for you all day long."

She let the shirt fall to the bed. He was being honest, and she would do the same. She wasn't some teenager who didn't understand the world. She knew how it worked. Despite her deep love of happily ever afters, she knew the most she could hope for was a happily ever now. She did kind of wish that organic cotton bras came in more attractive fashions. Hers was pretty industrial looking.

"Slowly. Take it off slowly."

She reached around and managed to unhook it. She was deeply aware that she was awkward, but Henry didn't seem to mind. And neither did little Henry, and by little Henry she meant big penis. He pushed aside his pants, kicking them away and freeing his cock. Henry's cock was large and gorgeous, with a beautiful bulbous head. Thick and purple, it pulsed in his hand as he stroked it up and down. His big hand gripped his dick, running from the base to the bulb as his eyes watched her.

She peeled the bra off slowly, her nipples peaking in the chilly air. She'd been naked plenty of times. Her mother loved it up here at Mountain and Valley. They came up for social hours and parties, and Nell never had a single qualm about getting down to her birthday suit, but it felt different now. She felt his eyes on her. Her nipples were hard pebbles. She was going to lose her virginity. She was going to lose her heart. It suddenly hit her that she would love Henry Flanders after this, and he hadn't promised her anything.

But nothing was certain. Nothing in the whole world. And love was worth the risk. She couldn't know that he wanted her for anything more than a night. She could only try. She wanted him. She thought she might be able to really care about him. And if he took her without any caring, that was on him, not her.

But not trying would be on her.

She'd waited for so long, but this was the right man.

She let the bra fall away.

Henry's sigh filled the room. "You are so fucking gorgeous, baby."

His beautiful dark eyes were sleepy and yet laser focused on her breasts. She felt them like a hand caressing her. His voice was a deep rich chocolate, and she could hear the approval in it. It ran down her spine, a sweet shiver that went straight to all her girl parts.

"I think you're lovely, too, Henry."

A slow smile crossed his face. "You would think that." His hand ran up and down his thick cock. "Take off your pants. I want to see your pussy."

Her whole body flushed. How could he talk that way? He didn't have a single problem with dirty words. She'd always found them repulsive until they came out of his mouth in that dark voice of his. Her hands moved almost of their own volition, curving under the waist of her undies and pushing them down. She tossed them off the bed, and she was completely naked and open to Henry Flanders's eyes.

He sighed, the sound a long, wanting brush against her body. "That's just about perfect. You shave. Why?"

"I don't like the whole hair thing." She frowned. She sometimes felt she was in the minority in the protesting world. She knew a couple of very smart women who could probably braid their underarm hair. She'd never seen a lack of grooming as a good protesting measure. "I know it's weird, but I feel better like this."

"Oh, you look better like that. If you were mine, I would have you lasered. I don't want anything between me and my pussy." His hand ran up and down his cock, the length of flesh hard and unrelenting. There was a pearly drop at the tip. His hand flicked over it, using it to make his strokes flow more smoothly. She responded to the sight. Her pussy seemed to pulse as though she could feel everything he was doing to his own cock.

It was wrong. She shouldn't allow some man to tell her what she would do, but she kind of wanted to, and making the decision for herself was the very essence of feminism. She wanted to play with Henry Flanders. She understood what it meant going in, so she wasn't fooling herself. He was here for a brief time. She could have him while he was here. She wanted any time he could give her.

Maybe it made her pathetic to be willing to take so little, but it also made her human and a woman. Women never knew what they would get going into a relationship. Women simply cared and hoped for the best and, when they were smart, forgave themselves if it all went to hell. That last bit was the most important part of all. Forgiveness began at home.

"You look so serious, Nell. This is supposed to be fun."

"It's supposed to be sacred."

His face fell. His hand came away from his cock. She'd said the wrong thing. Silence encroached, and she was deeply aware of how vulnerable she was.

"You're right," he replied slowly. "It's a sacred thing for a woman like you. I want to be here with you. I want it more than anything I've wanted in a long time, but I don't know that I can stay here, and I know damn well I won't bring you into my world. I feel more for you than I've felt for any woman in years, but I won't take something from you that you would rather wait to give. I'm not a good man. I'm rather awful, but I promise I'll take care of you as long as I'm here. I won't look at another woman. I'll only think about you. I'll be yours one hundred percent while I'm here."

Could she ask for more? He was being honest. He couldn't stay and she couldn't go. She had to take care of her mom. Her mother needed her. She and Henry were worlds apart, but they wanted each other. It was so much harder to be honest. He could have promised her to stay or to take her with him, but he'd been brave. He'd tried to set her expectations. He'd been a real man.

"I still want you, but I'll be honest with you, too. I can't go into this telling you that it won't mean anything to me. It will. I'll remember you always. You'll always be my first lover."

He stood up, and for a second she worried he would run out the door. "I won't forget you, either. I know you might not believe me, but you're different from the other women I've been with. Even when I leave, you should know that I won't forget you. All you have to do is tell Bill you need me and I'll come back. I meant what I said. I'll take care of you. If you give yourself to me tonight, it means something. It *is* sacred."

She couldn't ask for more than that. "I would like to be with you. For however long you choose to stay."

His skin flushed, the first real palpable emotion she'd seen in him. He moved toward her, the most serious look on his face. "I'll stay as long as I can. I want you to believe that. I really want you. I think I need you."

For the first time since they'd begun, she was the aggressor. She put her hand out, grasping his, pulling him toward her. She was going to be with Henry Flanders tonight. She was going to be his lover. "Come and kiss me, please."

He needed the politeness. She could see that now. She'd handled him all wrong. People needed different things, and it was wrong to withhold them. Henry needed to be needed. He craved it like a flower needed sunshine. And Nell needed to give. She gave so much, but often to people who didn't want her there. What would it feel like to give to someone who truly wanted her?

Henry stared at her like she was some indecipherable mystery, but his knee met the bed and his hands found her skin. Warmth spread across her as he filled the space between them. He took her into his arms.

"You're screwing up all my plans." Despite the words he said, she could feel a smile spread across his lips as he kissed her cheek.

"I don't mean to." She didn't mean to screw up anything, but she loved the way his arms curled around her. It felt like caring and protection. It utterly disarmed her. She had nothing to put up between them, no arguments, no talk. What could she say to him besides the obvious?

His forehead nestled against hers. "You might not mean to, but you're the sweetest bundle of chaos I've ever come across. You're like Pandora. I can't fucking resist you. I think you might be my downfall."

His hand came up and cupped her breast and she couldn't breathe, much less respond. And, quite frankly, she'd always appreciated the Pandora myth. In Greek mythology, Pandora had been the first woman, their Eve. She'd been the one to bring strife into the world, but also she'd been the one to save hope. Humans were nothing without some struggle. Humans fought and overcame and won. Life wasn't meaningful without a fight.

Love was a fight. Love was something to work for. She wasn't as naïve as everyone thought she was. She knew that even with a little luck, real love took work.

She wouldn't get that from Henry. He would leave, but she could have connection, a momentary bond that could prove that love might happen to her someday. And even if it didn't, she would know what it felt like because she thought she just might love Henry Flanders and that was a beautiful thing.

His lips found hers. She didn't hesitate this time. She flowered open beneath him. She let him in, his tongue surging past her lips to find synchronicity with hers. His tongue rubbed, lighting her up. His mouth slanted over hers, his hands twisting her body in a sweetly bossy way.

Her nipples brushed against the light dusting of hair on his muscular chest. They tightened, pointing out and becoming ridiculously sensitive. Every touch of his flesh seemed to run along her skin. He pulled her close, sweeping the space between them away, closing all distance. The slightly distracted man he'd been was gone, and now he seemed fully in the moment with her. All doubt washed away.

She let her hands wander. He was a deliciously masculine playground. He had muscle after muscle, each one encased in smooth, perfect flesh. She explored his shoulders, so broad and straight. His arms curved, flowing from hard biceps into perfectly curved forearms. His chest was a marvel. He was a mystery, and she so wanted to solve him. She allowed her fingertips to brush his perfectly tight abs.

"Lower, Nell. Touch me." Henry's voice sounded slightly strangled. He took off his glasses and tossed them to the side.

He wanted her to touch his penis. She'd sort of kind of touched one before. Well, she'd felt one with undies between them, but she didn't hesitate. Her hand knew exactly where it wanted to go. She stroked down his stomach to his penis.

"Touch my cock, Nell."

His cock. He wasn't polite. He didn't sit there and hope she did what he wanted. There was a sort of joy in that. She knew exactly what he wanted. She looked down between their bodies. His penis—his cock—was standing at attention, practically begging for a pet. Yes, she could please him. She could be enough for him. She let her palm enclose that big cock of his. So hard and yet so soft. Like the man.

"Fuck, that's it. That feels good. Yeah. Stroke me."

The deep timbre of his voice spurred her on. She liked this whole "talking during affection" thing. Before it had been awkward. She hadn't known where to kiss or touch and she'd pretty much lain back and hoped for the best, but Henry told her what he wanted. He kind of demanded it, and she was happy to comply.

He'd spanked her and ordered her to undress, and he'd fought for her.

She knew it was wrong, but it felt right.

She stroked his cock, her fingers fumbling. "I don't want to hurt you."

His face was a mask of arousal. "You won't hurt me. A cock is solidly built. Stroke me hard. Be rough. I'll like it. I'm going to be a little rough with you. Not tonight, but later. Later, I'm going to play hard, but I promise I'll make you like it. I'll make you fucking crave it."

She already craved him, and she hadn't truly had him yet. She gripped his cock harder, but even flexing her hand, she barely managed to close her palm around him.

He hissed slightly. "That's it. Stroke me. Get me hard and ready to fuck."

He already seemed hard. She wasn't sure how much harder he could get, but she was game to try. She let her hand run the full, long length of his cock. She had zero real experience, but he was so lovely. She stared at the cock in her hand, studying it with eager eyes. Numerous anatomy classes hadn't prepared her for how pretty it was. A long purple vein throbbed under her palm. He was neatly trimmed, with a hint of hair that led down to his balls. Perfect round globes that sat tight against his body. He was beautiful in every way.

"Lie back on the bed and spread your legs for me." His voice had taken on that sweet, bossy tone she'd come to associate with his sexual arousal. And his protectiveness. They seemed to go hand in hand.

She let go of his cock. When he got that tone of voice, he meant business. It was the mistake she'd made at her cabin. She hadn't handled him properly. She could see that now. Henry needed to be in charge of certain things, and when he wasn't allowed to be, he struggled. He'd wanted to protect her, and she'd chosen to defer to the men she knew. At the time, it had seemed like the right thing to do, but Rye Harper had never picked her up and carried her down a hall. He'd never tossed her on a bed and demanded she undress.

She owed something to her lover, no matter how long she'd known him.

It took every ounce of bravery she had, but she spread her legs and let him see her.

His hands found her ankles, brushing restlessly against them. His chest let loose a long, happy sigh as he stared right at that part of her that seemed to start so many political debates.

"Damn, you're lovely." He pressed on her ankles, pushing them up so her knees fell apart and she was fully on display. "I don't understand how you could possibly be a virgin. How can no man have claimed this?"

"I didn't want anyone until you." She wouldn't hide from him.

"I'm glad, baby." His hands started a long, slow crawl up her legs, warming her skin everywhere he touched. "Tell me what you've done. You've kissed, right?"

Not like he kissed her, but she had done something that could be called kissing. "Yes."

His hands were on her knees, moving to her thighs. "Had you ever touched a cock before? Ever taken one in your mouth?"

Henry liked to talk a lot. He hadn't seemed that way earlier. When they were in the car, he'd allowed her to talk the whole time. At dinner, he'd interjected a comment here or there, but for the most part, he'd kept her talking. Now he seemed to really want to talk. "No. I mean, I touched one through clothes, but I certainly didn't do the mouth thing."

"I went too far, didn't I? I went straight from kissing to oral sex. How about second base?"

She shook her head. "Oh, I didn't play softball. I wasn't big into sports."

A laugh came out of his mouth, and she finally got to see a brilliant smile on his face. It made him younger, lighter, so much more dangerous. His hands came out, and his fingertips lightly brushed her nipples. "I was talking about your breasts. Have you had a man play with your breasts?"

She felt a grimace cross her face. "Just some groping in college, and I didn't like it. He pinched me."

He moved on the bed, shifting and getting behind her. "Lie back between my legs."

Nell felt awkward, but she did as he asked, allowing him to get behind her so his back was to the headboard. She scooted toward him, not quite sure what he was planning. His arms came out, drawing her toward him so her back was cradled against his chest, his legs surrounding hers. She was suddenly completely wrapped in strong arms and legs, the intimacy piercing in its sweetness. He'd meant what he'd said. He was going to take care of her. She'd spread herself open for him, given him every indication that she was ready for sex, but he hadn't jumped on top of her. He was giving her real intimacy. He was making the moment special.

He pushed her hair to the side and kissed the nape of her neck, causing her to shiver. "I want to play with your breasts. I want to show you how much I like them, how important they are."

"I don't think they're very sensitive."

"Let me be the judge of that." His big hands came up and cupped her. "Your breasts are like all the other parts of your gorgeous body. They need attention."

His palms moved across her breasts, not groping or grasping but touching and stimulating. She couldn't help the gasp that came from her chest. His fingers played on her nipples, little touches that made her squirm and then long, gentle squeezes. All the while, his lips played at her neck, kissing and licking. She could feel his erection against the small of her back. He was so hard, but he kept playing with her, making her hot. His ankles caught hers, spreading her legs.

"Tell me what you're thinking." He breathed the words against her throat.

"I'm not thinking." It was true. She wasn't thinking at all. She wasn't formulating arguments in her head or going through all the things she needed to do. She was simply feeling.

"That's what I want to hear." His fingers twisted her nipples.

Nell gasped. Pain flared but it quickly turned to heat that coursed through her veins and made a direct line to her pussy. Her legs moved restlessly against his.

"I think you're beginning to understand," he murmured. "This is supposed to be good for you. I can make this very good for you."

It felt good. It felt spectacular. "Yes, Henry."

"Trust me. Put yourself in my hands. Let me take care of you." He pinched her nipples again, his lips on her ear. "Submit to me. Just here in the bedroom. Submit. Tell me I'm the Master here."

He really was the master. "Yes, Henry."

He hissed, his body going hard behind her. "I want you. I'm going to take you."

She found herself flat on her back. One minute she was in front of him, and the next he had flipped himself over and covered her. His weight pressed her down into the bed. Heat from his body poured into hers. She loved the way his chest brushed hers and how they fit together. She felt drugged as he kissed her. His lips caressed hers and then went lower, nuzzling her neck.

"No one's ever sucked your nipples." He sounded like he was talking more to himself than her. As though memorizing an inventory of everything he was taking.

His tongue came out, curling around her nipple. She shivered and then let her hands find his hair as he licked her. He played with her, laving and sucking and then biting down with a sweet sharpness. He switched to the other nipple, giving it the same attention.

"No one's loved your belly." He moved down, his tongue delving into her belly button. He was running his tongue over her, his hands moving her to suit his needs. She didn't have to do anything, just let him adore her.

"And no man's ever gotten a taste of this sugar." His mouth was right over her pussy. Her heart rate tripled. She could feel his heat as his lips hovered. "Tell me no one's ever put his mouth on this pussy and eaten you until you screamed."

Her voice came out in a low huff. "No. No one's ever done that."

And suddenly she really, really wanted someone to do that. Oh, yes. His breath played over her flesh. Anticipation made her body go taut.

"You're going to remain very still, Nell. I want you to reach above your head and grasp the slats on the headboard. You're going to hold on to them, and they will help you to not move while I play with you. You're mine right now. You're going to obey me."

She should be arguing with him, but, no, her hands didn't seem at all interested in protesting what was an obvious male grab for power. Nope. Her arms drifted up, and her suddenly submissive fingers found the headboard and curled around it. Obedience wasn't necessarily a bad word. She obeyed things like traffic laws and karmic laws and the rules of recycling. She was just obeying the rules of sex, and Henry seemed to be an expert. Yes, she could justify it that way.

And then she wasn't thinking at all as Henry's tongue came out, and he licked a long line along her pussy.

She gasped, her hips shifting.

Henry's head came up, his handsome face frowning. "Be still. I'll stop and spank you if you can't obey."

She didn't want him to stop. Maybe this whole sex thing didn't have to be a pure partnership. Or maybe she should rethink her idea of a partnership. It didn't always have to be fifty-fifty every minute of the day. Maybe it could be a sweet symphony where each partner did what they did best in order to please the other. What did Henry need? He needed to be in control here. He was telling her exactly what he needed and not prevaricating about it. It was a great thing when she thought about it.

"I'll be still. But it's hard because it feels so nice, Henry. You're very good at that."

He stared for a minute, his jaw dropping slightly. "Thank you. I've never actually been told that. Not in a verbal fashion."

He needed praise. "You are very, very good. I love the way it feels. I've never felt anything so good."

A slow smile crossed his face. "Oh, I can be even better, love, but I appreciate the praise. You taste so good. You taste incredible. Pure and…fair. You taste fair and right."

She couldn't help but giggle. He was trying. It was actually sweet of him. "I'm so glad. Please won't you kiss me again? I promise I'll be still. I'll try to."

His face, so hard before, softened. "I can handle your enthusiasm. We'll work on it, baby, but for now, I want to eat you up."

His head lowered again, and he made good on his promise. His tongue licked and loved and his lips sucked. His tongue was everywhere, spreading affection. Nell had to concentrate, forcing her legs to stay still. It felt perfect. He ate her like a dessert and for the first time in her life, she felt adored.

Over and over he ran his tongue along her flesh, and his hands left her thighs as though he knew she would stay still. She looked down her body, Henry's dark head at her core. He glanced up, tilting his head slightly. His eyes met hers and he sucked one petal of her labia into his mouth.

She felt the connection flow between them. This was why she'd waited all this time. She'd waited for a man she had a real connection to. He'd annoyed her and tempted her, but she'd felt something electric between them the minute she'd seen him. She might never find this again.

"Tell me how this feels, love." He teased a finger against her pussy.

"So good." She whimpered. It was so hard to stay still, but she'd promised.

"Do you want more?"

She needed more. She needed more than that finger. It dipped in and out of her pussy, teasing inside. "Yes."

"I can give you so much more." The words were warm on her skin. "But you have to give me something first. I want your orgasm. I want to hear you come."

His finger dove deep, and he settled his mouth over her again. He sucked her clitoris into his mouth, and she nearly screamed. Pleasure raced across her skin, heat filling her.

She was bigger than she'd been the moment before. She cried out, calling his name. She was less alone, happier.

Every cell in her body came alive, and she knew she'd found something important.

She settled down. Henry's head came up. "Please make love to me. Please, Henry."

She was ready.

Chapter Six

*P*lease *make love to me. Please, Henry.*

The words rang in his head. Bishop didn't make love. Bishop fucked. He picked his partners for their willingness to fuck and often preferred to pay for the privilege. He'd fucked prostitutes and sometimes he'd fucked for information. Not a single one of those women had looked up at him with clear brown eyes and politely asked him to make love to her.

Not one of them had praised him for the simple belief that they thought he should be praised for his skills. Nell Finn wasn't trying to manipulate him. She wasn't trying to maneuver him into a position where she had the power. She was being her sweet self.

And she wanted him to make love to her, to take her virginity, to be her first man.

John Bishop didn't make love, but maybe Henry Flanders did.

"I'll take care of you." He was shocked to discover he meant every word. He would take care of this woman for as long as he could. She was foreign to him, utterly alien, but so beautiful, and her beauty came from inside. He'd known many more gorgeous women than Nell Finn, but none had challenged him the way she did. Oh, a couple had tried to kill him, but not a single one had made him think the way she did. Her ideas were naïve, but she believed them and maybe, just maybe, she was right. Maybe it took a woman like Nell to change the world, even in the smallest way.

Bishop had spent most of his life fighting in a bloody war to keep the status quo.

Her lips curved up, her hands finding his hair. "I know."

"Nell, I…" He felt a need to reiterate the truth to her. He didn't want to lie. He didn't want to set false expectations. He wanted her more than he'd wanted anything in his life, but he couldn't steal this from her.

Her dark eyes softened, her fingers smoothing his hair back. "I know."

She knew he would leave. She knew he would walk away from her, and she was still offering herself up. She was telling him it was okay to leave her, that she would only take what he had to offer.

What the hell did he have to offer her?

It didn't matter because he was going to be a selfish bastard and take her anyway. He was going to take her because she was payment for everything he'd done. She was his prize. This tiny time with her would carry him through all the rest of the crap he had to do. For the rest of his career, he would know that what he was really protecting was Nell Finn. They would be a million miles from each other, but he would be fighting for her.

He dragged his body up, the taste of her still on his tongue. She'd tasted so good. He normally never ate pussy. His exchanges weren't so intimate, but he wanted Nell to experience everything. He had an overwhelming desire to be her first—her first real dirty kiss, her first intimacy, her first oral, her first sex of every kind. He was craving her. He had days to teach her everything.

But this first time, he was going to teach her how good it could be.

He let his body cover hers. She was small underneath him. He loved how silky smooth her skin was, how she contrasted to him. He suddenly had a deep desire to be the man she needed, a man she would admire.

He wanted to spread her and take her, his cock dominating. He'd never wanted to dominate a woman the way he wanted power over this one, but it wouldn't serve her. He kissed her long and slow, the argument playing out in his head. His cock and his brain were at war. His cock wanted to fuck her until she screamed, but his head wanted to serve her properly, to bind her to him in a way he'd never been bound before.

He kissed her nose, his brain taking control. He wasn't going to be selfish, not tonight. There would be plenty of time to play his games later, but he was going to give her tenderness tonight. She was warm and wet and willing, but he wanted this to last.

"Tell me you want me." He breathed the words against her cheek, adoring the way her arms had wound around him. He was surrounded by Nell, her skin touching his, the smell and taste of her filling his senses. He needed to hear the words. He couldn't take this from her. She had to give it.

"I want you." She smiled up at him. "It's going to be okay. You're going to do great. I know it. Has it been a while for you?"

He felt a grin cross his face. She surprised him at every turn. "It's been a while, but I think I can handle it."

He could handle her. She was so fucking sweet, but it was obvious she needed someone to watch out for her. She was the kind of woman who could get lost in a cause, whether it be her protests or her friends, and forget to truly take care of herself. She needed a strong top, though the top would likely need to be stealthy. Nell would need to feel like she was in control outside the bedroom, but she desperately needed someone looking out for her.

The fact that she was in bed with him was proof of that.

His tongue tangled with hers, taking it slow and easy. He rubbed his chest against hers and felt the way her legs spread further to accommodate him. She made a place for him, cradling him between her thighs. His cock was ragingly hard, but he kept it under control, content with rubbing himself against her. She was soft and warm, and so, so wet.

He inhaled her, letting her scent wash across his senses. He let his fingers find her hair, and he fisted it lightly. He was going to teach her so much while he was with her. He would show her how he liked his cock sucked. He would thrust his cock into her mouth and spill himself on her tongue and watch her drink him down.

His hips started to move. He couldn't wait longer or he would be inside her without any protection, and he didn't want that for her. The need to spill himself inside her was riding him hard, but he couldn't take the chance. If he came inside Nell, he would have to wait around. He would have to stay to make sure she didn't get pregnant.

She would let him. She wouldn't stop him because she wasn't really in control of herself any longer. He was in control. It would be the simplest thing in the world to let nature take its course and within minutes, he might be able to bind her to him in a way she couldn't deny even if she ever found out what a fucking bastard he was.

Bishop pulled away abruptly. He couldn't. He had to protect her.

"What?" Nell asked, her eyes wide.

"I need a condom." He fumbled. He never fumbled. He was always precise, in his movements, in his actions, but she was making him clumsy. His hands were actually shaking as he opened the bedside stand and reached for the condoms he always carried.

"Thank you. I'm not on birth control." She was staring up at him like he was some kind of hero. Her hands were on his waist, rubbing up and down, soothing him. "I never had to be before."

"We should take you in and get you on the pill." He didn't want to wear the fucking condom. He wanted to spill himself inside her. He wanted to know she was walking around with his semen tucked away, a piece of himself that would stay with her.

"All right," she agreed.

Yes, she needed a keeper. She'd just agreed to get on the pill for a man who had said he would leave her.

But Nell Finn was smart. She wouldn't wait around for his dumb ass. She would find someone. Maybe not the person she needed, but she would find someone who would take all her sweetness. She would forget about him eventually and she would need those pills, because a woman as sensual as Nell couldn't stay alone for long. After he was gone, she'd find another lover.

He tore open the condom, the movement a bit savage. He hated the idea. He was getting possessive. He was starting to think of Nell as his, and that was a dangerous thought.

A moan came out of his mouth as he started to roll the condom on. Nell's hand joined his, her small palm working the latex over his dick. He loved her hands. They were real. She didn't wear nail polish, but her nails were kept neat. Nell's hands worked. She used them to plant her garden and to type out her books. Now she used them to make him ready for her.

He nearly lost that iron-willed control he was known for. Bishop had to take a deep breath or he would come right then and there like he was fifteen again and making an idiot of himself with one of the teens who shared his foster home.

For the briefest of moments, he wished he'd never done it before. Looking down at Nell and the wonder on her face, he actually wished he was a virgin again, sharing this with her, being in the moment with her, young and fresh and staring at a future with the woman underneath him. Nell was so young. Oh, she was twenty-five, only ten years younger than him, but he was centuries ahead of her in damage.

She finished tugging on the condom, and her hands smoothed along his chest, bringing him back into the moment with her. Regrets didn't matter. There would be time for them later. If there was one thing Bishop had learned it was that regrets had a way of finding a man, even when he tried to outrun them.

The only thing that mattered now was pleasing Nell Finn. He let the melancholy thoughts flit away and concentrated on her.

"I'm going to go slow, baby. I don't want to hurt you." It was the last thing he wanted to do. He got to his knees and fit his cock to her pussy. His cock looked like a brutish marauder against that pretty pussy, but the head was already coated in her cream. She wanted him. He let his focus laser in on the sight as he pressed in, his cockhead disappearing, slipping just inside her.

She gasped, her hands tightening on him.

"It's all right." Slow. Easy. He pulled back out and then surged in again, gaining ground each time. "You were made to take me."

"You're going too slow." She was restless underneath him. Her hips shifted up, trying to take him deeper.

"Nell." He hissed her name, a warning that she didn't heed.

"I want more." Nell thrust up.

It was way more than he could take. He surged inside, thrusting in one long passage until she'd taken him to the root.

Her whole body tightened, and her face flushed. Her breath came out in pants. "I shouldn't have done that. I'm sorry. I've always been impatient. You should get it over with now. It's okay. I can take it."

She was so frustrating.

"Stay still. You'll get used to me." He looked down at her, his heart seizing. Tears pooled in her eyes. This was damn straight why he didn't deal with virgins. He didn't have the patience for it. He should do exactly what she said. He should finish quickly and let her go.

"You're not hurrying, Henry."

There was only one way to shut that mouth of hers. He kissed her gently, a soft request that she focus on something else. Nell's brain seemed to work too fast, to never shut off. He had to give her something else to concentrate on. She softened again, her arms moving around him once more. Her mouth opened beneath his, and he could feel the minute she relaxed. He let his body sink against hers, feeling the way her breasts pressed against his chest. He let his tongue do a lazy dance, rubbing hers slowly.

He took his time, even though his cock was dying. Patience. She might not have any, but it was his stock-in-trade. He held back, kissing her over and over, trying to drug her with pleasure. After a long while, he moved his hips again, and this time she didn't wince.

"Better?"

Her eyes had taken on that dreamy look again. She nodded. "Yes. Do it again, Henry. It feels so good."

It felt incredible. He'd never been in a tighter pussy. Nell gripped his cock, every inch a pure pleasure. He pulled out and very carefully thrust back in, making sure his pelvis ground down on her clit. He swiveled his hips and began a slow rhythm. In and out and all around. In and out, grinding down. That was the way to make sure she loved it.

He held back the rising tide, thrusting inside her with great care. Later he would let go. Later he could fuck her hard, but not tonight. Tonight was for her.

A low moan came from deep in her throat, and he let her pussy clamp down around his cock, milking him and sending him over the edge. The orgasm hit him like a lightning strike, making him shake and groan. He lost control and just fucked her for a few blissful moments, everything else slipping away until she was the only thing real in the world.

He thrust one last time, giving up every ounce he had, and then slumped over, his body pressing hers into the mattress.

Peace. Calm. He let her warmth and sweet scent surround him. Now was the time when he would normally get up, go shower, and walk away after a polite "thank you."

Nell's cheek nestled against his, their faces rubbing together in a perfect intimacy. "Henry, that was so beautiful."

She was beautiful. He shifted, hating the moment when his cock slipped out of her body. He rolled to the side, not quite knowing what to say to her.

It struck him quite forcefully that he'd never actually slept with a woman before. Oh, he'd fucked plenty of women. He'd spent the night with a couple. Mostly for work. There were several women out there who he'd screwed for the simple reason that he needed information from them and he'd either gotten it through pillow talk or he'd waited until the chick was asleep and downloaded her laptop or her phone. But he'd never slept beside them.

Not once in his life.

He was a sleeping virgin.

"Should I go?" Nell's eyes were wide, and Bishop wondered how long he'd been sitting there thinking about the past.

It would be the easiest thing in the world to help her out of bed, get them both cleaned up, and politely walk her back to her room.

103

"No. Give me a minute." He rolled out of bed. No matter what he did, he had to get rid of the condom. He stalked to the bathroom.

"You have a very nice backside."

He felt himself blush. Fucking blush. Like a goddamn schoolboy. "Thanks."

He slipped inside the bathroom and closed the door. What the fuck was he doing? Why was his heart racing? Why did he feel so weird?

Heart attack. He was obviously having a heart attack, and he was going to die right here on Naked Mountain. Would Bill even bother to dress him for the funeral or would he toss his naked butt in a nice comfy hole in the ground? Did nudists have burial rituals?

He was acting insane. He rolled the condom off and tossed it away. He cleaned himself up and got ready to walk out there and explain to Nell that he'd had a great time, but she should go back to her room. They needed to keep things casual.

Yes, that was what he would do.

He opened the door, ready to gently herd her out. And his heart did that stupid-ass flutter thing again because Nell's eyes were closed, and she had an arm wrapped around his pillow while she slept. Strands of chocolate brown hair covered her shoulders and a nipple peeked out.

He turned off the light and slipped into bed, moving her arm so she was cuddling him instead of the pillow. It was nice. Warm. Comfortable. It was better this way. It was her first time. She required some tenderness. He eased down, feeling his every muscle sinking into the bed.

She was only his for a few nights, a week, maybe. Perhaps two. He could stick around for a couple of weeks, but that was all. Maybe even a month. Yes, he could work it so he could have a month.

He could stay here with Nell. Maybe eventually he would get used to sleeping with her.

He yawned. Something about the heat of her body and the soft skin against his own was having a drugging effect, and he was slipping into sleep.

But he was going to have to see a doctor, because there was definitely something wrong with his heart.

* * * *

Nell came awake slowly, turning over underneath the blankets. She felt the sun on her face and blinked in the morning light.

Not her room. She was in Henry's room. And she was naked. So very, very naked. She reached out carefully, letting her arm creep behind her. Nothing. She was alone in bed.

Had Henry left? She sat up, holding the covers to her breasts.

"Good morning. There's a pot of hot water over here. I have Earl Grey, oolong, and green tea."

Henry was sitting at the desk, and sure enough, there was a tray beside him with a white ceramic pot and two mugs. It looked like he'd found some muffins.

He turned in his chair. He seemed to be working on a computer. His lips curved up in a small smile. He was devastating when he smiled. "The muffins are vegan. Blueberry and raspberry. I thought you might like them."

She nodded slowly, not quite sure how to handle the fact that he was wearing a T-shirt and sweatpants and she was totally naked. Where were her clothes? Should she take a shower? She definitely needed to brush her teeth.

"Nell?" Henry stared at her expectantly. "What tea would you like?"

Tea. He was offering her tea. She loved tea. "Green."

He sighed and crossed his arms over his chest. He looked different with his clothes on. He looked almost normal. When he'd been naked, with his glasses off, he'd been superhero hot, but he was back to sweetly attractive. Except his chocolate brown eyes went frosty. He was even hotter when he got his caveman on. She knew it was wrong, but she went all soft and gooey on the inside when Henry went dominant. "What is wrong with this picture, Nell?"

She had no idea. She pulled the blankets up, feeling every minute of her awkwardness. Maybe she should brazen her way through this. She spied her clothes across the room. Or she could run to the bathroom and start the shower.

"I asked you a question."

And she hadn't known the answer. She didn't like not knowing the answer. She always had the answer. She'd been champion of the debate team. "Everything seems fine to me."

"Why is that blanket around your neck? I have the heat up in the room. I made sure it's nice and toasty. Come over here and get your tea."

"Can you pass me my clothes?"

"No. That's not the way this works. We're alone so you're naked."

She stared at him, feeling a frown cross her face. "You aren't naked.

That doesn't seem fair."

"This isn't about fair," he replied, not giving her an inch. "This is the way it is. I want to watch you walk around naked. When we're alone, I want to know you're available to me."

"Again with the not fair."

"It isn't about fair, Nell. And it is fair when you think about it. When we're not alone, I'll do pretty much whatever you want me to as long as it doesn't put you in danger. Why do you think I brought the vegan muffins? I ignored the bacon. I know you said it didn't bother you if I ate meat, but I watched you last night and I think it did. I love bacon, but I think you would prefer I eschew it around you. I prefer you leave off your clothes. It's a trade."

When she really thought about it, it was an excellent trade. Henry wasn't a tiny man, and he seemed to have a good metabolism. He'd eaten two burgers and a whole bunch of fries the night before so she was sure he could have eaten a lot of bacon. She was saving a pig. Sure, she was potentially scaring him off. He'd seen her the night before, but that had been during sex. Men probably saw a woman differently when they were in sex mode. This was tea mode, and he might notice her cellulite.

She had to balance her need to stay sexy around Henry with her deep desire to save a pig. Pigs were intelligent creatures, but they were also known to eat just about anything. Pigs weren't the nicest creatures in the world, but that didn't mean that they should be horrifically murdered and then cut apart for various meats.

But her boobs did sag.

"I would give a lot to know what you're thinking right now." Henry's smile had moved from a little uptick of his lips to a brilliant, sunny thing.

"I was thinking I might be able to save a pig by showing off my boobs." It was a good cause.

"Yep. You should get up and come over here and sit on my lap, otherwise I might go and devour the first pig I see." He patted his lap. "I'm utterly willing to give up meat to obtain your submission."

There was a word she'd never liked before. Submission. "I don't know that I like the thought of submitting."

"Only because you're thinking about it the wrong way. You think submitting makes you weak, but I know it takes a strong woman to submit to a real man. It's an exchange and like all exchanges, you get something out of it. You promise me that when we're intimate, you'll obey me. I promise you that almost every other time, I'll follow your lead."

106

That was practically insane on his part. She couldn't see him in her world. Except she would love having him there. "I'm into some crazy stuff."

"Yeah, I know." He gestured toward the computer he'd been looking at. "Did you really need to protest that kid's birthday party?"

He had her computer? "That's private."

"Nothing is private anymore. Drop the sheet. I have some questions for you." He picked up a delicious-looking muffin. "Come on, baby. You know you're hungry. I didn't turn up the heater before we fell asleep so this place was arctic this morning. I woke up to my penis trying to crawl back into my body, but I braved getting out of bed to feed you."

She glanced out the window. The world was covered in white. The storm Stella had predicted had come in, and she bet the room had been mighty chilly before Henry turned the heat up. And she noticed that she had been carefully tucked into the blankets. Henry had put another blanket over her body while she'd been sleeping, making sure she was warm and comfy. He might be a rat fink computer thief, but he'd been incredibly tender the night before, and, it seemed, this morning as well. And he had it all toasty and warm in the room which she would usually protest, but this morning she was feeling a little selfish. She had Henry all to herself for this brief time. The earth would forgive her.

She let the sheet drop and held her hand out for the muffin. There was something deeply intimate and loving about eating breakfast in bed naked with her lover. Henry Flanders was her lover. She took a deep breath because tears were threatening. The last thing she wanted was to mar this time by crying. "I will take a raspberry muffin, thank you. And I wasn't actually protesting that boy's birthday. I was protesting the way the zoo treated its bears. When the conservancy that the bears came from gave them to the zoo, they also gave the zoo a large donation that should have gone toward a new, larger environment for the bears, but the zoo used the money to put in a carousel. I was protesting the carousel, which also happened to be the site of one Austin Jacobson's fourth birthday party. I also might have mentioned to his mother that the balloons she had bought would kill a ton of birds. Conversely, I performed the Heimlich maneuver and saved Austin's dad when he nearly choked on a hot dog. That wouldn't have happened with a vegan substitute."

Henry passed her the muffin and started to pour her tea. His eyes briefly found her breasts, and he sighed as though enchanted by the sight. "All right then. He probably isn't the one who broke into your cabin."

She took the tea mug. "You're looking through my e-mail to try to find the crazy gentleman?" Wow, that was sexist. "It could be a female. Females can be every bit as crazy as males."

"You're preaching to the choir, baby." He turned back to the computer. "And yes, I've been combing through your e-mails to see if anyone had sent you threatening letters. I was surprised at the volume."

She'd kind of gotten used to it. People tended to not like it when she protested their businesses or housing developments or zoos. She'd become accustomed to nasty e-mails and letters and the occasional phone call. "I get it a lot. I ignore most of it. Except for the box that looked like a bomb. I had to call the sheriff for that one. But the Farley brothers promised me that it was so poorly constructed, it would never have actually gone off. They're super smart. They're just kids, but they were much more informed about bomb making techniques than their elders."

"Someone sent you a bomb?" Henry was looking at her, and the temperature in the room seemed to have dropped again.

Maybe she should have kept that part to herself. She choked a little on the muffin. "Uhm, like I said, it wasn't a very good bomb. I also have gotten the occasional box filled with poop. Those didn't explode, either, thank god."

His face was flushed, his jaw a hard line. He seemed to take control of himself, his voice so much softer than his expression, as though he was working hard to try not to scare her. "Nell, sweetheart, I'm going to need the names of the people who sent you those packages."

"Oh, they don't tend to leave a return address." Henry seemed a bit naïve. Nell munched on the rest of her muffin. He probably didn't get a lot of threatening letters as an academic.

"But the sheriff tracked them down, right?"

"Law enforcement is pretty laid back here. It's kind of a no-harm-done thing."

Henry said something about harm under his breath, but Nell didn't catch all of it. His eyes closed briefly. "All right, then. We'll start fresh. Do you know where the skinny kid lives?"

"Logan or Seth?" They didn't like to be called kids, but she was sure that was who Henry was talking about.

"Seth."

"He's spending winter break with his grandfather. He lives on the outer edge of the valley. Logan's place is two doors down. You can't miss Logan's place. Teeny and Marie like gnomes. They're kind of everywhere. Seth and Logan will be either there or at Seth's place. They're pretty much always together though."

"Good." Henry stood up. "I think Bill told me he has a couple of snowmobiles. I would like to have a talk with the young man. I think he might know a thing or two about tracking someone down with a computer."

She passed back the napkin. "Thanks for the breakfast. It was delicious."

"I wouldn't know. I haven't had any yet." The temperature in the room shot right back up. Henry was staring at her like she was the best-looking muffin in the world. "How sore are you, baby?"

Just like that her heart tripled. One look from Henry and her whole body went soft and willing. "I'm good."

He pulled his shirt over his head and tossed it aside. "Excellent, because I'm very hungry. Spread your legs and let me have some breakfast. I need some honey."

Nell lay back and started the morning out right.

Chapter Seven

Bishop hopped off the snowmobile and stared at the small cabin in front of him. It was covered in snow, but someone had painstakingly shoveled the walkway from the front porch to the driveway. Three cars were parked along the circular drive—a tiny VW bug, a big-ass SUV, and a truck that had seen better days.

And everywhere he looked, he saw the evidence of the aforementioned gnomes. Their pointy red hats stuck up out of the snow. Bishop would bet that during the summertime, this yard was filled with flowers and ceramic gnomes would rule the valley.

A memory from his childhood washed over him. His mother had kept a small garden in the back of their house. The tiny home he'd spent his first years in had been in a trashy part of the town he'd grown up in, but she'd been proud of it. She kept it clean and she'd made a little playground in the back for him. It hadn't been much, just a ratty old swing set she'd bought secondhand and had to clean rust off of, and a sandbox she'd dug herself. He would sit there and watch her as she worked in the garden. His mother's hands had been callused from work, but she'd been the tenderest woman in the world.

Nell's hands were callused. Nell worked.

Bishop took a long breath and banished the unwanted memories. He wasn't sure why they had surfaced. He'd grown up in the heat of Houston. He'd never seen snow until he joined the military. But something about the cabin in front of him took him right back to that time when he'd been safe and warm and loved.

"Hello! Can I help you?" A small woman peeked out of her door. She was thin and warmly dressed, her graying hair in a neat bun. She had a slightly hooked nose, giving her an almost birdlike appearance, but the woman in front of him wouldn't be a hawk or an eagle. She was a little dove. "Come on inside. It's freezing out here. I have some cider warming."

He nodded her way, pocketing the keys to the snowmobile Bill had given him not twenty minutes before along with his promise to watch after Nell. He made short work of the distance, eager to be inside. This world was too cold, too white. Even dressed and away from the resort, he still felt a bit naked, as though all that pristine snow couldn't cover up the fact that he didn't belong here. A man needed camouflage to survive, and there was none to be had in this town. This woman proved it. She noticed a strange man in her front yard and invited him in for cider.

He thought about giving the older woman a stern talking-to. He could be a serial killer. He could be an Amway salesman. He could be anyone. But it wasn't his place. If Logan's mom wanted to get herself horrifically murdered, then that was her business.

Damn, that cider smelled good.

Bishop pushed through the door of the cabin. There was a small wreath hanging on the door. Underneath was a painted sign declaring this home to be the Green-Warner Homestead. Bishop wasn't sure if the woman currently heating up cider was a Green or a Warner, but she turned in the kitchen and motioned him in the door.

"Come in. Come in and sit a spell. That was a nasty storm last night, wasn't it?"

The cabin was warm inside, a fire raging in the fireplace illuminating the space. Bishop shrugged out of his coat, settling it on a peg beside the door. "It seems that way to me. I'm not from around here. This could be perfectly normal and I wouldn't know."

The older woman placed a mug on the bar and gestured Bishop to join her in the kitchen. "We get one or two big storms a year. My wife and I like to refer to this as snuggle weather. So you're Bill's friend. Mr. Flanders, isn't it? Where are you from?"

Perhaps the lady wasn't looking to be murdered. He'd forgotten that small towns thrived on gossip. It was on the tip of his tongue to say Houston. It sat right there in Bishop's brain that he could talk about his house in Houston and how the cabin reminded him of his childhood. But that was Bishop's childhood. Not Henry Flanders's.

"I'm originally from Ohio." It was a suitable Midwestern state. His accent was flat and could be mistaken for any number of Midwestern states. "Now I work at a small university in Washington State."

"A professor! How very nice. My name is Teeny Green. I suspect you're looking for the boys. Logan told me he helped you out yesterday."

Bishop was fairly certain Logan hadn't mentioned that the help he'd provided came in the form of a bar fight.

The boys in question had started to walk down the hall. Bishop heard the door open and then the low conversation between friends. Logan emerged first, a smile on his face. The smile abruptly disappeared as he realized he wasn't alone in the cabin. Logan took one look at Bishop standing at the bar, turned, and started back down the hall.

Seth Stark didn't run. He put his hands on his lanky hips and attempted to stare Bishop down. "What are you doing here?"

There was a small gasp that came from Teeny Green. Her eyes narrowed as she looked at the young man. "Seth, surely your momma taught you better manners than that."

Seth didn't back down at all. "My momma is from the Upper East Side. She doesn't believe in manners."

Teeny Green simply stared the young man down. After a few moments of maternal judgment, Seth sighed. "I'm sorry, Miss Teeny. Mr. Flanders, how can I help you?"

It was obvious the kid didn't want to help, but he wasn't going to be given a choice. "I have Nell's computer contents on a thumb drive. I don't have the time to go through every lead. I rather suspected that you might have some software that could cut that time down for us."

The minute the word "software" came out of Bishop's mouth, Seth lit up. "Hell, yeah." There was the sound of a foot tapping against the floor. Teeny Green didn't seem to like swearing either. "Sorry. What I meant to say was yes, Mr. Flanders. I can certainly help you with that."

A brilliant smile came over Teeny's face. "Well, you boys go on back to Logan's room. I'll bring you some cookies when they're done."

Bishop wondered for a moment if he'd gone down a rabbit hole. Seth turned, walking back toward the room he'd first come out of. Bishop grabbed his mug of apple cider. There was no use in wasting it. It smelled delicious, and now that he thought about it, the cookies smelled pretty good too. If he had to spend time in teenage hell, at least there were cookies.

Seth opened the door to Logan's bedroom, and Bishop followed.

Logan's room was a temple to the chosen object of his worship. Posters lined the wall, making a tapestry of superheroes and villains, all in vivid colors. Comic books. At the last group home he'd been in, one of the boys his age had had a collection of comic books. Chris Johnson. Bishop hadn't thought about Chris Johnson in ten years, maybe more. Though they'd been the same age, Chris hadn't spent as much time in the system as Bishop. He'd tried to share those comic books, but by then Bishop knew there was no such thing as a superhero.

A wide-eyed Logan sat on the bottom bunk. "Dude, did you tell my mom? Because I told her we helped you out with directions to the library. I totally did not mention the bar. I'm not supposed to go to the bar. Not just that bar in particular, but any bar. I get to go to juice bars, but not if they sell alcohol."

It was obvious his parents kept Logan on a tight leash. "I didn't mention the unfortunate incident. Here's the hard drive, Seth. Now, what do either of you know about threats against Nell?"

"Are you talking about the shit bombs?" Logan giggled and then his mouth turned down. "Could you not tell my moms about the cussing?"

"Yes, I am talking about bombs of all kinds." Did anybody take this seriously? "You know most people get scared when someone sends them a bomb in the mail."

Seth was already sitting at the small desk, his hands flying across the keyboard. He never looked up, and Bishop realized that this was Seth Stark in his natural environment. The kid's whole attitude had changed the minute he sat in front of that keyboard. "From what I heard, Will and Bobby said it was a lame attempt. And the bomb wasn't full of shit. Nell has received packages of crap, but the bomb was full of…well, it was full of bomb stuff. I don't know what really, but it wasn't shit."

Yeah, the kid was trying to pretend, but Bishop was pretty sure he knew exactly what he was talking about. "You should be careful or the feds will show up on your front doorstep this time."

Logan snorted. "Dude, that happened by the time he was ten."

Seth shrugged. "I was a curious kid. Can we get back to the problem at hand? Okay. I've narrowed the search parameters down to three names."

"How the hell did you do that?" Bishop had come to get a list of anyone who had sent her a threat. He'd expected to spend days combing through her e-mails and placing potential suspects on a list.

Seth turned back, a superior grin on his face. "I built out an algorithm that matches up names, dates, and then searches the Internet for any information on those names. It then places the potential suspects in order of probability of violation. I have various filters for money lost, position at the beginning of the protest, position at the end, how many keywords they used in the various e-mails."

Bishop could imagine what those words were. Words like "murder" and "kill" and "rape" and "die." He'd read a couple of those e-mails, his blood pressure threatening to hit new heights. He had to be careful about his tone and the words he used himself. "And this thing works? I've never heard of software that works like this."

Seth shrugged, an oddly arrogant gesture. "That's because I wrote the program. It doesn't exist anywhere else. And it won't tell us who did the crime. It merely gives us a list of suspects in the order of probability. And here's our list of suspects."

There was a low hum as the printer started up and began to work. A single sheet came out, and Seth handed it over with the smirk of a person who knew how good they were at their job. "What would take the police several weeks, I managed to do overnight."

"Overnight? I just gave you the e-mails."

Seth snorted. "Oh, I hacked her e-mail server after we finished our *Battlestar Galactica* marathon."

"Dude, you can't tell my moms about that either." Logan seemed to have trust issues with his moms. "They told me I couldn't commit any felonies or I won't get the deputy job and I'll end up having to work at Stella's. Stella scares me, and I've seen what Max Harper can do to someone who gets his order wrong."

"Why won't you just let me pay for your college?" Seth's eyes rolled. "Dude, my parents won't even notice that the money's gone."

A stubborn look settled over Logan's face. "I'm not a charity case."

Ah, rich boy and poor boy had some issues themselves. Bishop understood what it meant to not have money. He'd gone into the Army when he'd aged out of foster care because he'd had no other place to go. At least this Logan kid had a home. Bishop understood pride, though. He wouldn't have taken a handout at Logan's age either. Sometimes all a man had was his pride. He was pretty sure Logan shouldn't go into law enforcement though. He seemed really attached to his mothers' apron strings.

"All right, man." Seth conceded easily as though he wished he hadn't opened his mouth in the first place.

"I'm going to start working and save some money and I'll get there on my own. Now who's on the list? Who wants to hurt Nell?" Logan asked.

Bishop looked down at the sheet of paper. There were twenty names on the page along with an assigned risk percentage. No wonder the feds had been interested in the kid. This software wouldn't make cases for them, but it could, when the right information was present, point the way to a list of suspects. He immediately decided to focus on the top three names. They were the only ones with a risk assessment of over sixty percent.

Jim Miller, Mickey Camden, and Warren Lyle.

"Why no women?" Logan asked, looking over Bishop's shoulder.

It bugged him, but he couldn't do what he would normally do which was to pop whoever wasn't respecting his space. Killing a kid for getting too close might break his cover. If Logan's moms didn't even want him to curse, they would likely object to his quick, though painless, death.

"Do you know how few women actually plan out killings?" Bishop doubted the perpetrator was a woman. It wasn't that women couldn't get pissed off and tear through some shit, but they rarely did it over business.

"Women tend to be moment-of-passion killers," Seth explained. Logan stared at him. "Sorry, I watch a lot of TV."

Yeah, Bishop bet the kid did. "I need to take a look at these guys."

"Do you want me to print out their dossiers?" Seth asked.

"You're kidding me." He needed this fucker out in the field. He could get his jobs done in half the time, force Seth to do his paperwork, and sneak off to spend time with Nell.

He couldn't think like that. Not even in a joking way. He would have a brief time with Nell and then he had to do what he did best—disappear. It could be dangerous for her if he kept up a relationship with someone like Nell. It would be far too easy for one of his numerous enemies to follow him and find out that he had a weakness to exploit. No. Once he left Bliss, he would never come back. Everyone was safer that way.

But before he could leave, he had to make sure she was okay by taking care of whoever wanted to hurt her this time.

There would be a next time, a voice in his head was whispering to him. He could save her this time, but she wasn't about to give up the crusades. Women like Nell got more active—not less—as time went by. Sure, she would eventually get married and probably have a kid or two, but she wouldn't give up trying to change the world, and there were a lot of people out there who were perfectly happy with the world the way it was.

Nell would always be in danger.

"So do you want me to print it, Mr. Flanders?" The Stark kid was looking up at him, a curious expression on his face.

"Yeah, yeah sure." The printer began humming again, and Bishop was left feeling unsettled.

There was a brief knock, and the door came open. Teeny Green waltzed in carrying a tray of cookies.

"There's some fresh milk if you boys want some." She left the tray on the desk. Logan and Seth immediately dug into the cookies, but Bishop's mind wasn't on his stomach.

When the printout was done, he grabbed it off the printer and got ready to leave. The quicker he solved this, the quicker he could be on his way. Nell was dangerous. She was dangerous to herself, and she was definitely dangerous to his sanity. He needed to leave as soon as possible. A man could get comfortable in a place like Bliss, but Bishop had made a decision long ago. He could call no place home. He had to stay sharp, and he couldn't do it in a place filled with lovely brunettes and women who made homemade cookies and apple cider.

He nodded to the boys and started to make his way out. There was something too homey about the small cabin. Everywhere he looked he saw a family and their lives lovingly documented in photos and award certificates and mementoes. He couldn't help but notice an old family photo that had been framed and mounted on the wall of the living room. It showed two women and a baby boy. He recognized Teeny Green, younger though no less radiant. She was wearing a white dress with a lacy collar as she smiled at the camera. A baby probably no older than eight months sat in her lap, his mouth opened in a big toothless grin. A stout-looking woman stood behind them, her hands protectively on Teeny's shoulders. She was a bit grim, but something about the picture fascinated him. Though the woman in the back wasn't smiling, there was a pride in her stance. This was her family.

Lesbian couples might be accepted in big cities these days, but in small-town Colorado two decades ago? What kind of courage had those women had to start a life for themselves here? What kind of fortitude had gone into building this small cabin?

"My wife's name is Marie." Teeny walked out of the kitchen, wiping her hands on her apron. She sighed as she looked at the picture. "I know a lot of families like to keep a current portrait up, but I like to look back and remember where we came from. I love this picture. It was the first one we had done. A traveling photographer took it. We couldn't find a studio who would take it for us. Things were a little less tolerant in this part of the world back then. Bliss didn't have a portrait studio, so we had to make our own."

He was curious. "Why would you stay here? You could have gone to San Francisco or New York. People would have accepted you."

She shook her head. "This was our home, and here in Bliss, we never had a lick of trouble. We were pioneers in our way. Marie's family came out here from back East. Her family's held this land for almost a hundred years. Besides, if we all go and hide in the city, no one would ever get to know us."

That was the point. "And they would never get to hurt you."

"Nothing good in life ever came without a struggle. When Marie and I opened our store, there were people from some other towns who said they would never buy anything from people like us. We almost went under that first year, and then the Circle G started buying all their supplies from us even though it would have been less expensive to get them from one of the big stores in another town. And Albert Lang walked in and bought every piece of fishing equipment we had. You have to understand, Al was a judge, and he was the head of a very wealthy and influential family. He should have been one of the people trying to push us out, but he told me to hang on for a year or two and before long, no one would care because we would just be a part of the community. And he was right. The Harpers finally started buying from us and before we knew it, Max and Rye were coming in and begging for treats and playing with our kid. Things don't change unless you make them change, Mr. Flanders. You can't do that by running away every time the going gets tough."

A low voice broke through the moment. "No. You do it with the business end of a shotgun. You want to know how to change people's minds, shove a shotgun in their gut and then see how fast they suddenly don't care what your sexual orientation is." The stern lady from the photograph walked through the cabin door. She was as broad as Teeny was slender. And she damn straight looked like a woman who could wield a shotgun. "Who the hell are you?"

Finally, someone he could relate to. "Professor Henry Flanders."

Marie frowned. "Is he here for Seth? That boy always seems to have some intellectual types sniffing around him."

Teeny wagged a finger her wife's way. "Be more polite. People are

117

going to think you don't have an ounce of manners, Marie Warner."

Marie stared at Bishop, shaking her head at her wife. "I never did have a lick of manners, but I got a real good nose for trouble. I don't like the looks of this one. I would bet a lot that he's hiding something."

Bishop had to give her credit. He was hiding pretty much everything, but he simply shrugged and gave her a harmless smile. "I'm trying to figure out who trashed the Finn cabin."

A long moment passed and finally Marie nodded. "Good for Nell. You let me know if you need an extra gun. I'm damn good at taking a son of a bitch down."

"Marie!" Teeny threw her hands up.

Marie finally cracked a smile and sent a wink her wife's way. "He's good with me if he's helping out Nell and her momma. They need someone to watch out for them. Nell's too good to see real trouble coming her way, I always said. Now, I smell your cider, darlin'. You always know how to warm me up."

She enveloped the smaller woman in a bear hug.

"God, Mom, can you stop with the gross affection stuff?" Logan made a vomiting sound as he grabbed another couple of cookies from the table, but Bishop caught sight of Seth watching the two women, a wistful expression on his face.

Poor little rich boy.

"Thanks for everything, ladies." Bishop grabbed his coat from the hanger and buttoned up.

Teeny pressed a bag of cookies into his hand, for the "road" as she called it. He walked out of the house feeling deeply unsettled because he'd liked it there far too much.

He managed to make it out the door and halfway down the drive when Seth Stark came running out. He hadn't put a coat on and he stood on the porch, his hands shoved in his pockets. "Someone looked into your cover story. It was probably Stef Talbot. He checks into everyone who comes to town for any length of time. I think it'll hold, though. He didn't look past the surface stuff. Are you on the run?"

The snow couldn't be any colder than Bishop's gut in that moment. He forced himself to smile. The kid couldn't possibly know anything. "What are you talking about?"

Seth hopped off the porch, his teeth chattering just a bit. "It's a good construct, but I know how deep to go. The information about you appears to begin at your birth, but it was uploaded to various databases a week ago. You see, the truth is always in the code if you know where to look for it. So I'll ask again. Are you on the run or are you undercover? You could be a con artist, I suppose."

He was surprised that criminal hadn't been the first possibility on the kid's list. It would have been the first thing Bishop would have thought of. The kid was far too smart for his own good. "It wasn't the feds who came for you, was it? It was the Agency."

A single shoulder shrugged. "I've done some work for them. Damn it. You're Agency. That's why you were able to take out all those guys in the bar fight. Well, it makes me feel better. I was worried you were going to try to take Nell for all she's worth. It's not much, by the way."

Perhaps a nugget of truth was called for. After all, he wouldn't be using the name Henry Flanders again after a week or two. He would need to come up with another cover because he didn't trust just having the one in place, but he'd already known he would get rid of the Henry cover last night. He couldn't leave it out there for Nell to potentially find one day. "I'm on vacation. I'm only here for a few days."

"And you thought you would sleep with Nell while you're here?"

Or maybe he would have to take the little fucker out anyway. "I like her, but I'm not the right man for her. I don't live a life that she could possibly understand or accept."

Seth's eyes seemed to find something in the snow. "Yeah, well, sometimes we have to accept who we are deep inside."

At least the kid was reasonable. "Yes. And Nell wouldn't like that version of me very much, but I do care about her. It's why I want to make sure she's safe. I can handle this problem for her and then I'll disappear. I'll be nothing more than a nice memory for her. Of course, if you tell her, she'll feel used when I'm really not trying to use her. I genuinely care about the lady. Can you leave things be at least long enough for me to figure out who's trying to hurt her?"

Seth nodded. "Okay."

"Get back inside. Your lips are starting to turn blue."

"I only said sometimes, you know."

Bishop sighed. "What are you talking about now?"

"Sometimes we have to accept who we are and sometimes we just have to change who we are so we can get what we want. I play a lot of D&D."

Bishop snorted. "I bet."

Seth shook his head. "Don't be a snob. You can get really attached to a character in D&D, and then you miss one saving throw and bam, your character's dead and you have to start all over again. But you don't stop playing. You keep going, and a lot of times you find out that the character you end up with is way better than the one that came before. Sometimes you gotta keep going until it's right, until the skin fits finally. That's all I'm saying. Let me know if you need any more help." The kid turned and ran back inside.

Bishop stared at the cabin, wondering if he'd ever felt right in his own skin.

Chapter Eight

Nell sighed as she eased into the hot tub. This was exactly what she needed. She'd lied to Henry. She was sore, but not so much that she wanted to miss a minute of his lovemaking.

She closed her eyes, letting the soothing sound of the tub lull her. Her body felt well used, as though she'd finally figured out what it had been made to do. Henry had been voracious this morning, using his mouth on her and then working his cock deep inside.

If only she didn't have that ignorant man trying to hurt her, she would probably still be in bed with Henry.

"Hey, are you up for some company?" A soft voice brought Nell out of her reverie.

Nell opened her eyes and smiled. Callie walked in followed by a tall, handsome man with dark hair and slate gray eyes.

"Hello, Stefan," Nell said, sitting up more properly. "When did you get back from New York?"

Stefan Talbot was the richest man in Bliss. He had an undeniably soft heart when it came to the women of the town. Nell had made a study of the artist. He was a rather fascinating character. Tall and lean with icy eyes, he could look every inch the ruthless king of all he surveyed, but the minute someone was in trouble, Stef was on hand with an open heart and an even more open checkbook. On several occasions, Nell had managed to squeeze a huge check out of Stef for a good cause.

"I got in late last night. I enjoy the city, but I have to admit, it's good to be home for a while. The light here is different than anywhere in the world. It's softer. I paint better here." Stef dropped his robe, and Nell couldn't help but admire him. He was an extremely attractive man, but her eyes turned down almost of their own accord. Somehow it didn't seem right to look at someone else now that she'd been in Henry's bed.

Stef slid into the water with a long sigh. "Apparently I came back into town at just the right time. Callie called me last night to tell me about all the new people we have hanging around."

Callie winced as she, too, dropped her robe and got into the hot tub. The resort was clothing optional with the singular exception of the pool and the hot tub. No bathing suits allowed for the tenants of the Mountain and Valley Naturist Community. "Sorry, I have a problem with the gossip bug. I don't really think of it as gossip. It's more like sharing fun stories about the people I love."

"Yes, I love it when you share stories about me," Stef said with only the mildest hint of rebuke. Callie made up for her lamentable gossip addiction by being one of the nicest people alive. And if Callie was a sweet-hearted gossip, then Stef could be a very nice, overprotective older brother. "So, tell me about this Henry person."

The last thing she wanted was for Stef Talbot to decide that she needed someone to watch out for her. "He's a nice man. He's a history professor, and I like him."

Stef's eyes narrowed. "You like him?"

She'd heard stories about Stef's private life, mostly from Callie. Stef practiced BDSM. From what Nell had learned, he'd started at a fairly young age and now had relationships with women that were purely based on Dominance and submission. Stef had gotten her started reading BDSM romances. Oh, he would never ever admit that he even knew they existed should someone ask. He'd told her if she ratted him out, he would stop helping her favorite charities, but Stef was the one who'd bought her a set of books when she'd admitted she was curious.

Henry was interested in that lifestyle, at least when it came to sex. It was right there on the tip of her tongue to ask Stef some questions, but she held back the impulse. Henry wasn't staying around. He would be gone, and sooner than Nell would like. She didn't want to be seen as the poor virgin who got left behind.

"I like him. It's not a big deal. He's a tourist. He's only here until the semester starts up again."

Stef let a moment pass, his eye pinning her. "Nell, are you sleeping with him?"

"Stefan!" Callie admonished, frowning at her best friend.

But Nell had known the question would come up the minute he'd walked in the door. "There was some sleep involved."

Callie's jaw dropped open. "Are you kidding me? I...I didn't think you would actually sleep with him. Nell, are you sure? I don't think that's such a good idea."

She hadn't expected Callie to react that way. She'd kind of thought she could talk to Callie. Callie was really the only one close to her age. Most of the other women around were closer to her mother's age, and she couldn't talk about sex with her mother. Oh, her mother loved to talk about sex. Her mother was a deeply open woman who thought she should talk to her daughter about everything. When Nell had first gotten her period, her mother had thrown her a party celebrating her womanhood.

Yeah, Nell didn't want her mother throwing a *Punching Out Her V-Card Party*.

She'd thought she might be able to talk to Callie. She'd gotten close to her, but Nell hated the look in Callie's eyes now. Callie looked slightly horrified at the idea of her sleeping with Henry. "Well, I will admit there wasn't much thought behind it. It's a fun fling, you know?"

"I'm sure it seems fun now." Callie stood up, reaching for her robe. "I bet it won't be so great later. Uhm, I remembered I promised my mom I would help her out with something. I'll be back soon."

She hurried out, knotting her robe around her.

Humiliation washed over Nell. She had no idea what had just happened, but she hated the way she felt now. Vulnerable. Alone. "I guess I should go, too."

Stef put a hand out, his eyes warming with sympathy. "Please stay. Callie wasn't judging you. She was feeling the weight of her own decisions, and I'm pretty sure she needs a good cry. Look, I shouldn't tell you this, but the last thing either of you needs is a rift in your friendship. Callie lost her virginity to a couple of friends of mine."

She felt her eyes widen as his words sank in. "A couple? Like Max and Rye?"

Stef shook his head. "Not Max and Rye, though I'm sure the desire for a ménage came from her childhood crush on those two. It was hard on Callie being the only girl around here. We didn't make it any easier, but that's neither here nor there. I think Callie's worried about you. She doesn't want you to be in the same position she's in. She thought she could handle one wild weekend, and she fell for them. Now they're gone and her heart still hurts."

Callie hadn't said a word. "They were stupid to leave her."

A frown crossed his handsome face. "Yes, and if I could find the little fuckers, I would very likely get my ass kicked because they're not so little and I'm pretty sure Zane was found in some Paleolithic cave and unfrozen for scientific purposes." He leaned forward, his eyes softening. "I'll find them one day. I know one of them quite well, and if he didn't fall for Callie, I'll eat Max's hat. I know where it's been, so that's a bet I don't want to lose. I just want you to know she's not judging you. I think she's judging herself."

Her heart ached for Callie. Callie seemed so very alone even though everyone in town adored her. She knew the feeling. Bliss was a wonderful place, but she still felt the weight of her solitude. Meeting Henry had pointed out how lonely she'd been. "I'm so sorry to hear that. She has nothing to be ashamed of. It's not wrong to love someone, even if they can't love you back."

"You keep believing, Mary Sunshine. I mean that. I know you've only been around for a couple of months, but I already can't imagine Bliss without you here."

"Well, I'll certainly stay as long as Mom…" She couldn't say it.

Stef leaned forward. "Nell, after your mother passes, you have to stay. This is your home now."

She loved this place, but there were problems she hadn't been able to solve, and they weren't going to go away. "I'm afraid Mom pays all the bills. I have to find a job, and even then I likely won't be able to find one where I can make a livable wage out here. There's not much call for a woman with a degree in social work in a town of a couple of hundred people."

It was what she'd been avoiding for months—the thought of having to leave after her mom was gone. Losing her mother would be hard enough, but losing this place, too, would be terrible. She couldn't imagine herself in a city now that she'd lived out here, but that was where she would have to go.

"What about your writing?" Stef asked quietly.

Nell snorted. That was a pipe dream. She'd been writing since she was a kid. She'd started out writing little stories, faery tales really, about the other world her mother loved to talk about. Then she'd grown up and realized she needed to write adult books, books that could change hearts and minds. Well, they might be able to change them if anyone ever actually read them. "Uhm, apparently no one wants to read thrillers about social justice. I thought it was a good idea at the time. It's sort of a Steve Berry–meets–*Les Misérables* story all set around the man-made disaster that was the Dust Bowl. An intrepid farm girl finds the clues to saving mankind buried deep in Oklahoma, but she has to fight dust storms and misogyny and rabid politicians to save everyone. I really thought it would sell."

For the first time since she'd met him, Stef seemed at a loss. Yeah, that was pretty much the way every agent and editor she'd submitted it to had reacted. "I, well, I could make a call."

She sighed and let her head rest against the back of the hot tub. "Don't bother. I think I'm pretty much doomed to failure on the writing front. Unless someone starts picking up my *Doctor Who* fan fiction, I'm pretty much out of luck."

"You write *Doctor Who* fan fiction?" The question came out of Stef's mouth on a laugh.

She let a smile curl her lips up. "It's erotic fan fiction. I think multicolored scarves are intensely sexy. I also find British accents soothing."

His jaw dropped for a minute, and then a long laugh boomed through the space. Stef laughed for a good long while, the sound filling her with joy. Stefan Talbot didn't laugh often. It was a good thing to give the young artist a bit of respite from what seemed like a too-serious life. She often thought that was why he'd stayed in Bliss, though he likely belonged in New York or Paris. He stayed in Bliss because he could laugh here. He took a deep breath. "I'm going to have to look that up online."

"You'll have to find me. Good luck. I don't write under Nell Finn."

"All I have to do is look for the story that has some message about recycling."

Damn him. He knew her too well. "I'm sure I'm not the only activist who writes fan fic."

His smile dimmed slightly. "What do you know about this guy?"

She stared at him.

"I'm not going to be protested, Nell. You don't have a dad and your mom can't protect you the way she would like. That means the men of this town have to look out for you."

The men of Bliss seemed united on that front. "There is so very much wrong with that statement."

He held his hands up. "Would it help if I told you I would do the same for Logan? Hell, I'm trying to convince Noah that he's in trouble. I don't like the woman he's dating. She tried to hit on me two days ago, but Jamie doesn't think Noah is willing to listen."

So it wasn't a completely sexist "protect the women" play. She couldn't exactly protest if Stef was treating her the same way he treated Noah. And Noah was in for some trouble. She'd met Ally, an actress working with the Bliss Repertory Theater, and Nell hadn't been impressed. Ally had seemed very interested in moving up the social ladder, and she needed money for that. Noah had recently come into a trust fund and Ally had moved her attentions from his brother, James, to Noah.

But she didn't have Noah's problems.

"Henry isn't after my money," she assured him. "He knows I don't have any."

"I'm not worried about him being after money. You have plenty of other attributes a man could want."

Oh, yes, now she was curious. "Like?"

Gray eyes rolled. "I don't need to go into that."

"Yes, you do."

"Come on. Don't make me say it."

She was pretty sure she knew what he was talking about. "Is this the submissive thing?"

"Yes, Nell. It's the 'submissive thing.'" He used very sarcastic air quotes. "It's not a thing. It's reality. You would most likely be very happy if your sexual relationship was controlled by a strong partner."

Stef was a true believer. Unfortunately, in this case, he was also right. "I know."

A long sigh came from his chest. "A lot of men would love to take advantage of your nature. I think you would be happier with a Dom. Not a full-time D/s relationship. I think that would be too confining for you, but you need a partner who can be patient because he loves you and adores you for the unique woman you are. He needs to be able to understand you."

"Jeez, you've just described like one person in the whole world. Where on earth do I find this saint?" She felt like crying. Henry couldn't understand her. He'd said it last night. They were so far apart when it came to their ideals. Henry was smart, but he didn't seem to care about the same things she did. He would put up with it during their affair, but he would be gone in a week or so and he would find someone who wasn't as difficult as she was, someone who could get along with people and who didn't protest businesses on a regular basis.

Someone who wasn't so weird.

"I can introduce you to some people," Stef offered. "Give me a couple of weeks and we'll go to Dallas. I have a friend there who's quite good at matching submissives with well-meaning Doms."

She shuddered in horror. The thought of getting set up was awful. She was about to tell Stef all the problems with that scenario when a low voice cut through the quiet bubbling sound of the spa.

"She has no desire to go to Dallas."

"Henry." She looked up and realized he'd stepped into the spa room, and she hadn't noticed. She'd been so involved in conversation with Stef that she hadn't realized they weren't alone.

"Mr. Flanders." Stef didn't look put out. He actually stood up and held out a hand. "It's nice to meet you."

"Is it?" Henry stared at Stef's hand, but made no move to shake it. "Tell me, what sort of protocol do you follow that you feel perfectly comfortable being alone and naked with another man's sub?"

"Henry!" That wasn't polite at all. Henry looked positively territorial as he stalked forward.

Stef squared his shoulders, too. "I follow the protocol where a Dom puts a collar on a sub and then she's off-limits. Until then, she needs the men who give a damn about her to watch her back and make sure she's taken care of. Honestly, even if she's got a collar on, I would still look after her if she needed it."

The testosterone was flying around. She needed to calm the situation down. "I can make my own decisions."

They completely ignored her. Henry had a small bag in his hand and looked delicious. He'd shed his coat and wore only jeans and a T-shirt that showed off his leanly muscular arms. "You can't expect a man to put a collar on a woman the day after he meets her. These things take time and honestly, I think putting a collar on this one will be tricky."

"I wasn't aware you had that kind of time here." Stef stepped out of the hot tub. If he was uncomfortable being naked around a clothed man, he didn't show it. He simply reached for a towel and took his time drying off.

And Henry stepped between them, obviously trying to eliminate her line of sight. "And I was unaware I needed to ask you if it was all right to have a relationship with Nell."

Stef slipped into his robe and turned back to Henry. "She's special."

Nell sat back, well aware that those two really didn't want to hear from her. "Special." Yuck. Everyone said that. She kind of worried they meant it in a "she's not altogether there" way. The other men of the town could talk about her specialness all they liked, but none of them had ever made her feel the way Henry did. She resented Stef's interference the tiniest bit. Not enough to actually protest him because his heart was in the right place, but certainly enough to sulk a little.

But then she also resented the fact that Henry had walked in acting all caveman like. He was leaving soon so she wasn't sure what was up with all the possessiveness.

Of course, on the other hand, the possessiveness made her feel cherished and beloved, but she rather thought that was her vagina talking. She'd recently learned that sexual activity had caused her vagina to revert from its pure feminist roots to something primal that didn't care about anything but getting some more sex from the right man. Perhaps when Henry was gone, she could find her vagina a proper organic, earth-friendly vibrator that ran on rechargeable batteries. Maybe then it would stop screaming at her to pounce on Henry.

"Earth to Nell." Henry had turned and stared down at her.

"Sorry, did you say something?"

Stef chuckled. "We worked a few things out while you were thinking. You'll find she can drift away at the oddest times."

"She's a writer. She's creative. It's only to be expected." Henry's voice had gone a little gruff while he defended her.

And her vagina was talking again. Yep, it didn't seem to want to shut up while he was around, and it didn't like the idea of an organic vibrator. It wanted the real thing.

Stef crossed his arms over his chest. "Well, all right then. Nell, you take care. Henry, if there's anything I can do, I'll help out."

Henry didn't miss a beat. "You can figure out a way to lock the door when you leave."

He couldn't be thinking that way. Nell looked up at him. "This is a public space. It's meant for everyone."

But Stef simply smiled. He walked over to the small closet where the towels were kept and reached toward the back. He produced a sign. *Closed for repairs.* Someone had drawn two naked people climbing into a hot tub and then placed a large *X* across them. "You're not the first, Flanders. You won't be the last. I'll hang it on my way out. You've got an hour before they'll be in here setting up for the Hot Tub Fun Spa party.

You want to be out of here by then. I hear they're waxing some of the men in an effort to keep the Squatchers off them."

The door closed behind Stef.

"Dare I ask?" Henry pulled his shirt over his head, and Nell couldn't help but watch. She was mad at him, but gosh, he was pretty. She knew she shouldn't think like that. He was a human being, and he deserved more than to be seen as a sexual object.

She forced her eyes away and concentrated on the question at hand. "The wax thing or the Squatchers?"

She heard the rustle of clothing being folded away. "I get the wax thing. Hairy guys, lots of pain. Yeah, the Talbot guy is right. I should avoid that at all costs. What the hell is a Squatcher?"

"It's a sort of cryptozoologist."

"So a scientist of some type?" She heard the smallest splash as Henry slid into the hot tub.

"Yes. They study Sasquatch, or as the creature is known in other circles, Bigfoot." She felt comfortable enough to look at him again. She shouldn't have. It wasn't merely his hunky body that got her heart racing. His face was so handsome, all square-jawed and warm brown eyes.

Those eyes widened slightly. "Bigfoot? Seriously?"

"Henry, are you being judgmental?"

An innocent look crossed his face. "Not at all, sweetheart. Bigfoot is probably very serious around here. Now why don't you come over to my side of the tub and give me a kiss?"

She wasn't ready to melt in his arms. "You can't treat my friends like you just treated Stefan."

All innocence was gone, and his jaw formed a hard line. "He was naked in the tub with you."

"It's a nudist resort. They don't allow clothes in the hot tub. What did you expect? That he would hop in wearing a turtleneck and jeans?"

He didn't seem willing to give on this subject. "I would expect he would respect a few boundaries. You're lucky I didn't start a fight."

She couldn't help the way her eyes rolled. "See. That's why this can't work. Violence isn't the answer."

"It can be, but I'll give you that this time it wasn't. The minute he stepped out of the tub, I had all the answers I needed. I have to admit, the naked thing can be useful at times."

She shook her head. "I don't understand."

Henry leaned forward, his hands finding her knees under the water.

"He wasn't hard. He doesn't want you that way. He really is just looking out for you. And he's a lifestyle guy. Serious from the looks of it. If he says he'll take care of you, he means it."

Nell gasped and pulled away. "You were looking at the size of his penis to decide if he was interested in me?"

Henry pulled her back. "No, I was looking at the state of his erection. You see, I've been hard since the moment someone told me you were in the hot tub. A man who wants you is going to have a hard-on whenever he thinks about how soft your breasts are or how good it feels to slide inside your pussy or how much he wants to fuck your mouth."

Her vagina was definitely threatening to take over. His hands moved up her thighs. "Henry, anyone could walk in. Shouldn't we talk about what you found out? Is it safe for me to go home?"

She had to start cleaning up. She needed to find a job. She had to sell her computer. Surely someone would pay a few hundred bucks for it. She would miss her computer. She had a whole community of friends on the Internet, and she would have to go without them.

"Hey." Henry pulled her close. "Don't disappear on me. No. It's not safe to go home, but I have a list of suspects I want to check out. I don't want you to worry." His fingers came up and brushed away tears she didn't know she'd shed. "Don't cry, baby. I'll take care of everything."

He would try. She had no doubt he would find the culprit and try to make things safe for her before he left, but then she would be alone again. Her mother would still be dying. She would still have to move, and she would do it without any support this time.

And that wasn't Henry's problem.

"You're killing me, Nell." His arms wrapped around her, and just for a minute, she felt safe. She let her head find his shoulder. "Tell me what to do. I don't know how to help."

He didn't sound like a man who wanted to get his happy fun time in and leave. He had a job to do, but maybe they could keep in touch. She cuddled close. "Take my mind off things for a while."

It was all she could ask.

"I can do that." Henry's lips touched her forehead. "I want to play. Will you play with me?"

Submit. He wanted her to submit to him. She hated the word, but her vagina was once again loudly stating its opinion. It wanted to submit and, when she thought about it, it was just another choice to make. Henry hadn't done anything to her that hadn't been pleasurable, so why not "play" with him?

"Yes. I want to play."

He pulled lightly on her hair, forcing her to look up at him. "Do you have any idea what you do to me?"

She couldn't help but smile. She could feel what she was doing to him. His cock was hard and poking at her belly. She let her legs drift around his muscled hips. She would like to watch him work out. "I'm trying very hard not to turn you into a sexual object, but you make it difficult for me."

A low chuckle rumbled from his chest. She loved that she could make him laugh. She rather thought he didn't laugh often. "Don't try at all. I want to be your sexual object. Don't turn this into an intellectual thing. This has nothing to do with your brain. This is chemistry, baby. This doesn't come along very often."

"Doesn't it?" She was curious. She had almost no experience. "It's not this way with your other lovers?"

He shook his head as he rubbed their noses together. "I'll be honest with you. I would have told you this differently before I met you, but now I am pretty sure I've never had a lover before. I had women. Plenty of women, but they weren't meaningful. You're meaningful. I don't want you to get the wrong idea, I have to leave, but I don't think I'll ever forget you."

It was all she could ask for at the moment. He had to get back to his job, and she had to take care of her mother. One day she would look him up. If he wasn't in a relationship, maybe they could try again. But she had today and a couple of tomorrows.

"I won't forget you either."

A look of sadness crossed his face. "You will and that's all right. The most I want is to be a distant memory. I want you to be happy. I don't think I ever wanted anything as much as I want that."

He seemed to be struggling with something. She wanted to ask, but this wasn't something she could push for. He had to be ready to talk to her. Maybe Henry needed to forget his troubles, too. They could give each other that much. She brushed her lips to his. "Did you bring the condoms?"

She wanted to feel him moving inside her. For those brief moments, there was no aloneness, no singularity. They were together without question when he was making love to her.

He calmed a bit and a hard look came into his eyes. She was starting to associate that look with sex and pleasure. "I brought them, but I won't use them until I'm ready."

He could be so bossy. "I'm ready right now. You're ready right now. Let's go."

He shook his head. "Are you trying to take charge of this? You know what happens when you do that. Turn around. Put that ass in the air."

Yeah, she'd been kind of going for that. Henry had liked spanking her and she had to admit, she'd liked it, too. He seemed to get even hotter when she was a little bit bratty. Nell turned, her body relaxing for the first time since he'd walked out the door this morning. She stood up on the seat of the hot tub and leaned over, shivering as she placed her ass in the air.

He moved behind her. "This is a count of twenty. Who's in charge of sex?"

"You are, Henry."

"Damn right, I am. I'm not going to let you forget it."

Nell nearly screamed as his hand met her backside. The heat of the water had softened her skin, making the smack so much more intense. Pain flared, racing across her skin as Henry began spanking her over and over again. Tears squeezed from her eyes, but just as she was about to call a halt to it, heat spread, engulfing her. Her pussy was so wet as he smacked away. The tears that came out felt purifying as though all the troubles of her world were slipping away as they fell from her eyes. Over and over again he slapped her ass, making her muscles weak. She lost count, trusting him to keep it. She would be sore tomorrow because he wasn't holding back. She would feel this moment every time she sat down, and she would remember the way it felt and how it sounded. She would remember the startling sting and how it turned into something so much sweeter when she was patient.

"God, baby, your ass is pink." Henry groaned as he spoke. "It's gorgeous. Stay like this. Don't move."

She didn't even want to. That was all? She'd been in a happy place. She wasn't sure she wanted to come out of it yet. But then Henry's mouth was on her skin, kissing the very place he'd just smacked. He kissed her all over, from the small of her back, grazing kisses along her cheeks to where they rounded down to her thighs. It was a sweet torture because what she wanted to do was to tilt her hips up and spread her legs wide so he could slip between them and play with her pussy. But he'd told her not to move, and she was trying to be a good girl.

"Stay that way. I have something else I need to do."

He left her there. She could hear him get out of the hot tub, water dripping from his body as he made his way across the tile. There was the sound of a zipper coming undone and then a rustling as his hands moved probably into the bag he'd brought with him. She closed her eyes and imagined him as he walked back to the tub with the condoms in hand. He was so masculine. His clothes hid it well, but he was covered in lean muscle. There wasn't an ounce of fat on Henry Flanders. He was her own personal Superman. Clark Kent by day, unassuming and, to the people who didn't look closely, a bit bland. But when the clothes came off, oh, he was a god of a man. And any minute now, she would hear the condom wrapper open and he would move behind her. His big cock would be on the edge of her pussy. She would shiver because he seemed so big, too big, but then he would ease his way in and they would be together.

She felt Henry move behind her. Her whole body went taut with anticipation.

"Nell, honey, I'm going to need you to relax." Henry's hands moved along her curves.

She couldn't relax until he was deep inside her. She took a long breath, trying to calm herself. She waited for the sound, but what she heard was more of a popping. Then his hands were back on her cheeks, spreading her wide.

"This is going to be cold. But I'll warm you up fast," Henry said.

Something wet and cold slid between her cheeks. Nell gasped, the feeling foreign. "What's going on? Oh my god. Are you doing what I think you're doing?"

"Well, sweetheart, if you think I'm about to shove a plug up your ass, then you're the big winner." There was a low, sexy laugh that came from Henry's chest. But Nell wasn't laughing because now she could feel something pressing against her anus. "It's only a plug. It's nothing to worry about."

She wasn't so sure about that. After all, Henry wasn't the one about to have something shoved up his ass. She'd been a virgin the day before. She wasn't sure she was ready for this. She tried to look back. "We should talk about this."

"You say that because you don't understand protocol. The real time for talking is afterward." He continued what he was doing, pressing the tip of the plug against her far-too-small asshole. He was working the plug in little circles. "Unless of course you're in some sort of pain or you're scared. This is a small plug, so I doubt you're in pain. And you're such a brave girl. You've faced down screaming crowds. I can't imagine one tiny plug is going to scare my lady."

Manipulative bastard. He was pushing all the right buttons. She couldn't back down from that challenge, but she could ask a simple question. "Do you want to explain why you feel the need to insert a plug up my rectum?"

The plug slipped inside, a brief foray before the circles began again. Pressure. An oddly erotic pressure seemed to be building, and it centered on her asshole. He was opening her up, teasing his way inside, making her ready for something quite larger. "All the better to fuck your ass, my dear. I do believe I told you when we started that I wanted to take you every way a man can take a woman. I don't want to leave an inch of you untouched."

She couldn't help the whimper that came out of her mouth when the plug slipped in again. Henry pressed it farther this time, sliding it in an inch or so before slowly pulling it back out. He stretched her, forcing her to accept the small piece of plastic. If he had his way, one day very, very soon, it would be his cock foraging up her rectum. He would know every inch of her body. He would have her in every way he could.

And she wanted it. She wanted for Henry to know every inch of her. She wanted to be able to feel him everywhere.

"Lean forward," he commanded. "Flatten your back."

She stretched, going into a modified Flat Back pose. It was a little like yoga, this whole sex thing. She needed to get into the right position and then he would slide in easily. She flattened her back, giving him access to everything. And she remembered how much he liked to hear his name. "Yes, Henry."

"Yeah, baby." His voice had gone all deep and guttural, a sure sign that his cock was engaged. She loved the fact that she now knew his tells. She could tell that he was getting hot when his eyes went slightly sleepy and his hands grew languid as they stroked her body. "That's what I want. Do you know how gorgeous you are? Do you have any idea how crazy you get me?"

She knew how crazy he got her. He had her to the point that she was pressing back against that darn plug, waiting for it to invade and conquer. She moved her hips and felt it slide deep inside, a thrill of victory overtaking her.

"Beautiful." He let her cheeks fall back together, but his fingers stroked lower, playing in her pussy. "I can fill up all your holes, baby. I can shove a vibrator in your pussy and my cock up your ass and you'll be so full."

She could imagine. He would try to master her in every way he could. She could feel the plug stretching her, holding her open, filling her up. She felt deliciously stretched and now his fingers were playing in her pussy. Every inch of her flesh felt lit up, humming and happy. "Please."

She needed more than he was giving her. She needed him to make good on his promises, to fill her with his cock.

A single finger pressed inside. "I'll give you everything. Everything, but you're going to obey me first."

He would push her until he was satisfied. It was maddening, but she knew he would come through in the end. He would make sure she had everything she needed. "All right."

She relaxed, giving over to him. There was such peace in the decision, such comfort. She didn't have to be in control because Henry was. She could let go here. She could float along and simply enjoy. She was always in control. She was always making decisions, but being with Henry allowed her to let it all go. At first, she'd thought he was asking for something wrong, but she'd realized what a beautiful gift this was. Submission wasn't a compromise.

His fingers delved deep, fucking upward inside her, making her writhe. She held herself as still as possible, letting Henry control the penetration. She could feel the pressure of the plug. It had been foreign at first, but every second that went by made her more comfortable with it. Nell could feel the press of his lips on the small of her back as his thumb made circles around her clitoris. Pleasure built, threatening to crest. But every time she got close to the edge, he pulled back. Over and over he brought her higher, retreating just as she thought she would drop over.

"Not yet, baby. We're not even close yet. We have a whole hour and I'm going to use it. I've been thinking about this all day. I've been thinking about it from the minute I came last time. This is what I do now. I'm either fucking you or I'm thinking about all the ways I'll fuck you. You're a witch, Nell Finn."

Not according to her mother. According to her mother she was a faery, but they had some magic, too, right?

She heard him moving behind her, the water splashing all around.

"Maybe I should give you a taste. You've been such a good girl. You stayed here. Sure, when I came back, I found you naked with another man, but I know you. I wasn't worried about you at all. You're too good for me, but I'll take you anyway. Let me make you feel good, baby."

He pressed on her clit as he forced two fingers high into her pussy. He rubbed her from the inside and the outside, sending an orgasm screaming through her system. She couldn't help the moan that came from deep inside.

Everything wrong floated away as she gave herself up to Henry.

Chapter Nine

Bishop prayed the sign Stef Talbot had placed outside the door would work because there was no damn way he was stopping now. If someone walked in, they were going to get an eyeful of the sweetest ass cheeks ever created, and suddenly Bishop didn't care. When he'd first realized there was a man in the tub with Nell, he'd thought about how easily he could kill Talbot. He'd gone over about a hundred ways to kill the motherfucker, and he knew exactly where he wanted to bury the body. But the man truly wasn't after her, and Nell wouldn't go with him even if he had been. She belonged to him.

Well, she belonged to Henry Flanders.

Nell's skin had flushed a gorgeous shade of pink as she'd come. He could still feel her pussy muscles clenching, trying to hold his fingers inside.

She'd taken the plug beautifully. The fact that the plug he'd bought just for her was now nestled deep in her body made up for the fact that she wasn't wearing his collar.

"Henry, Henry." She called out his name as she came down from the high.

He pulled his fingers out of her pussy and sucked them inside his mouth. He loved the taste of her. "Come on, baby. It's my turn. You're going to take me in that sweet mouth of yours. I want to feel your tongue wrapped around my cock."

He helped her turn and then took her place, sitting on the side of the tub while she knelt in the bubbling water. What a fucking life they had here. A man could get used to it. No clothes, no worries. Just a gorgeous woman in a hot tub. No blood. No guilt. Only love.

"Henry?"

He shook off the fanciful notion. No blood? His life had been nothing but blood for years. This was a brief respite, and he wasn't going to waste time thinking about things that couldn't happen. Nell was staring up at him, her brown eyes filled with concern. She was a gorgeous nymph with her breasts barely popping out of the water. He reached out, touching her hair and drawing her in.

"I want you to lick me." His cock was already hard enough to fuck. Hell, it seemed to be the only thing he wanted to do anymore. He wanted to fuck Nell and lie around in bed listening to her talk.

"All right, but I should warn you. I've never done this before. I might be perfectly horrible at it." She licked her lips as she stared down at his cock. A look of sheer determination crossed her face and Bishop suddenly realized that he was in for a wild ride. Nell made love with all the passion and heart she put into her protests. It seemed to be the only way she knew how to live. There was no holding back with her. Life kicked her in the crotch, and she stood up and got back to trying to change all the bad shit around her.

She was kind of a hero when he thought about it.

"I think you'll be the best. I think you're always the best." His voice broke a little as he said the words, emotion choking him. He meant it. Somehow she had turned his thinking around, and now he wondered if he wasn't the fool. He certainly was the imbecile for even thinking of leaving her, but he had made his choice a long time ago.

"I'm going to try." Her lips curled up in a smile that seemed to light up the whole room. "It's hard though. The plug thingy wants to come out. I think it wants to be free."

Oh, that wasn't happening. He let his fingers tighten in her hair. He was only in charge in one damn place with her, and he wasn't about to give that up. He would likely spend the next several days eating fake meat and vegetables no one but rabbits should put in their diets. She was keeping that plug inside. "Clench tight. If you lose that plug, I'll find a bigger one."

"I'll try my hardest then." There was a mischievous grin on her face as she leaned forward and kissed the head of his cock.

That was exactly what he needed. Nell pressed small kisses all along his flesh. Her lips were a soft butterfly landing on every inch of his cock. He hissed, trying to maintain control. It had never been a chore before he'd met Nell. He could have sex while plotting his next move and thinking three steps ahead, but with Nell he was lucky to remember to breathe.

"Use your tongue now. Lick me all over."

Her tongue came out and started a long, slow glide over his dick. He took a long breath as she seemed to find a place she liked. Her tongue caressed the underside of his cock, rubbing and loving it. A pulse of arousal escaped from the slit, and Nell lapped it up like it was candy.

Not good at this? Hell, it was the best oral he'd ever had.

He set his hands on her hair as she sucked his cockhead into her mouth. Her tongue whirled around.

"Suck me in. Relax your jaw and take me inside. I want you to take more of me." He leaned back and watched as she complied. His cock started to disappear inside her mouth, her lips wrapping around him. Heat flared along his skin. He let his head fall back and gave up. He didn't have to be in control all the time. He could relax with Nell. Nell wouldn't hurt him. Nell wouldn't betray him. Nell only wanted to please him.

And she seemed to take some deep pleasure in doing just that. Nell looked utterly peaceful as she set about her task. She sucked him hard and then licked her way back down. Her hand came up, touching his balls, softly at first, and then rolling them firmly as she became more comfortable.

"That's what I want." What he wanted was her. He loved watching as she became more and more sure of herself. She was becoming a sex goddess right before his eyes.

How long would she wait after he was gone? How long would she mourn him before she realized he hadn't been worth the gift she'd bestowed on him? How long before she realized she should move on? And how long would it be before the males around her got their heads out of their asses and realized what a true treasure she was?

Would it be the deputy who claimed that loving heart of hers? Or maybe Talbot?

Someone would want her and that someone wouldn't be stupid enough to leave her.

That someone better pray he was good enough for her, because Bishop intended to keep watch. He couldn't be with her, but he could take care of anyone who tried to hurt her.

Pleasure curled up his spine as Nell opened wide to try to take him to the root. He gently tangled his hands in her hair, guiding her forward. His hips moved, fucking into her mouth in short strokes.

He was right there on the edge. He could almost feel the back of her throat. It would be easy to come right then and there, but he wanted more. He wanted her pussy.

"Stop, baby. I don't want to come yet." He only had so much time before the hairy brigade took over their love nest.

Nell kissed his cock one last time. "Does that mean I did it right?"

He didn't take the time to answer her. He pulled her close and kissed her, rubbing his chest against hers. His tongue invaded, dominating hers as she softened for him. He gripped the cheeks of her ass, pulling her into the cradle of his thighs. His cock cuddled up to her belly.

He inhaled her. He kissed her over and over again, wanting to mark her. It wasn't fair to her, but he wanted to mean something to her. He wanted to know she would still think of him years from now. She wrapped her arms around him, surrounding him with her unique warmth.

His cock was going to explode if he didn't get inside her soon. He forced himself to stop and reach for the damn condoms. He'd placed them by the tub. He might be a bastard, but he wasn't going to leave her alone with a baby.

Nell watched with eager eyes as he rolled the condom over his straining cock. She never played coy. Her emotions were always right there for him to see, to believe. She put a hand on his, helping him sheathe himself.

"Come on, baby. Get on your knees, facing away from me." He slid back into the water and helped her around. He loved tracing her curves with the flat of his palm, memorizing every inch of her. "Spread your knees. Let me inside."

Her knees moved, opening herself up to him. He could see the light purple plug peeking from between her cheeks, preparing her for his cock. He would fuck her ass until he made her love it, until she knew what it really meant to be possessed, that there was nothing civilized or fair about it.

He moved between her legs, lining his cock up. Her pussy was wet from the orgasm he'd given her, but she was still so damn tight. He pressed up, pushing his cock inside, forcing his way. He gripped her hips, guiding himself in.

Not only was she tight, the plug made her tighter. He could feel it dragging on his dick, a pure pleasure, but he was determined to take her over the edge with him.

"I feel so full." Her head dropped forward as she dragged air into her lungs. A hot groan came out of her mouth, and Bishop could feel it all along his cock.

"You're not even half full yet, baby." He forced another inch in, his skin singing everywhere they touched. *So good.* She felt so fucking good. He took his time, patiently working his cock inside. Her pussy muscles squeezed, threatening to send him over the edge, but he forced it back.

Not yet. Not yet. He didn't want it to end yet.

God, he wasn't sure he wanted it to ever fucking end, and he wasn't thinking about the sex.

He pulled back, the drag on his dick nearly making his eyes cross. Nell's pussy clenched, trying to keep him in, threatening his control, but he was a man on a mission.

He let his hand slide around her body, his thumb finding that nubbin that brought her so much pleasure.

Nell gasped as he pinched at her clit, and he knew he wouldn't have to wait long. She was close. He fucked her hard, picking up the pace. He rammed his dick in while he worked her clit. Over and over, he fucked inside, losing himself completely. She was the only thing that mattered in that moment. They were the only two people in the whole fucking world. There was no job to return to, no mission to complete beyond sealing the bond between them. There was Henry and there was Nell. He didn't have to be John Bishop here. He didn't have to be the kid no one wanted, the boy trying so hard to fit in. He could be Nell's man. Henry Flanders fit in here. He fit with her like a puzzle piece long forgotten but found and locked into place, complete once more.

Nell's shout filled the small space, echoing off the walls. She clamped down hard, her orgasm forcing his own. It raced up, bubbling from his balls, causing his whole body to shake as he gave up.

She slumped over, her torso resting on the marble floor. Bishop's hands shook as he rid himself of the condom, tying it off and shoving it into his bag.

He was in far too deep. He was falling for the girl, and he couldn't afford to do that. She was a distraction. She was a liability. She was a weakness.

He should walk away now. It would be best for the both of them. He could turn over all the information he had to Rye Harper and pray the man was a better law enforcement officer than the sheriff. He could tell her he would be back, towel off, get dressed, and then walk away. He could be on a plane in two hours, and he would never have to think about her or Bliss again.

"I don't think I can move." Her face was turned toward him, those lips that had loved him curled up in a satisfied grin.

"You don't have to." He picked her up and settled her on his lap. He smoothed back her hair as she laid her head on his chest.

This was where he wanted to be, cuddled close to Nell.

He would stay just for one more day.

* * * *

Nell slipped the sign back in the closet as a group descended to set up for the spa party. That had been a close call. Henry had only just washed everything up after taking the plug out. It would have been truly uncomfortable to have gotten caught with that plug.

The door opened and Pam and Bill walked in carrying a massage table. Callie followed behind them with a large box.

Henry moved quickly to take it out of Callie's hands. And he didn't even try to hide the fact that he wasn't wearing a stitch. He was getting comfortable.

And she was falling deeply in love.

"Henry, it's nice to see you're settling in." Bill set the massage table down and shed the coat he was wearing. He toed off his boots and grinned up at Henry. "I have to admit, I rather thought you would run by now."

Henry's broad shoulders shrugged as he placed the box on the table. "I'm finding I can be adaptable when I want to be."

A light hit Bill's eyes. He reached out and patted Henry's arm. "Yes, you can. You can adapt to just about anything, son, and happiness is damn easy to adapt to."

Henry cleared his throat. "Well, I'm not quite as scared of all the naked stuff as I thought I would be."

It was good to see him being open and tolerant. And, at the same time, it kind of hurt because she was pretty sure he was still leaving. He was opening up and becoming a man she would be so proud to love, and he would walk away and another woman would get that big heart all to herself.

"Oh, you're not a coward at all, Professor Flanders." Nell's mother stood in the doorway, a thick robe wrapped around her body. "I think you're special."

"I don't know about special, Moira," Henry replied. "But I am okay with the naked thing."

Her mother gave Henry a very thorough once-over. "Well, any man who looks like you should be. Henry, dear, could you get me a lounger? I'd rather like to rest while we're waiting."

Her mother looked pale, fragile, but she smiled at Henry as he leapt into action. He didn't hesitate, didn't take time for small talk. He nearly ran across the room to grab one of the lounge chairs stacked at the back.

"He's a good man, your Henry." Her mom put an arm around her shoulder, resting their heads together. "I like him a lot."

Tears immediately sprang to her eyes. She wanted more time. It was going too fast, like time was speeding up and she wanted so desperately to stay, to hold the moment. So sweet. So fleeting. This was life. It had to be savored because it was over quickly. "I think I might love him, Mom."

Her mother's smile was soft as she looked at her. "Of course you do. He's your soul mate. I can see it very plainly."

"Moira, where do you want this?" Henry was holding the heavy chaise like it weighed nothing.

"Oh, I want to be close to the action. We're waxing Sasquatch, after all. You know we call them trolls where I come from. Such an odd place, the Earth plane." Her mother pointed to a spot close to the massage table where Callie was starting to heat a pot for the wax and Pam was setting up a pedicure station. Henry moved to do her bidding, and Moira squeezed Nell. "I think I would like my toes to be purple this time. One thing I love about this plane is the technology. The vampires have it, too, but it's so much more personal here."

Henry didn't seem to notice the crazy talk. He was busy placing the chaise and talking to Bill. A tendril of guilt sparked through her system. Henry should love her mom, too. There was nothing wrong with her mother. A little insanity never hurt anyone. Moira Finn had been a wonderful mother.

"I think purple would be great." Nell leaned over, pressing her lips to her mom's cheek. Time was short. She wouldn't hold back on her affection. Love was never wrong. Love was never wasted. Her eyes strayed to Henry. Even if he couldn't love her back, she was better for loving him. Her mom had taught her that. "I love you, Mom."

"I love you, baby. You're the best thing I ever did. I wish you could have known my cousin. The good one, not the asswipe. Seamus was a good man. He had his flaws, but I loved him. Torin was a little shit. I don't know how he came from the same family as the rest of us."

"Here you go, Moira." Henry held a hand out, guiding her to the chaise. "Maybe you can put the robe down so you're more comfortable. It's nice and warm in here."

He patted the chaise as though it wouldn't bother him if her mother dropped her robe and made herself comfortable. He'd come so far. He could go farther. Henry Flanders could be such a great man if he only allowed himself to be. He was capable of such deep love and acceptance. He was on the cusp of being a great man, and she couldn't help but wonder at it.

Her mother didn't have a problem with shedding her robe, either. She shrugged out of it and handed it to Henry, who kept his eyes squarely on her face before laying the robe out on the chaise for her.

"Here you go," Henry said gallantly. "Nell, honey, I'm going to head into town for a couple of hours. I'll be back before it's time for bed, okay?"

She nodded. He was very likely going into town so he could work on her case. She wished he wouldn't take it so seriously, but that was the way Henry thought. Her mom squeezed Henry's hand as she took her place and then Nell wrapped her arms around him.

She loved the feel of him. His hands found her waist and she felt surrounded, beloved. He hadn't said it, probably never would, but she felt adored when he held her like that. "Have a nice time. Call me if you need anything."

He looked down at her. "Go to my room when you're done. I want you in my bed. If you aren't there, I'll hunt you down."

He would, too. He was ridiculously possessive, and it occurred to her to talk to him about it, but the truth was, she kind of liked it and she liked having a key to his room. She got the idea he wouldn't give it out to anyone but her. "I'll be there. I don't have any plans. I'll stay here with Mom and then have dinner and head to bed. Your bed. I know it's a nudist resort, but it's actually quite staid."

"See that it stays that way." He brushed his lips against hers. "Is it wrong that I feel weird grabbing my pants?"

She shook her head. "Nope. You should always be naked."

He frowned. "Yeah, we're going to have to negotiate that, baby. Be good."

He walked out, picking up his bag as he left and grabbing his clothes. She couldn't help but watch as he walked away, his backside on perfect display.

"That is a very attractive man."

"Mom!"

Her mother shrugged. "I'm old, honey, not dead. He's got a lovely physique. It's obvious that your Henry believes in a healthy amount of physical activity."

The door closed behind him, and Nell sat down on the edge of the lounger. It was as good a time as any to have this discussion with her mother. The last thing she wanted was for her mom to get the idea that this thing with Henry was going to last. "I really like him."

Her mom frowned. "I think it's more than like. You're sleeping with him."

Was there no privacy anywhere? "How does everyone know that?"

"Callie saw him whisking you away last night. She said it was very romantic. Did he really carry you down the hall like you weighed less than a feather, dear?"

"Callie!"

Callie turned, wincing. "Gossip is my only flaw. And it was quite lovely, though I'll be honest, I thought you would make out with him. I wouldn't have told your mom if I actually thought you were sleeping with him. Please don't protest me."

And it had probably made Callie think about everything she'd lost. "I think I can forgive you. Besides, I hear you're going to be the one to wax Roy Ferguson."

Callie nodded. "He's tired of the Squatchers hunting him. They send out mating calls and everything. How do they know the mating call of a Sasquatch if they've never actually seen one? It makes a person think." Callie shook her head. "I'm going to need more wax. We'll be back in a minute."

Callie left with her mom, and Bill nodded as he followed them.

"I wish I could help more, but I'm so tired these days." Her mother lay back. She looked weary, but there was a secretive smile on her face.

"It's the chemotherapy." Nell held her mom's hand. "When this round is over, you'll feel better."

"No, love. I stopped the chemo about a month ago."

Nell felt her whole world shift. She'd thought Pam was driving her into Alamosa for treatments all this time. "Mom! How could you do that?"

"Because it's time." There was a weak squeeze to her hand as her mom gripped her fingers. "Don't be angry with me, sweetheart. There's a time to fight and there's a time to go out with grace. If we hadn't found this place, if I wasn't sure you would be all right, I would still be fighting. And I would still be in pain. I can rest now, Nell. I can go and see your father again. I've been so far from home."

Nell's heart threatened to break. The thought of losing her mother was almost unimaginable, but she'd been in pain for so long, and not merely physical pain. "Do you honestly believe you'll see him again?"

Clear brown eyes held her own. "Oh, yes. I know everyone thinks I'm crazy. It's been nice being here in Bliss, but they put me in the same category as Mel with his aliens. They think there's something wrong with my brain or that I had a loss that I couldn't accept, but I know my truth. Honey, there are more worlds out there than you can imagine. This world is just one. This time is just one. My husband is waiting for me. He's my soul mate. We didn't get our chance in this life, but there will be another. I have faith."

"I don't understand how you can believe that. You have no evidence that we get another chance. What if we die and this is all there is?" She didn't want to believe that, but faced with the reality of her mother's passing, fear threatened to take hold, fear that this was all that existed, that the great mystery of life could be solved with a resounding blank space of nothingness.

"That's why they call it faith, Eleanor. If we had the answers, there would be no reason to believe. Do you remember when you were young and I took you to see that one play everyone raved about?"

Nell groaned. "*Peter Pan.* How could I forget? You tried to tell the actors that they had everything wrong and that they didn't know the difference between a pixie and a faery."

"Well, they were using the wrong names. It was a bit insulting. Humans like to be called the proper names. Why wouldn't they think a pixie would? Tinker Bell was obviously a pixie, right down to the fact that she can hold a mean grudge." She shook her head. "I'm getting away from my point. I remember watching you when the little pixie was dying."

She smiled at the memory. "They told everyone if we clapped hard enough she would come back to life."

"If you believed enough. It's an object lesson. You have to have faith. You have to believe. Maybe things won't turn out the way you thought they would. Maybe your dreams won't all come true, but if you have faith and put good things out into the world, then you've done your job. Be patient, my love. These things tend to work out in the end. Even if it takes a few lifetimes." She laid her head against the lounger, a long sigh coming from her chest. "Death is nothing to be afraid of. It's merely a doorway to the next phase. And when you take that door one day, your father and I will be waiting on the other side. We'll be together again. We're always together. That's been the joy of my existence."

Nell held her mother's hand and tried not to cry. No amount of faith would keep her mother here. No amount of faith would keep Henry here.

"If he's your soul mate, you'll find each other." Her mother had always known what she was thinking. She'd never been able to hide. "And I'm not gone, yet. We still have some time, but Nell, no more treatments. I want to enjoy the time I have left with you. I want to make some precious memories."

She nodded, tears filling her eyes. "I want that, too."

Her mom reached up, brushing away her tears. "And don't count that man out yet. He obviously has some decisions to make. I believe he'll come around in the end. Happily ever afters run in our family."

Nell frowned. "I thought war and thieving uncles run in our family."

Moira waved that off. "That was just a blip on the map. It will sort itself out in the end. We Finns always find our happiness. Sometimes we have to fight for it, though."

The doors opened again and Callie walked through, carrying an even bigger tub than before. "I've got to get this heated. Nell, will you go and let the pedicurist in? She's at the gate, but she needs to be buzzed in. And hurry. We don't want to lose her. She's the only one at Polly's who's willing to touch hobbit feet, as they call them."

"Hobbits." Her mother huffed. "She should try trimming an ogre's toenails. Sometimes the damn toenails fight back."

Callie laughed, and her mother was off talking about all sorts of creatures. Nell went for the door. She glanced back and saw her mother smiling.

Despite everything, her mother believed things would work out. Maybe it was time for Nell to believe, too. She grabbed her robe. Normally she wouldn't bother, but it was awfully cold outside. She slipped her phone into her pocket. Henry might call. He'd only been gone for twenty minutes or so and she already missed him. She dragged on her boots because there was a lot of snow between here and the gate.

She jogged outside, following the tracks Henry's truck had made in the snow. She was going to have to get him into a more earth-friendly vehicle. Snow fell as she raced to the gate. She could see Kelly Hansen's compact had made it up the mountain. Kelly was Polly's oldest daughter and seemed to be following her mother into the beauty business.

Nell hit the button and the gate began to swing open, but Kelly's car stayed where it was, not moving. Kelly's face stared out the front window, her hands on the steering wheel.

Was something wrong? Kelly had trouble with mild epilepsy in the past. Was she having a seizure? Nell ran out, trying to remember what she should do. The driver's side window was open.

Kelly's hands were shaking, her face a stark white. "Nell, I'm so sorry."

A man sat up from the back seat. There was a nasty-looking gun in his hand, and he pointed it straight at Kelly's eighteen-year-old head. Kelly was just a baby, but Warren Lyle was a full-grown man. The former CEO of Lyle Waste Management Systems sneered her way.

"Get in the car or we'll see what the inside of this kid's head looks like."

Well, at least she knew who had broken into her cabin now.

Kelly muffled a cry.

"Why don't you let her go?" Nell asked, her heart pounding in her chest. The grounds were completely empty. Everyone was inside. An eerie silence filled the yard around her.

Lyle placed the gun right against Kelly's head, the metal butting her forward. "You have three seconds or I'll kill the both of you right here."

"Please, Nell. Please help me." Tears poured down Kelly's cheeks.

Help me. Two words guaranteed to bring Nell Finn running.

Two words that might get her killed this time.

Nell calmly got into the car.

Chapter Ten

Bishop sighed as he sat down at the "Internet Café." It was not the center of technology he'd been hoping for. He shouldn't have expected more. Night was falling and the Bear Creek Lounge and Internet Café was filling up. Luckily, the crowd seemed way more interested in a beer than in checking their e-mail since the Café portion of the place consisted of one small table and a wretchedly slow dial-up. Dial-up. He didn't realize that was even a thing anymore.

He bet the Stark kid had way better access.

"Hey, it's Henry, isn't it?" A familiar redhead walked up wearing black slacks and a white shirt. She had a tray of drinks balanced on her hand.

Holly, the lonely heart. A man really couldn't blend into the background in a town this small. "Henry Flanders. Nice to see you again."

Holly flushed prettily. She was a lovely woman, but she couldn't compare to his Nell. "Sorry about hitting on you at Hell on Wheels. I didn't know you were involved with Nell. I like Nell. I wouldn't try to come between the two of you. She's so nice. Well, until you forget to recycle and then, boy, can that girl give you a lecture."

He'd already decided on how to handle that particular problem. When Nell got mouthy with him, he would shove his cock between her lips and the problem would be solved. Or maybe a ball gag. She would look awfully cute in full bondage. "It's okay. I'm only here for another week or so. Maybe two. I plan on spending all my time with Nell."

Holly nodded. "I'm glad. And I can't thank you enough for helping out with the whole bar fight thing. Max has too much fun with stuff like that, if you ask me. He would have taken forever to end it. We were lucky you were there because that Laura lady was in some pain. I don't know why a woman who recently had surgery would go hitchhiking across the country, but she doesn't want to talk about it."

Bishop didn't want to talk about it either, but Holly could come in handy. "Hey, is there any way to boost this signal? It's awfully slow."

Holly groaned. "Yeah, it gets that way when my boss uses up the signal to watch Internet porn."

A bald head popped up from behind the bar. "Don't tell Anne. She gets real mad about that."

Holly's eyes rolled. "I won't mention it if you'll get back to work. We're filling up in here, Lonnie. I need two Manhattans and that fellow over there was asking about a martimmy. I think he means martini, but he has a weird accent. And stay off the Internet. We have a paying customer."

Lonnie immediately started pulling down bar glasses and bottles of liquor.

"It should work better now. How about a Scotch? Lonnie keeps a fifteen-year around for Stef Talbot, but he won't miss a couple of fingers."

Finally, civilization. And it didn't hurt that it belonged to Talbot. "Make it three fingers and I'll forget all about your boss's porn problem."

She winked and walked away. Sure enough, the speed picked up. Thank god. He'd read the dossiers Seth had put together, but he wanted to look these asswipes up himself. Sometimes there were things out there that didn't fit into a twenty-year-old's version of a file.

It didn't take too long before he'd completely discounted Jim Miller. Miller ran a company that had gone under when Nell had proven that the small restaurant chain named Tasty and Healthy actually used lard as a regular ingredient. Miller had been embarrassed on network television and had vowed revenge on the group that had taken him down, but Seth had neglected to look at the asshole's personal page. His wife gave birth to a new baby the same day Nell's place had been broken into. There were pictures of the former CEO holding the tiny girl.

So it came down to Mickey Camden and Warren Lyle.

Camden previously had run a small pharmaceutical firm. Nell had decided the lab animals needed their freedom. It should have been a simple open-and-shut case with Nell going to jail for breaking and entering, but while she was freeing the rabbits and monkeys, she also discovered that Camden was trafficking drugs for a cartel.

Camden was awaiting trial. Nell had paid a small fine.

He was going to smack her ass for that. She'd gone in alone. Anything could have happened to her. She was a chaos magnet.

Camden was one to watch. Lyle, too. Lyle's firm specialized in storing nuclear waste. They handled everything from biomedical nuclear waste to large energy firms. Nell had managed to prove they were cutting corners and the EPA had taken his ass down. Lyle's wife had left him.

Two people. Seth was damn good. Without Seth's program, he would still be going through Nell's computer, still be sifting through the hundreds of protests she'd participated in or organized over the years. Now he only had to deal with two assholes. He needed to figure out where they were.

But he needed better Internet. He couldn't hack anything with this piece of crap. And it slowed down again. He glanced up. Lonnie had disappeared behind the bar again.

An odd pinging sound zinged through the air. Bishop looked back and a man in a trucker hat was walking through the lounge area with a small handheld device that was pinging and lighting up as he waved it around.

Bishop packed up Nell's computer and pulled out his cell. He'd gotten Seth's number from an e-mail. He quickly texted the kid with the two names he was concerned about.

Lyle and Camden. Run their credit cards. I'll be at your place in twenty.

He moved over to the bar. He could use that drink. Holly set the Scotch in front of him. Seth would need half an hour or so to get his task done. He could take his time. Nell was very likely getting her toes painted by some naked person. Bishop took a long sniff of the perfectly oaky liquor and gave a silent prayer of thanks that Stef Talbot had excellent taste in Scotch. He took a nice sip, the flavor familiar and comforting.

Like Nell. When he closed his eyes, he could still taste her on his tongue, still smell the spicy scent of her arousal, feel that soft skin pressing against his.

"Could I get a beer?" a deep voice asked. Bishop felt someone move into the seat beside him.

Lonnie grabbed a longneck from the cooler and quickly popped the top. "Fred. How's it going?"

A man in a Western shirt with pearl snaps sat on the barstool beside him. Bishop quickly estimated his age, status, and likely field of employment. Gray hair peeked from beneath a cowboy hat that had seen a lot of wear, but the shirt was of excellent quality and the watch around his wrist was easily worth a couple grand. He was around sixty-five, had some money, and worked in the sun if the deep lines on his face were any indication. He likely owned a ranch.

"I'm getting by, Lonnie. That's all I can ask right now."

The barkeeper frowned, concern obvious on his face. "I heard a rumor that Noah might be getting married."

"I don't know about that, but I sincerely hope my son gets his head out of his ass before he does something he shouldn't." The rancher took a long drag off his beer. "I don't think this would be happening if my Ellen was still alive."

Lonnie patted the bar in front of him. "Yeah. I still miss her. How's Brian doing?"

A long sigh came from the cowboy. "He's comfortable. That's all we can hope for now."

"If there's anything Anne and I can do to help, let us know. I'm going to go grab you some pretzels. I keep the kind you like in the back."

Maybe Lonnie wasn't such an ass. Bishop sipped his Scotch and wondered where he would be at this time next year. Colombia? Argentina? Would they move him to the Middle East? Fuck, he might not even be alive next year.

Who would be watching after Nell?

"You got any kids?"

Bishop nearly cringed. Damn. The last thing he wanted was to get into a discussion with a complete stranger. "Nope."

The cowboy sighed. "Well, you're still young. One day you'll have kids and, let me tell you, you need to remember that they *will* drive you to drink." He chuckled. "I will say that it was easier when my boys were little. All they wanted was a taste of whatever their momma was cooking and for their dads to play some ball with them."

"Dads?" He couldn't help it. He knew he shouldn't ask, but it came out.

"Fred Glen." He held out a hand.

Bishop shook it. "Henry Flanders."

"Well, Henry, I own a ranch. I was married and had a son. James. My wife was killed in a car accident when Jamie was just a toddler. My best friend had a kid, too. Noah. Brian's wife left him and he came to live out on the G with us. That's where we met our Ellen."

Was he saying what Bishop thought he was saying? "You shared her?"

A brilliant smile crossed the man's face, and he touched the gold band on his left ring finger. "We married her. She was Jamie's and Noah's momma. We had a good twenty years together. She died a while back. Brian's not going to last long. He's got a bad heart. I think it broke the day our Ellen died."

What the hell was worth that kind of heartache? Nell. A vision of her looking up at him with perfect trust in her eyes assaulted him. He should keep quiet. The guy would stop talking eventually. None of this meant anything to Bishop. "Would you do it again?"

He nodded. "Oh, god, I would do it in a heartbeat. I wouldn't change anything."

"But she died. He's going to die." Nell could die. It was better to walk away, to not feel anything. His mother had died. It was what people did. They died. They left. They failed.

"I'll die one day, too. But if I hadn't loved Ellen, if I hadn't shared a life with Brian and our kids, well, I wouldn't have lived. This ache in my gut, it means I lived, son. I loved. I built something. I don't regret a minute of it. Not even the end. Brian and I held her when she passed and then we had each other. No. My only problem is my boys. They have a woman coming between them. My youngest is going to make a very big mistake and I can't stop him. He thinks he's in love."

A long moment passed. "How can you tell?"

Fred Glen turned slightly. "How can you tell if you're in love?"

Was he in love with Nell? He'd never felt anything close to the way he felt when she walked into a room. Was that love? "Yeah."

"When you can't think of anything but her." A mysterious smile curled his lips up, like he was lost in some ridiculously sweet memory. "When she's the only thing in the world that matters. When you realize you want to be a better man, make the world a better place, because she's in it. When the choices you make, about yourself, about the kind of man you are all boil to one thing—will she be proud of you? That's when you know."

Bishop took a damn long drink this time.

There was a loud beeping behind him. Holly rushed around the bar.

"Oh, dear, this is going to get bad," Holly said, worry plain in her voice.

Fred Glen's face lit up. "Oh, this is going to be fun."

Bishop opened his eyes, and the redhead was putting down her tray.

She looked behind the bar. "Damn it, Lonnie. Get out here. We have real trouble."

Lonnie poked his head out of the back and quickly disappeared again. "It's just Mel."

Holly practically vibrated as she stared out into the lounge. "I swear to god, I'm going to quit one day."

"Who's Mel?" The only thing he knew about the man named Mel was that he believed in aliens and had a thing for beets. Bishop took another sip of the Scotch. He tried his damnedest to stop thinking about what Fred Glen had said. He didn't love her. He was just sleeping with her. He'd been her first man and he felt a responsibility toward her. That was all. He wanted her.

If he played his cards right, he could find the bad guy and be back in time to have dinner with Nell before they explored a little bondage this evening. He was going to tie her to the bedposts, spreading her arms and legs wide, splaying her open for his very delicious torture. He would lick her from head to toe. He would get her so hot she would be begging for his cock. He might even clamp her nipples. That would be pretty.

"Mel's a legend around these parts. He considers himself an alien hunter. Notice that he's got tinfoil under that hat of his. Claims it keeps the death rays from taking him." Fred was grinning, his weariness fading for the moment.

Bishop turned in his chair, watching the action out in the lounge. Mel was the man in the trucker hat with the weird beeping thing. It was going off like crazy as he stood in front of a young man with a shock of dark hair. His face was unlined, his eyes wide as he looked up at the lanky man. He had been talking to a pretty brunette who moved away the minute Mel walked up as though she knew disaster was about to happen and wanted to get clear of the blast radius.

"All right, you. You know damn well you're not supposed to be here," the man named Mel accused.

The younger man shrank back a bit, clutching his glass. "I am only trying to enjoy my martimmy. Go away."

Dude did not come from here. What was that accent? Croatian?

Mel didn't seem to give a crap about the weird accent. "Not on your life, buddy. You are in direct violation of Intergalactic Council Order 100923-4821. This is protected ground. You're not allowed to breed here."

Holly rushed up, an envelope in her hands. "Oh, god, he's talking about breeding. I am so sorry. If we don't let him kick someone out about once a month, he gets antsy, and that's bad for everyone. The town got together a couple of months back and put together this nice package for Mel's victims."

"Holly, he ain't a victim. He's a Sibalian male of mating age. That ain't even his real form," Mel explained.

"What is this man talking about? I'm here on vacationings. This is ridiculous." The man set down his drink, his face flushing. "I demand to talk to the management."

Holly pressed the envelope in his hand. "Management snuck into the kitchen to watch Internet porn. I'm so sorry. There's no charge for the drink and the Trading Post has a free quarter pound of fudge for you. You can get your oil changed at Roger's Garage for nineteen ninety-nine. Polly offers a free wax, but I kind of think she enjoys that. She's a little sadistic if you ask me. And there's free coffee for you at Stella's. Please don't sue us."

The man huffed, grabbed the envelope, and stalked out.

"Nothing to worry about here, people." Mel held up his detector thingy. "You're all safe. You don't have to worry about being overrun with Sibalian young. Whew. That was a close one. The vodka in the drink would have triggered his mating pheromones and then no woman would be safe. No need to thank me."

Mel tipped his foil-lined hat and waved good-bye, his job apparently done.

"Nope." Fred Glen was smiling broadly. "Wouldn't change a damn thing. This is the place to live, son."

Bishop slapped some bills on the counter. He needed to get to Seth's and then get home to Nell. Well, get back to his room. Nell was waiting for him and he had plans on how to spend the night. It did not include watching an alien hunter threaten tourists. "Thanks, Fred. It was good to meet you."

He grabbed his case, put on his coat, and headed out. Night had fallen and the cold blasted him. He wanted to be back with Nell where it was warm.

His phone buzzed, a text coming in.

It's Lyle. Used a credit card in Alamosa two days ago.

Bishop sighed. One assignment down. He could find the fucker tomorrow and then bury him. There had to be plenty of places to bury a body out here. It had been a couple of weeks since he'd killed someone.

Nell would protest him if she knew. He could hear the lecture on how he should rehabilitate criminals, not internally decapitate them. But he was really good at internal decapitation. It was his signature move. Bloodless. Usually no one had time to scream. And, when he thought about it, it was fairly painless. Killing with kindness. Nell would approve.

And then she would protest.

Any way he looked at it, Nell would never be able to accept the real John Bishop. And what the fuck was he thinking anyway? That he could take Nell with him? He worked deep-cover assignments with some of the most dangerous terrorists and drug dealers in the world. He'd worked with female agents before. He'd used them as cover. They were beautiful and deadly and knew when to keep their mouths closed.

Nell would protest the terrorists and get her gorgeous ass shot in five seconds flat.

There was a quick, loud, sucking sound and Bishop's eyes were flooded with a blue light. It was gone in an instant, but a cold wind blew him back. *What the fuck?*

Mel walked from around the side of the building. "He's off. Gotta make sure with those boys. When they get the mating heat, they can take out whole cities. You ever seen the episode of *Star Trek* with the tribbles? Yeah, that's what it's like. Luckily I have a direct line to MI17, and they can open a wormhole."

Bishop shook his head. What was the proof on the liquor again? "MI17?"

Mel nodded as though all of this was perfectly normal. "Sure. The Brits don't acknowledge they have an MI17, but that's just silly. Who else would have put down the Great Invasion of '89? It sure wasn't going to be that Star Wars defense project. Hell, no. Mayonnaise. That's what scares those Orcanians."

Bishop was pretty sure he was the one who had landed on a different planet.

His phone rang as he watched the deeply odd man walking toward an old pickup truck. He slid his finger across the screen to answer. "Yeah?"

"John?"

Bishop froze.

"It's Bill. I'm alone, but you need to get here and quick. Nell is missing, son."

His heart threatened to stop. "What do you mean? She was with her mother when I left her."

"It's been chaotic around here. We didn't realize she was missing until a couple of minutes ago. Callie asked her to go and let in Kelly, Polly's girl. The gate can only be opened by residents and guests who have keys. Nell went out to manually open the gate."

"Where is this Kelly person?"

"That's just it. She's not here, either. She was in her car at the front gate, and now she's gone. I'm trying to pull up the security tapes right now. Pam and Callie are with the others searching the grounds, but I have a very bad feeling."

Bishop ran for his car. "I'll be there in ten minutes. Call the sheriff."

"I called him before I called you. Rye Harper's on his way and the sheriff's going out to Polly's to make sure Kelly didn't go home."

"How long has she been gone?"

"It's been about half an hour since anyone saw her."

Nausea threatened to take over. That was practically forever. If all Lyle wanted to do was kill Nell, he likely would have shot her and left her body lying there, but he'd taken her. Bishop had to hope that Lyle wanted to torture her for a while. He couldn't even believe he was thinking the words, but she had to be alive. He could help her, put her back together, anything—just as long as she was still alive.

"John, she's alive." It was like Bill could feel his anxiety over the line. "If we haven't found her body, then she's alive. We need to figure out where he would take her."

Bishop didn't know the land. He didn't have any idea where the hell the fucker would go. And he needed a goddamn piece. He wasn't carrying. He'd locked his SIG away back at the resort because he didn't want Nell to catch him with a gun. He didn't even have a knife on him.

Mel was suddenly beside him, the older man moving almost silently. "Is everything all right? You went real pale there for a second. Are you remembering a past alien experience? It happens to me all the time. I got some tonic that helps."

"I don't need tonic. I need a gun."

"Shotgun, handgun, stun gun? You're going to have to be more specific." Mel straightened his trucker hat, the tinfoil crinkling. "Do you know the nature of the creature we're hunting?"

The guy was a nut, but maybe he had some guns. And he probably knew the area. "It's not a creature, just a giant asshole. He's got Nell Finn, and I'm worried he's going to kill her."

"Come with me," Mel said. "I've got a kit in my truck and a radio. I'll get the crew on this. How long's she been gone? Do we know what type of vehicle she was taken in? The snow's been coming down hard all afternoon, so they wouldn't get far on foot."

Now the man suddenly sounded competent. He strode back to his antique pickup and opened the bed as Bishop followed along. He could already see a full gun rack through the back window. He counted a shotgun and a rifle. Maybe this Mel guy could track more than fake aliens. "Bill said she was likely in someone named Kelly's car. I don't know her."

"Kelly Hansen. Nice girl. Crappy car. It's going to struggle in this snow, especially coming down off the mountain. I've been out here for about forty minutes trying to make sure the order to MI17 had gone through before I threw the Sibalian out." He pointed at the place where the road from the resort met the highway. "Unless they tried going down the other side, this is where they would have come out and I'm telling you, Kelly's brakes wouldn't make it down the other side. Once you get past my place and the Harpers', the grade is too steep. I haven't seen anyone come off the mountain so they're either still up there or they're at the bottom of the other side."

Fuck. It seemed like there were a whole bunch of ways for Nell to die tonight. "Can you get me up there? We should be able to follow the tracks in the snow. Most people around here drive trucks and SUVs. If this Kelly's car is smaller, we should be able to tell where she's gone."

A large tool kit sat in the back of Mel's truck. He worked a lock and then flipped it open, and Bishop's eyes widened because he wasn't even sure what half that shit was. The tinfoiled man had guns of all kinds, knives, a short sword, what looked like a medieval mace, some hair spray, and several items that Bishop was pretty sure he didn't want to touch. But there was a very staid-looking semiautomatic, and Bishop felt better the minute the weight hit his hand. He checked the mag. The gun was in perfect order. It would blow a nice hole through Warren Lyle's head.

Reality settled on Bishop as Mel opened his driver's door and started talking on a radio. He'd been in too many fucked-up situations to honestly believe that this would go well. His brain worked through all the scenarios and almost none of them played out in his favor. Almost every single one ended with Nell dead in the snow and with Bishop seeking revenge.

He loved Nell Finn. It was stupid. It was wrong. It could only end in complete disaster, but he was in love with Nell, and he suddenly understood that if he allowed Nell deep into his heart, she would change him forever. It had probably already happened. He was probably ruined for any other woman, but then it didn't matter because he wasn't the kind of guy who got married and settled down in a small town. He was a killer. He was a tool, and the United States government wasn't going to allow an asset like John Bishop to ask for a mulligan and walk away. They would come after him, and Nell would get hurt.

If Nell was even alive.

"I just got some info on the radio. Max is on the case. He's talking to Rye, says they have confirmation that Nell got into Kelly's car and they started back down the mountain. He's calling some people he knows on the other side to see if they remember Kelly's car rolling by. Bill Hartman is going to send some of his folks out on snowmobiles to see what he can find."

So everyone was looking for her. He wasn't alone. There was an odd comfort to that, but no one would look for her the way he would. No one else would keep going until they found her. Even if it took forever because the world was suddenly utterly meaningless if one brunette with soft eyes and a softer heart wasn't walking around in it.

Bishop took a nice-looking hunting knife out of the box and pocketed it, too.

"Are you ready to go? I figured we would drive to the base and see what we can find from there." Mel slapped at the side of the truck. "Let's get going."

A buzzing sound came from the highway, and in the distance, Bishop could hear his fake name being called.

"Henry! Henry! Stop!"

Not Nell. Bishop looked out and saw a single headlight breaking through the twilight. Was that a motorcycle? It was too small. Dirt bike, maybe. And it had at least one too many people on it. He counted two heads as the dirt bike turned into the parking lot.

Seth Stark hopped off the back and started running toward Bishop. Logan parked the bike and slid the helmet off his head. The lanky teen had a hunting rifle strapped to his back. "Please, Mr. Flanders…"

Bishop growled. He didn't need this distraction. "I won't tell your moms. What is it Seth? I have to go. Lyle has Nell."

Seth had his own version of a weapon in his hands, a state-of-the-art laptop. He opened it, the light glowing from the screen. "I know. I overheard the sheriff and Rye Harper talking on the police radio. I figured she probably had her phone. Almost no one walks around without their phone out here, and Nell's been really careful since her mom got sick. She always carries it."

A spark of hope lit through him. "You talked to her?"

Seth shook his head. "No. She's not answering, but I think I got something better. I hacked into the cell company's computer and I have a signal on her. She's up on the mountain." He frowned. "The signal's not moving. We need to hurry because any minute the company's going to realize that someone else has control of their satellite and the feds are probably going to come after me again."

"I won't tell Logan's moms about that either. Ditch the dirt bike. Get in the truck." They could all squeeze in. He needed Seth, but he had a feeling Seth wouldn't leave Logan behind and besides, an extra gun never hurt.

They piled into the truck, and Seth started giving instructions on how to get to the signal.

Mel turned the truck down the highway.

He'd worked with the top SEAL teams and with the best intelligence operatives from across the globe. God, what he wouldn't give to have Tennessee Smith or Taggart backing him up. No, he was stuck with an insane alien hunter, a kid who would either take over the world or spend a lot of time in jail, and Logan, who just didn't want his moms to find out anything. This was his team.

He prayed they had what it took. John Bishop wasn't a man who prayed. He figured God had left him alone a long time ago, but for the first time since he was a child, he reached out to whatever was out there in the universe.

Just let her be alive. God, just let her be alive.

Chapter Eleven

The cold hit her first and then the pain.

Confusion ruled her brain. Where was she? What had happened? Why was her head pounding?

But it was the cold that got to her. She'd been warm before with Henry's arms wrapped around her. All she had to do to get warm was to look at him, to remember how he kissed her, like she was the only woman in the whole world. She'd been toasty warm in the hot tub, his skin as hot as the water.

Now everything was cold. It invaded her bones. She was shaking and it was so, so quiet that she could hear her teeth chattering.

The accident. She'd been in an accident.

It came back in flashes, small scenes that brought Nell back to reality.

Kelly crying as she drove. Lyle spitting bile. The horrible sound the car had made as it began to roll.

Kelly had tried to tell him that she couldn't make it down the far side of the mountain. Her hands shook even as she tried to steer. Nell had been sitting beside her, trying to keep everyone calm even while Warren Lyle told her all the things he planned to do to her.

You cost me everything, bitch. I'm going to make you pay.

He'd pulled her hair, yanking at it, and she'd had to stifle a scream. She couldn't give in to her fear. She had to stay calm. No matter what happened, she wouldn't go out in fear. She would go out doing what she always did. She would try to make things better. She would use reason.

Warren Lyle had been one of the vilest cases she'd ever had the privilege of working. He'd owned a firm that specialized in dealing with medical waste and was about to be handed a deal to store waste for one of the biggest nuclear plants in the country. His firm had been going places, but Nell had discovered he was exceptionally sloppy about his storage techniques. He'd already had a resounding effect on the ecosystem by the time Nell called in the EPA.

It's a fucking desert. No one gives a fuck about the desert.

Nell did. She'd tried to explain to him that it wasn't just the desert he was polluting. There were underground rivers that connected all the way through the country. His radioactive waste could have gotten into drinking water. It could have hurt a lot of people. It could have hurt his own children. She'd kept calm, though tears had been streaming down her face.

Lyle had slapped the side of her head. His wife had left him. He didn't see his kids anymore, and it was all Nell's fault.

And then the world had upended and gone black.

An accident. Yes, she was clearer now. They had been in an accident. The car had careened off the road. There had been screaming and terror, and all she'd been able to think about was Henry. They'd had so little time together. How could she lose him now? She'd prayed that her mother was right and that soul mates found each other again and again because she'd found her home and now she was dying.

Home wasn't necessarily a place. It was a heart that mated to her own.

She forced her eyes open and a wave of nausea hit her gut. Something was wrong. She couldn't see and something was floating around her eyes. She reached up. It was her hair. Why was her hair hanging like that?

Now she could feel the seat belt cutting into her chest. She flexed her hands, moved her toes. She was freezing, but everything seemed to work. She took a long breath. She needed to get out of here. She had to get help.

There was a low moan that came from her left.

Nell forced her head up despite the pain. She was upside down, suspended by the seat belt. She needed to get out, but if she did it too fast and the car was on the edge of a cliff, her weight dropping could shift the car and cause them to roll again. Patience. She couldn't panic. She had to stay calm.

"What happened?" Kelly asked.

"Shhh. We need to be quiet. I think he's still out." Above all else, they needed to get out of this car and away from Warren Lyle. They couldn't be too far from the main road. She could make her way back up the mountain to the resort or around it to the Harper Ranch or Mel's place. She had to find some help, but she couldn't do that if the jerk face was shooting at her.

And she had to find a way to help Kelly. Kelly hadn't done anything to draw Lyle's anger. She was completely innocent.

"I hurt really bad, Nell. I'm scared."

There was no way to figure out where they were without getting out of the car. She forced her legs to straighten, pointing her toes until she could almost touch the roof of the car. Luckily, Kelly was a considerate driver. She drove a compact that was fairly earth friendly if one ignored the whole fossil fuel–use thing.

She reached across her chest and let her hand find the cool metal of the seat belt. Pressing the button, she let her feet find the roof and stopped her fall by shoving her hands out and bracing against the ceiling.

"Can you move?" Nell asked quietly.

"I think so. Are we upside down?" Kelly whimpered as Nell reached across her body. The lights were still on, but the top of the car was buried in snow. A spark of illumination shone out over the bank they had rolled into. The driver's side door was crushed inward, glass coating the roof. It was hard to see, but she thought it was a tree they had banged into. It had likely stopped their roll down the mountain and saved their lives. So much for deforestation. It was always bad. There was nothing at all good about it.

"We are. I'm going to unbuckle you. You're going to fall. I don't want you to hit the steering wheel so I'll leave my arms here, okay? I'm going to catch you." Nell clicked the buckle, and Kelly's body slumped forward. Her slight weight hit Nell's arms.

Kelly moaned, a deep sound that came from her chest. "I can move."

"I'm not going to leave you." She'd gotten Kelly into this mess. She had to get her out.

"I'll be okay. I can definitely walk, maybe even run. We need to go." Kelly started to move. "Damn, it's so cold."

Kelly was wearing a parka. She shouldn't be complaining. Nell was in a robe and it was a flipping satin robe. She was wearing a pair of boots, but her legs were uncovered. Her knees were knocking together in a vain attempt to stay warm.

"Yes, it is cold, but we need to move. I don't think he's awake yet."

Even as Nell said the words, a low groan came from the back seat. It made all the hair on her arms stand up straight screaming danger.

They had to get out of here and now.

She pushed the passenger's side door open using her right leg to force it. A blast of cold air filled the small cab of the car, threatening to freeze her lungs. How far away was she from the resort? They had driven away from the resort, but she'd been concentrating on talking to Warren, on making him understand that what he was doing wasn't logical. She hadn't been paying attention to how far they'd gone.

The door squeaked as she threw it open.

Another low groan came from the back seat. Panic threatened to overtake her. She had to get them both out. She thought about looking for the gun, but if he woke up, he could get it first, and she wouldn't know what to do with it anyway. She wasn't sure she could pull the trigger, but she could definitely run. She could run fast.

If she could get the feeling back in her legs.

She crawled out of the car, her skin protesting when her hands hit the snow. It was deep up here on the mountain. Every instinct told her to stay where it was warm, but she had to ignore them. She forced her way, her knees sinking into the snow. The moon had risen early, shining off the pure white of the powder. She couldn't tell exactly where she was. A labyrinth of aspens and evergreens surrounded her. Which way should she go? Once she started, she would be easy to track. There would be no way to cover the prints her boots would leave in the snow. She needed to get somewhere safe and fast.

"What the fuck?" A low voice groaned.

She reached back into the car and grabbed Kelly's hands. They had to go. They had to get out of here. She pulled and Kelly managed to crawl through, her teeth chattering.

Kelly got to her feet, shaking. There was a big bulge coming up on her forehead where she seemed to have hit the steering wheel. A trickle of blood was coming from a cut lip, but Kelly seemed to be able to move.

"Which way should we go?" Kelly's blonde hair hung limply around her brutalized face.

"I don't know where we are. I think we're about halfway down the west side. If we head around to the north side, we should find Mel or the Harper ranch. Max has a barbed wire fence up," Nell whispered as she adjusted her robe. God, she was so cold. Her boots were supposed to be cruelty-free, but it seemed they were definitely cruel on her feet right now. They did next to nothing to keep the cold out.

She'd talked to Max about that fence and how it was wrong to put up barricades, but now she would use it to find help. If she could get over that fence, all she would have to do was run until she caught sight of the house.

The car shook, the back door rattling as something from the inside started to pound away. Both women jumped back, their hands tangling together.

"Go," Nell said, pointing down the mountain. "Run that way. It should take you to the Harpers. If Max is there, tell him where we are. If he's not, find a way into the house and call the sheriff."

"I shouldn't leave you." Kelly clasped her hand. They were running out of time. The back door was starting to open. Kelly kicked out, viciously shoving the door back. There was a thud and a groan, and it seemed like Kelly had also managed to hit Lyle's skull. "Motherfucker."

A shot shattered the glass and pinged by Nell's head.

"Go!" She pushed Kelly the way she should run.

Kelly looked back once more, a frown on her face, and then took off, her boots leaving prints in the snow.

Nell's whole body shook. She wanted to run, but she had to make sure Lyle followed her and not Kelly.

Another shot fired out of the car, keeping her away. She thought about grabbing a branch and trying to clock him, but he could easily fire again. She inched away, trying to give herself a good head start, but leaving no way to mistake where she'd gone. Tears filled her eyes, nearly freezing to her skin. She had to wait. Just a minute. This was her problem, not Kelly's. She couldn't sacrifice the young girl to save herself.

Lyle emerged, his eyes on her. He lifted his gun even as he lay half in and half out of the car.

Nell took off as the shot sounded through the air, booming through the forest. She forced her legs to work, moving mechanically, almost without feeling. She ran, the snow up to her ankles, pristine as far as she could see, covering whatever lay beneath it.

"You can run, bitch, but you can't fucking hide."

She ran, not looking back. All that mattered was getting as far from him as possible. She had no idea how injured he was. He hadn't been wearing a seat belt. Apparently a seat belt would have cramped his kidnapping style, and she had to hope that it had also broken his legs. An unkind thought, yes, but she was pretty sure it wouldn't really affect her karma because the man was trying to kill her.

And he would if the cold didn't get her first.

She tripped, her feet hitting something solid under the snow that sent her whole body careening. She landed face-first, an icy blanket covering her cheek.

Get up. No time to waste. No time to hurt.

She pushed up on her wrists and got to her knees and then her feet. She could hear Lyle. He was getting close.

She ran again, this time through a thicket of trees, pine needles striking her face like tiny knives cutting at her.

A scream strangled out of her throat as she fell again. There was no way to tell what was under the snow and the forest was so thick here that the canopy nearly drowned out the moon's light. Nell stumbled against a tree, her strength waning. It was too cold. She'd nearly lost all feeling in her arms and legs.

"Got ya, bitch. Now let's have that talk we were going to have." Lyle's silhouette emerged from the trees. She could see the gun glinting from the sparks of moonlight that made it through the evergreens.

She braced herself against the tree. Which seemed to have fur. And which snorted as she held onto it.

A hot breath of air hit her cheek as the massive moose turned.

She was caught between the beast and a gun, and Nell couldn't see a way out.

* * * *

"The signal is up ahead," Seth said, pointing through the glass. "And down. Shit."

Bishop could easily see what the kid was cursing about. The tire tracks they had been following swerved and left the winding road ahead, dropping off into a white and black nothingness.

How scared had Nell been? Had she called out for him? Was she waiting for him to save her?

"They're off road." Mel brought the truck to a stop, tires crunching in the snow. He hadn't wavered for a moment, his hands steady on the wheel. He glanced to the two young men in the back of the cab, his voice perfectly even. No panic from the alien hunter. Bishop wouldn't mind being in the field with him. "You boys arm up or stay here. I taught Logan myself. He's a damn fine shot. He knows these woods. Seth, do you know how to use a rifle?"

A determined look came across the kid's face as Bishop hopped out and Seth followed. "I've spent every summer here since I was five years old. I stayed from the day after I got out of school right up until Grandad put me on a plane kicking and screaming. I know this place, too. I also know that Nell's phone is a hundred feet down that way."

Bishop walked to the side of the road. There was no guardrail, nothing at all to stop a car from falling off. He hopped down, unwilling to wait on the others. Trees surrounded him, but up ahead he could see a glint of metal. Bishop heard the others beginning to follow. It didn't matter. All that mattered was getting to Nell as quickly as possible.

He followed the path left in the snow by the car rolling down the mountain. He moved quickly, years of practice allowing for grace even with the snow and the grade he was running down. The minute he saw the car, he lifted his weapon, taking a firing stance.

And nothing.

"You said her phone was here." Bishop ran the last couple of yards to the site of the wreck. Even in the dim light, he could see how the car had rolled and crushed up against a tree. The driver's side was caved in, and there was blood in the snow, but he couldn't see bodies in the car. An eerie quiet settled around them.

"The signal is right here. She must have dropped it." Seth held a rifle in his hand, but he didn't look as competent as his best friend. Logan dropped to his knees in front of the window and reached in.

"It's here, but they're long gone," Logan said.

"And the tracks go two different ways." Mel ran his hand along an aspen tree's trunk. "Someone's been shooting. Looks like a .45 slug. Doesn't look like he hit anything except this tree though. Not enough blood. Just a little bit in the snow and on the car. That happened in the accident."

Bishop studied the scene, quickly coming to the same conclusion as Mel. If someone had been shot, there would be more blood. Unless this fucker had dumped her body, Nell was alive. There were three distinct sets of prints. One set, small, almost certainly female, went to the north. That set was alone, but he had the sudden certainty that those boot prints didn't belong to Nell. They were triangular at the toe. A cowboy boot and therefore made of leather. Nell would never allow that to touch her feet.

No. The small rounded-toe prints were hers, and he knew what she'd done. She'd drawn the asshole with the gun away from the other woman.

If she wasn't already dead, he might kill her.

Mel pulled out a walkie-talkie. "Max? You there?"

A crackling masculine voice came over the handheld radio Mel had switched to. "I am. Just found one of our missing girls. Kelly said Nell was still up there when she took off. Nell was going to run the opposite way."

Bishop didn't wait for further information. He ran, his feet following the line of the larger set of prints. He jogged easily through the snow, the previous runner having already plowed the path. Nell had survived the crash. She'd still been able to run. She was alive, and he had to find her before that changed.

A shot crashed through the forest, the sound seeming to come from everywhere at once. Bishop's heart threatened to pound out of his chest. That shot seemed to echo, pinging off the trees and straight through his system. Seth had made it to his side. His eyes were wide as the shot sounded. He opened his mouth to scream.

Bishop quickly covered Seth's mouth with his hand, the sound never making it past his lips. He kept his voice at a whisper. "Don't you dare scream. Don't make a sound."

He couldn't let the kid alert the shooter that they were here. Seth nodded, and Bishop let him go.

Mel didn't make a single noise as he moved in. He motioned toward the woods ahead, his hand making a chopping motion. Mel had some Army training. Bishop gestured around, silently telling Mel to take the flank. He pointed to himself and then in a straight line. He would go through while Mel and Logan went around.

"You can run, bitch, but you can't fucking hide." A male voice echoed through the woods.

He closed his jaw tightly to keep the growl that came naturally inside. Oh, he was going to take that fucker's head off. He would do it slowly. He would savor the way his neck crunched, but he wouldn't be satisfied until it actually came off in his hands and he could mount it on his wall.

"Stay here," he whispered to Seth and took off. The kid would confuse things. Mel and Logan were calmer. Seth was ready to panic. This was likely the scariest thing that had ever happened to the kid, but Bishop couldn't worry about him now. Seth had done his part.

Bishop moved forward. He wasn't listening to his instincts. They were telling him to run yelling and screaming for her. Like Seth, he was on the verge of panic. He was Henry Flanders in that moment, and he needed to be John Bishop. He pushed the fear down. It wouldn't help Nell. He was an iceman, a ghost. It was how he was able to do his job, but there it was—a horrible out-of-control feeling, like bile rising from the pit of his stomach.

He forced it down as he approached the spot where he was almost certain the sound had come from.

He heard a strangled scream and then a masculine voice shouting.

"What the fuck is that?"

There was a low sound, a huffing chuff that couldn't possibly be human.

"Holy shit! That's big."

"It's a moose." Nell's shaky voice whispered through the woods. "Try not to startle it. I think it's already afraid because of all the shooting."

"Well, we'll see if he's afraid of this."

"Don't!" Nell screamed.

Bishop stopped fighting his instincts. He took off running, not caring if anyone heard him coming because he knew that Nell was about to do something supremely stupid. She'd already put herself in danger to save Kelly. She would likely do the same thing for the moose.

A shot rang out again, the sound ringing in Bishop's ears.

Bishop entered the clearing at a dead run and stopped on a dime at what he saw there.

An enormous creature stood between Warren Lyle and Nell, his massive body a bulwark separating them. The moose huffed, and even from where he stood he could feel the heat coming off the large beast. It was bigger than anything he'd seen before, its magnificent horns at least as wide as he was tall. Lyle looked small compared to the huffing animal. Bishop saw how his hand shook as he raised his weapon.

It was an easy thing to walk up behind him. Lyle's whole being was focused on the beast that had him in its sights. The ground underneath them trembled as the beast stomped one mighty hoof, its antlers shaking.

He had an arm around Lyle's neck in an instant, the muzzle of the SIG placed firmly at the base of the man's head. It took everything he had not to pull the trigger, ending it all here and now, but he didn't want Nell to see the blood, the way the man's skull would split.

"Henry, you found me." Nell's voice was shaking. From what he could see she wasn't prepared for the weather, her curvy frame dressed only in a thin robe and her rubber boots. In the moonlight she looked pale, her lips almost blue. "You need to be still. The moose is gentle, but he'll attack if he thinks he's been threatened."

"Drop the gun or I'll blow your head off." It was what he wanted to do anyway, but Nell was probably right about the moose. The big-ass animal seemed to have had too much stimulation for one night.

"I can pay you a million dollars. Just get me out of here and let me have the girl. She took everything from me. I'm a rich man. I'll get you anything you want." Warren Lyle stood still, his voice a low, desperate rasp.

He was digging himself a deeper hole. "The only thing I want is to blow your head off. The only reason I haven't done it yet is because of that woman over there. Whatever she did to you it was because she was trying to help someone else."

"And because he was evil." Nell's teeth chattered as she spoke.

Where the hell was Mel? He was at an impasse. He needed to get Nell somewhere warm, but first he had to make sure he didn't get trampled by Bullwinkle.

"So if he's evil, I can kill him, right?" Maybe she would be reasonable about this.

She shook her head. "We can't sink to their level."

He'd already sunk. He'd likely killed far more than Warren Lyle could conceive of. Nell would be horrified. "Drop the gun or what she says won't matter to me. Do you understand?"

Lyle's gun dropped, falling to the ground.

Mel stalked up from behind. "You did real good, there, professor. Are you sure you haven't done some hunting in your time?"

Oh, he'd hunted a lot—terrorists, killers, rogue agents. "I got lucky."

Bishop kicked Lyle's gun out of the way as Mel walked straight up to the moose. Logan took his coat off and wrapped it around Nell. He was starting to like the kid.

"Go on, now. You've had your fun." Mel slapped at the moose's backside, and Bishop stiffened, waiting for the thing to strike.

It merely huffed, an arrogant sound, as it shook its horns out and started to walk away.

"That's Maurice. He's a jokester, that one. I swear, he's scared the crap out of more than one kid who leaned up against him thinking he was a tree. Logan, here, peed his pants once," Mel explained.

"Did you see the size of that thing? I was seven. We're lucky all I did was pee." Logan was surprisingly calm. "Rye's on his way. He just radioed Mel. Rye will take this jerk into custody."

Maybe the kid could do a deputy's job.

With deep regret, he relaxed his hold on Lyle. It looked like he would be going to jail instead of a fast grave. He couldn't bring himself to shatter

Nell's illusions. He was weak around her.

Of course, it would be easy to make sure the fucker never left his jail cell again. There were lots of ways to ensure that. All a man needed were connections and cash and he could easily have a threat removed forever, and Nell would never have to know how bloody his hands were.

She could still have her perfect vision of her college professor lover.

Well, maybe not perfect since he fully intended to make sure her ass was red once he figured out if she had frostbite.

"Take this asshole for me, Mel." He needed to get his hands on her. He wouldn't quite believe it was real until he held her in his arms, warmed her up with the heat of his own body.

"Is it over?" a voice asked from behind him, surprising them all.

Lyle kicked back and Bishop, who had been pushing him toward Mel, slipped, catching his foot on a fallen branch. Lyle moved fast, capturing Seth and wrapping an arm around his throat. Lyle had a hundred pounds on the kid. Seth dropped his rifle. It lay on the snow right at Lyle's feet.

Three guns came up, pointed right at Lyle, but now he had a human shield. Seth fought, but he was ineffectual against Lyle's muscle. He held Seth with one arm. His other hand reached into the pocket of his coat and came out with a large, wicked-looking knife.

"I was going to gut that bitch with this, but now I think maybe it's my ticket to freedom." Lyle's lips curled back. He held the knife right at Seth's throat. Bishop could see the way it pressed in, a delicate red line beginning to form.

"Let him go. It's me you want." Nell started toward the raving lunatic with the ridiculously large knife. "Let him go, and I'll go with you."

No way. No how. It made him a ruthless bastard, but he wouldn't sacrifice Nell to save Seth. In fact, he would do the exact opposite. It wasn't fair, but if he had a choice, he would always choose Nell. He wrapped an arm around her waist and pulled her close.

Lyle wasn't backing down. "Give me the bitch or I'll slit this kid's throat. You have no idea how much I'll sacrifice to see her pay."

He had a good idea. Lyle had lost his damn mind, and he would do anything to get his revenge, but he wasn't going to let Nell play the martyr this time.

"You have to let me go. I can't, Henry. I can't live with this." Nell tried to struggle, but he lifted her up so she couldn't fight him.

He looked back at Mel. "Do you have a shot?"

Mel shook his head. "No."

A brilliant blue flash came through the forest, followed by a flash of red. Rye Harper was here, but he might be too late. Nell kept up her struggle, pleading with him. Mel held his ground. Bishop wondered if he was going to watch Seth's blood spill on the ground. He was rather shocked to find out the idea made his gut turn. He gave a shit about that kid.

A shot rang out, and Bishop watched as a neat hole split Lyle's head, an unbelievable show of marksmanship. One inch to the left or right and Seth Stark would have died, but that shot had been sheer perfection. Seth stood still as Lyle dropped back, his body falling to the snow.

"Is he dead?" Seth asked, his eyes wide and his whole body shaking.

Rye Harper charged into the scene, his pistol up. "What the hell is going on? Who took that shot?"

Logan Green walked up to his friend, his rifle at his side. He put a hand on Seth's shoulder. "We can't ever tell my moms I did that."

Harper looked down at the body and whistled. "Damn, Logan, I was trying to come up with some way to keep you from applying for my job when I take over as sheriff. The job's yours, son. This is good work. And we won't mention this to Teeny or Marie. You boys get out of here. Go home. If I'm going to be the sheriff of Bliss, I might as well start learning how to cover shit up. It's kind of a way of life out here."

"You can let me down now." Nell's voice sounded hollow. She lay limp in his arms.

"No." Bishop clutched her close. He would have to let her go, but not tonight. Tonight, he would make sure she was safe. It was the only thing he could do for her.

He started to walk toward the car, ignoring everything else.

Nell was all that mattered.

Chapter Twelve

Two days later, Nell wondered if Henry was ever going to touch her again.

"Are you sure you want to do this?" Callie asked. She held up the handcuffs. "This stuff looks pretty serious. Where did you get this from? Never mind. I know the answer. Stef."

"He brought over a whole bag of toys. That's what he called them, but some of those things don't look like a ton of fun." She pulled out what looked like a riding crop. Stef seemed to have thought of almost everything.

Now she had to hope she could tempt Henry into using them.

For two nights he'd held her, stroking her hair until she fell asleep, but beyond kissing her silly, he hadn't made a move.

It was starting to worry her. She was starting to think that he would leave without ever making love to her again.

Callie helped turn the sheets down. "Has he said anything?"

Nell shook her head. This seduction scene was her last play. "No. He took me to the hospital, and even though they said I only needed some rest, he hasn't seemed interested. Do you think he figured out how much trouble I am? Is that why he doesn't want me anymore?"

Callie pushed her glasses up. "You aren't trouble. I think he still wants you. I've seen how he looks at you, and it's not like he's left you alone. I had to pry him away from you this afternoon. I think he's…thinking."

She was pretty sure she wouldn't like what Henry was thinking about.

She was pretty sure he was thinking about leaving. "I want one more night."

A long sigh came out of Callie's chest. "I hate to tell you this, but one more night won't fix anything if he's intent on leaving. Believe me. I know. One more night is just going to be something else to remember. Another memory that nothing else and no one else can ever compete with. It might be better to let him go."

"Would you do it? If you could go back, would you take away the time you spent with those guys?"

Callie stopped, pain etched on her face. She sat down on the bed, her hands in her lap. "Their names were Nate and Zane."

Nate and Zane were idiots because Callie was one of the sweetest women she'd ever met. What had called them away? "Do you wish you hadn't met them?"

Callie reached out and took her hand, squeezing it gently. "No. I would do it again. I fell in love with them. It wasn't their fault that they couldn't love me back. I dream about them every night. I just wish…I wish it would end differently for you and Henry, but I think he's going to leave."

Nell was pretty sure that would happen and never once had he mentioned her coming to visit. "I know."

"We're so dumb." Callie wiped away her tears. "But I'll be here for you. I want you to know that. We can cry together."

She reached out and hugged her friend, grateful that she wouldn't be alone. "Thank you. I'm afraid I'll take you up on that offer. I wish I could be more practical, but I want one more night."

She knew it wouldn't solve anything, wouldn't fix the problem, but she wanted it because she loved him.

"Okay. Get naked and I'll cuff you. God, I never thought I would say those words." Callie took a long breath and stood up. "Go on. Drop the robe, but don't expect me to attach these."

She held up two long dangly earrings. Nell frowned as she shrugged out of her robe. "Do you think those are diamonds? Why did Stef send me earrings?"

Nell settled herself on the bed and spread her arms out. She and Callie had carefully placed the handcuffs.

Callie leaned over, a smile on her face as she snicked the cuffs over Nell's wrists. "Not for your ears, hon. Those are nipple clamps, and I bet Henry loves them. He's a pervert, right? He looks all upstanding and professory, but he's a complete freak under that, I bet."

Nell felt a smile cross her face as she lay back. "He seems very interested in Dominance and submission. And he deeply enjoys spanking me. I would normally protest that, but it feels nice."

Callie laughed as she placed the spreader bar between Nell's legs. "This is totally insane. And your wax job is perfect."

"Polly. She was reluctant at first, and then she got into it. Now she has the Bare-Assed Brazilian on her menu. I mentioned that she shouldn't have used the word 'ass,' but she left it there."

Callie placed the last cuff and stood back. "Okay. I'm going to go and get him. I'll be fast because Stef would be so upset if I left you all bound like that for very long. I'm not into the lifestyle, but I know that much. Don't like die or anything. Someone will be right back."

The door opened and closed, and Nell was left alone and spread wide for a man who she hoped wanted to take her for pleasure.

Nell closed her eyes and hoped this worked. She wasn't dumb. She knew he wouldn't stay because she'd slept with him, but she had to let him know how she felt. It was dangerous, but she'd never shied away from that. She told it like it was, and she loved Henry Flanders.

It wasn't more than five minutes before the door opened and she heard a low, masculine curse.

"What the fuck is going on here?"

She opened her eyes, looking up at him. He was wearing sweats and a T-shirt, his normal workout clothes. Despite the clothing-optional nature of the gym on-site, Henry insisted that the leather seats on the weight trainers chafed his skin and the towels weren't big enough. He stared down at her, a deep frown on his face.

"You don't think I'm pretty?" She kind of thought he would like her like this. He'd talked a lot about bondage and tying her up. Had she been wrong? Had he decided he wasn't interested in her anymore? Was he staying close to her because he'd taken her virginity and he didn't know how to gracefully back out of the relationship?

His jaw tightened. "You're gorgeous, but I'm leaving tomorrow morning. I don't think this is a good idea."

She was totally open to him, and there was no way she could shrink back. She kind of got the lifestyle now. It didn't allow for her to hide. Her body was open so it was easier to open her heart. "I love you, Henry."

He dropped to his knees, his hands on her body—one on her thigh and one above her breast. "You can't know what that means to me."

Not exactly an exclamation of love, but he hadn't vomited either. "Maybe we could talk on the phone."

He pulled his hands back. "No. That's not possible."

"Why? Are you married?" She'd mentally run through every possible scenario and had determined that horrible thought was the most likely possibility.

He shook his head. "No. God, no. Nell, you're the only woman I've ever…felt this way about. Please don't think there's anyone else. There won't be, but I made choices that I can't back away from. Damn it. I've been thinking about this for days. I want to be with you. I want to be this man you need, the kind of man you can love, but I don't think I can be."

"Is it the vegan stuff? Because we can work on that." She wasn't going to lose the love of her life because he liked to eat a burger every now and then. "I don't think I can cook it, but I'm also very tolerant. I wouldn't force you to live like that."

The saddest look crossed his face and his hand caressed her cheek. "I know you are. This goes way beyond my love of a good steak. Baby, if I stayed with you, I would honor that. I wouldn't touch it again. But there are other considerations, and talking about it won't change things. Sleeping with you tonight won't make me stay. I'll still leave in the morning, so why don't you let me get you out of these cuffs and we can have a nice night together? We can go into town and have dinner."

Tears pooled in her eyes. "You don't want me?"

Henry stood up. "How can you even think that? Look at how hard I am."

She looked up and his sweats were tenting, his cock a long, hard line. He wanted her, but he wasn't willing to stay with her. She knew she should save herself the heartache, but she loved him and there wasn't anything wrong with it. Her love was valuable. Her love wasn't dependent on whether he could love her back. If he'd been cruel, she would have turned him away, but then if he'd been unkind, she wouldn't have loved him in the first place. "Play with me. I won't do this with anyone else so I want my last night."

She could have sworn she saw a sheen of tears in his eyes. "You will. You'll find someone."

She shook her head. "No. You're the love of my life and there won't be anyone else. It's all right. You have to believe what you will, but right now, in this moment, I know that I won't love anyone the way I love you. I'm asking you for one last night. I know what I'm getting into. I won't beg you to stay. I probably will cry. I won't be able to help it, but I'll let you go if that's what you need."

His head fell forward, and for a moment she was almost certain he would deny her. The seconds ticked away, the silence a drain on her soul.

And then his head came back up and his eyes were hot.

She would lose the war, but this battle had been won.

"Who cuffed you? If you say Stefan Talbot, I might have to pay a visit to him before we get started." Henry took a long breath and placed a hand on her head. He touched her hair, smoothing it back before his fingers started to trail a long line down her body. He started at her forehead, caressing her nose and lingering on her mouth before moving to her chin. "Answer me, sweetheart."

"It was Callie. Stef gave me the handcuffs and told us how to set it up."

"Excellent. He gets to live."

He could be so very possessive. She shouldn't find pleasure in that, but she was honest with herself. It was the only way to stay sane. The thought of another woman touching him made her sad. Maybe she was possessive, too. She had friends who were into the open-love lifestyle, but it would never be for her.

She wouldn't love anyone after Henry.

She shivered as he drew his fingers over her chest. Her nipples peaked as though begging for his attention. "He gave me a bag of sexy stuff. I don't know what some of it is."

Henry sighed contentedly as he traced his fingers over her belly. He was leaving a trail of goose bumps everywhere he touched. He drew his fingers lower, and she could feel her pussy start to come to life at the mere thought of him being close. Just a few more inches and the pads of his fingers would brush her clit and light her up. Just another second…

"I should see what he brought for us." He pulled his hand away, turning and picking up the leather bag Stef had given her.

"That was mean." She was out of breath and she hadn't moved.

The sweetest smile curled his lips up as he set the bag on the bed. "It's not mean. It's a little tease. I promise I'll touch that sweet spot eventually, but it will be on my schedule. Not yours. I want you panting for it."

This was something she didn't quite understand. "Why?"

He looked down at her, tenderness plain on his face. "Because it makes me feel good knowing that someone as beautiful as you will let me have my way. When I think about getting to play with you, it gets me so hard. God, all the things we could do, the things I want to show you."

He stopped as though he realized he'd been talking like they had a future.

"What kind of nasty toys did Stef send?" she asked, wanting so desperately to keep the smile on his face.

He turned back to the bag, unzipping it. There was that smile. "I like the way Stef thinks."

He pulled out a tiny tube and uncapped it.

"Should I ask what that is?" Nell asked.

"It's oil used to stimulate the clitoris. Don't worry, baby. I'm sure it's all organic and earth friendly. It's cinnamon and almond oil and some rosemary essence. It's going to plump this pretty jewel right up, and it'll taste nice when I suck on it."

"I don't know that I need any stimulation." She could barely breathe as it was.

"That's ten and you'll take what I give you. Are you telling me no?" He paused, the cap in his hand.

He was infuriating, and she would probably never tell him no. Somehow, being bound and trussed up, she'd never felt more free than she did when he was in charge. When Henry closed the door, it was like all the problems of the world drifted away, and she didn't have to worry about anything but finding pleasure with him.

God, she would miss him every second of the day for the rest of her life.

"I'm not telling you no and I'm looking forward to my spanking, Henry."

"Good. So am I." He dribbled the oil on her clit. It was cool and made her hips shimmy. His thumb closed over the spot he'd lubed up. "Such a pretty pearl. Soon it will be all soft and ripe for the tasting."

Sparks of pleasure shot across her skin as he pressed down and made long, luxurious circles.

And then stopped, proving he had a touch of sadist in there.

"Let's see what else Stef left us. Nice." He pulled out what looked like a plug made for an elephant.

"I don't think that's going to work." What had Stef been thinking?

"It's smaller than me, baby. It's going to work fine. It only needs some lube." He winked at her and walked toward the bathroom.

He was going to shove that enormous plug up her backside. There was only one reason to do it. He was going to make love to her ass. He was going to claim her.

And she was going to let him.

He was back quickly, his shirt gone and that big old plug in his hand, glistening with lubricant. She couldn't help looking at his chest. He was all hers. Everyone else could look at him and see the professor, but she saw the lover he was, the man he could be.

"I like you in a spreader, but if it gets uncomfortable, I want you to tell me," he said as he kneeled on the bed in between her legs.

"I am so uncomfortable, but it has nothing to do with the spreader." It had everything to do with the fact that he wasn't inside her.

He groaned, a sexy sound, as he set the plug on her belly and shoved both hands under her ass. He forced her hips up. "Fuck, I like having this much access. It's so hot." He pulled her cheeks apart. "I can see your pussy and your asshole. They're both right here, waiting for me. Waiting for my cock."

She would give him everything, so he was right. She was waiting for him. She might wait for him forever.

He picked up the plug and pressed it to her asshole. The pressure made her wince, but there was no pain, just a jangled feeling that caused her to whimper.

"Yeah, baby, I love that." He really was a pervert. She loved that about him. All the perfectly polite males she'd known paled in the face of his open honesty. He told her what he needed, and that made her feel so powerful. She didn't have to ask. He gave it to her. It was a gift. It made it all right to ask for what she needed.

"Henry, please. I need a kiss." She couldn't go another minute without his lips on hers.

He pulled the plug away and suddenly he loomed over her. "Baby, I love to kiss you."

He leaned down and pressed his lips to hers, the pressure so sweet she almost lost it. She wanted to wrap her arms around him but there was the problem of the cuffs. His tongue surged in, mating with her own, forcing her mouth open wide. His chest pressed to hers, and she gave over. He rubbed against her as he licked at her lips, filling her with desperate desire.

He pulled back, rubbing his nose against hers. "Now behave."

Her skin felt cold when he left her, getting back to his knees and winking down at her. She immediately felt the press of the plug against her asshole. He rimmed her, rolling the plug against the rosette of her ass over and over and over again.

He moved the plug in, foraging in shallow presses. Every push gained ground, opening her up until he shoved the plug home, gaining every inch she had.

"Beautiful." He was looking at her asshole.

"I'm glad you think so." She was panting, her breath sawing in and out of her chest.

"I definitely think so. Do you want me to show you how beautiful you are?" His palms were on her knees.

This was the only time she felt beautiful. "Yes, Henry."

"Damn, I love it when you say, 'Yes, Henry.'" He leaned over and ran his nose along her pussy. He teased her, lighting her up and making her heart pound. He breathed her in. She knew she should feel self-conscious, but she loved how much he liked her smell, her taste. He made her feel special, like she was a sumptuous dessert he liked to try over and over again.

"Yes, Henry." She would tell him that every minute of the day. "Yes, Henry."

He lifted up and reached over into the bag, his hands coming back with the nipple clamps. "Let's see how you feel after I've put these beauties on you. What do you say?"

He was torturing her. He'd been so close, his nose right in her pussy, and now he left her high but definitely not dry. She was sopping wet and dying, but there was only one answer to that question. "Yes, Henry."

"I wish I could always be this man." He palmed her breasts, his hands covering her. "I want to be so right for you."

He was, but she couldn't prove it with anything but her heart. "You are right. Even if it's only for tonight. You're the right man."

He was the only man.

He reached out and pinched her right nipple between his thumb and forefinger, twisting lightly. Her nipples were tight and ready. In an instant, he clamped her nipple, the screw holding her firmly and making her breathe out as it lit her up.

"So pretty. You're my little plaything." He twisted her left nipple and set the clamp on her. The jewels dangled from her nipples, pretty diamonds that marked her as Henry's lover. The clamps bit into her flesh, but it wasn't a real pain. It was an ache, a longing.

He leaned over, his tongue coming out, and licked at the exposed part of her nipples. Sweet heat flared through her. She'd been clamped and plugged and claimed. "My Nell."

He looked at her for the longest time, his eyes taking in every inch of her, raking across her body. He hopped off the bed and reached for the bag again. "I'll be right back, baby. I need to clean up and get a couple of things ready. Stay there like a very good girl."

She nearly rolled her eyes, but then caught sight of the crop in his hand and decided to play along. "Yes, Henry."

"Excellent. Good girls get treats." He pulled out a small egg-shaped device and twisted it so it started vibrating. "I'm not strapping it on, so you'll have to be very still if you want to keep it. Be good, baby."

He placed the vibe right on the mound of her pussy, barely touching her clit. Nell stopped breathing because it felt so, so good, but Henry was right. That playful vibrator was precariously perched. Any movement and it would roll off and she would be in trouble.

It shifted slightly, touching the top of her clit. The purr of the vibrator hit her already-stimulated clitoris, and she couldn't help but moan. So close. Little spasms of heat electrified her skin, and the spark threatened to become a fire. Just a bit more. She could move it just a tiny bit closer. If she could wiggle a fraction of an inch, she would have it.

And then it was gone, the egg rolling away. *Damn it*. Now she was cursing. She never cursed. Well, almost never.

"Oh, what a bad girl. She lost her egg." Henry stalked back into the room. He'd ditched the sweatpants and his glasses. He loomed over her, all predatory alpha male, every inch of his body corded with lean muscle. His cock thrust up from a nest of neatly trimmed dark hair. He held the crop in his hand, tapping his palm with it as he looked her over. "I believe I wanted that egg to be where I left it. You disobeyed."

Oh, what was he going to do with that crop? He couldn't smack her backside. "How about we negotiate? I'll take half the blame and the egg can take the other half. I think it might be a faulty egg. Seriously, I'm planning a protest."

A brilliant smile crossed his face. "I love to play with you. Well, my sweet sub, the egg has already had its punishment." He drew the crop down her body, letting the leather tip caress her skin. He pulled it down until it sat on the top of her clitoris. "That egg was happy right here. It had finally found a nice spot to call home. So we'll move on to your punishment."

Before she could protest that seemingly unfair circumstance, he tapped her clit with the crop. A quick slapping motion that made her scream. She could feel the plug in her ass as she clamped down. There was no real pain, merely a jagged sensation that made her deeply aware of parts of her body she'd never paid much attention to before. She was always so lost in thought that there was a beauty to the simplicity of being deeply aware of her own body.

He tapped her clit again, another jangly rush heating her skin.

"How wet are you, baby? Is this pussy getting soaked and ready for a cock? Or a tongue?" He slapped at her again, the sound worse than the sensation.

"I'm so wet." She struggled with the bonds. She wanted to touch herself, to relieve the horrible ache that was building. The oil he'd rubbed into her clit had her throbbing and ready to beg for release, but he kept up the slow torture.

"How about your nipples? Are they aching yet?" He flicked the crop across her breasts lightly.

"Oh, oh." The words came out on a puff of breath. Her nipples were tight, so tight. The jewels vibrated as he touched them with the crop.

"I could leave you like this. I could sit down and get some work done safe and secure in the knowledge that you're exactly where you should be." He frowned. "Not off somewhere nearly being killed."

She sniffled, tears forming because they were finally at the heart of the matter. She'd danced around the subject for days. She'd known Henry for a brief time, but she'd already learned that he didn't talk about things until he was ready to. She'd had to be patient, to get him to a place where he felt safe enough to open up. He felt in control now. "I'm sorry."

His jaw tightened, and he brought the crop across the fleshy part of her breasts. "I saw the tapes. The security camera watches the front gate. I watched that tape over and over again. You could have gotten away."

She shook her head. "No, I couldn't."

"Yes, you could have." He struck her thighs, the sound slapping, but the crop had a lot of play in it. Had it been a sturdier crop, she might have been screaming, but he seemed to know what he was doing. There was a sting and then a pleasant heat crept across her legs. "You could have run behind the security shed and called someone."

She could have, but there was a problem with that scenario. "I would have left Kelly alone. I couldn't do that."

He slapped at her other thigh. "Yes, you could. You're my sub. You do what I say and I say you save yourself."

She wanted to hold him, but he likely wouldn't allow it at this point.

"I can be your sub here, but I always have to be me. I love you. I can't tell you how much I love you, but you have to take me as I am, and I will always try to help. I could never walk away."

"You were ready to give yourself up. After I had already fucking saved you."

She still got cold thinking about the night. "But Seth was in danger, and I was the one Lyle wanted."

"He would have killed you."

"Not likely. You would have saved me again. I believe that. I know you think I'm naïve. I know you think half the things I believe in are stupid and silly, but this is who I am. I won't allow someone like Warren Lyle the power to change the core of my soul. I won't allow fear to do it either. If I had told you to kill him after he'd already been disarmed, I would have been reacting in a way that fear and anger shaped. I don't want to spend my life reacting. I want to act. I want to act on all the good things I can be. I want to act on my impulse to be kind, to be positive."

He stopped, his head down. "And if that gets you killed?"

"Then at least I lived the way I wanted to live."

His eyes came back up, deep brown orbs that held her own. "I don't understand you, but I don't want you to change. Not ever." He tossed the crop away and climbed between her legs, placing his mouth right over her pussy. "God, I'll never forget the way you taste."

He licked her clit, his tongue rubbing hard, and there was no way to hold the orgasm back. It shot through her system like a wildfire, and she screamed out his name.

He stayed right where he was for a moment, licking and petting her as she came down from the high and then he sat up, gently releasing her legs from the spreader bar.

"What are you doing?" she asked, barely able to get the words out.

"I'm releasing you." He grabbed the key Callie had left on the nightstand and started to uncuff her hands.

Nell held back tears because she wasn't ready for it to end.

She would never be ready for it to end.

Chapter Thirteen

The key to the handcuffs snicked softly as Bishop released Nell's wrists. He held her arm in his hand, checking to make sure the circulation was all right. Callie seemed to have done a good job. There was no chafing or red marks, just Nell's pure porcelain skin. He drew her hand to his lips, kissing her before moving to the next hand and releasing it, too.

He wanted to tie her up, to wind rope around her breasts until they stood up at attention. He would take his time, the rope his art and she his canvas.

He needed more time. He needed time to do everything with her, to take her to a club, to spend hours and hours fucking her, only stopping for short naps and food he would feed her from his hands.

He looked down at her breasts where the jewels dangled from her nipples. Her nipples were a nice ruby red, engorged with blood from the clamps. He hadn't been as kind as Callie. Nell would feel the marks of those clamps for days. Every time she moved, she would feel the ache as her nipples touched the fabric of her shirt. He knew it made him a bastard, but he liked the thought.

His hand trailed down to her breasts. The sadist in him was aroused at the thought of the bite of pain he was going to give her. He would never want to hurt her in any real way, but this was erotic, and he had a plan to soothe her. "This is going to hurt but only for a minute."

She drew her plump bottom lip into her mouth. He loved that mouth. He loved the way she sucked his cock. "I don't care about the pain. I don't want this to be over yet. You promised me a whole night."

How could she think he was done? He wasn't even close to being done.

She was a terrible submissive, and he wouldn't have her any other way. "I'm in control here. You'll take what I give you and not question me. You're angling for another spanking, but I think that's what you want. I'm not done, sweetheart. I haven't even started yet, but I can't leave you like this for very long. I know what I'm doing. I would never tell you how to protest, so leave the bondage to me."

"Okay." Tears sparkled in those clear brown eyes as she looked up at him, uncertainty plain on her face.

If she wasn't the perfect sub, then he wasn't exactly überDom when it came to her. Protocol didn't matter. Rules didn't matter. Nothing mattered but making her happy. He climbed onto the bed next to her and caught her lips with his. Sighing into her mouth, he pressed her body into the bed, covering her entirely. So soft, so open. It didn't matter that she questioned him. She was worried, and he wanted to make her comfortable. No concerns were allowed in the bed tonight. Just pleasure.

She could manipulate him with nothing but a few tears and those big doe eyes. He had fucking protocol when it came to his subs, and one of those rules was that his submissive didn't question him. His lovers accepted his discipline and his pleasure and thanked him for it. If a prior sub had forced him to stop his previous plans to explain what he was doing to her, he would have dismissed her.

But not Nell. He couldn't even think about dismissing Nell. The women who had come before had been casual, subs he'd picked up in a club or women he'd used as cover for his job. Some had been bought and paid for, some had betrayed him. Women in his world were kept at arms' length, but he couldn't do it with Nell. He couldn't push her away, couldn't hide behind rules or pretend that she didn't really matter. She wasn't exchangeable. No one else in the world could make him feel like Nell did.

She was his ultimate weakness. She could cost him everything. So why did he want to revel in her? Spend every second he could with her arms wrapped around him?

He was the badass. How did she make him feel safe? He kissed her softly, enjoying the intimacy of being pressed to her body, her legs spreading to welcome him inside. She never tried to hide from him. From the moment he'd met her, she'd opened herself up and invited him in. They had all night. He didn't want to waste a minute of it.

185

But first, he had to get her out of those clamps.

He shifted slightly, moving his head to her breasts. *Poor little nipples.* The teeth of the clamps bit into them, engorging them with blood, making them look like red jewels on her chest. They were so beautiful, and they were about to hurt like hell. "I'm going to take these off now, baby. Try not to scream."

He pinched the clamp off the first one, and her gasp filled the room. Before she could say a word, he leaned over and took the wounded nipple into his mouth. He tongued it and suckled gently, easing the pain of the blood racing back in. He tossed the clamp aside, spending all his energy on soothing the nipple he'd tortured. Her hands found his hair as she held him close. He could smell her arousal, still taste her on his tongue.

"You're not going to leave?" Nell asked, her voice small and vulnerable.

He would leave, but not tonight. He sighed, shifting so he could get to the other breast. "We have tonight. It's all I can promise you, but I won't leave you until I have to."

If he stayed much longer, he wasn't sure he would be able to leave at all.

His fingers moved nimbly, twisting off the clamp. His tongue was on her before she could scream. He moved back and forth between her breasts, loving and memorizing them so he could close his eyes and relive the moment later when he was far from Bliss. He couldn't tell her, but he intended to live with her memory, the vision of her the only thing he would ever be able to love.

He'd made all the wrong choices. He could see that now. He'd done what Nell hadn't. She acted on her love, her optimism. He had acted on all that was dark. She'd taken the bad shit that had happened to her and turned it into a positive. He'd used it as an excuse to indulge his darkness. He wasn't worthy of her. He couldn't be, but he could make her believe how amazing she was.

"You're so beautiful, baby. I've never seen anyone as beautiful as you." He kissed the top of her nipples one last time. Her breasts weren't the largest he'd ever played with, but he loved how round and perfect they were, how they nestled into his palm as though they had been made to fit his hands.

"That's sweet, but I'm hardly a beauty." Her hands moved in his hair.

He lifted his head, frowning at her. He wasn't about to put up with that. She was gorgeous. Perhaps not in a showy way. She didn't wear makeup. Her clothes had been designed for function rather than seduction. But her skin was porcelain smooth, her eyes so guileless he could lose himself in them. Her goodness practically glowed. "You're the most beautiful woman in the world to me. I'll never think anyone is lovelier than you. I'll never want anyone the way I want you."

His cock wanted her. So fucking bad. He was dying. His dick was so close to her pussy. It rested right up on her labia, getting coated in all that juice from her orgasm. It would be such a simple thing to let his cock go, and he could be inside her in a single thrust. There wouldn't be anything between them. If he fucked her without a condom, if he spent himself inside her, he would have to stay. He could buy them a couple more weeks to see if she was pregnant. And if she was pregnant?

The Agency would still come after him. An operative like him didn't retire to a sleepy mountain town and marry a sweet activist. The CIA had put a lot of money into training him, and he'd been a part of a whole lot of classified operations that the government didn't want anyone to know about. And that wasn't the only problem with this scenario. He'd made too many enemies, too many bad choices that could come back to haunt him and Nell. There were a whole bunch of nasty forces out there who would be thrilled to know John Bishop had a weakness.

If he wouldn't make a good husband, then he wasn't parenthood material either.

"Turn over." He couldn't take the chance, but he also was far too selfish to give up the idea of being inside her without anything between them. He'd had a physical, and she was perfect. There was nothing to keep him from this particular act. He wanted everything she would give him. He wanted to be her first again.

She allowed him to roll her over. That round, glorious ass of hers came into view. His mouth practically watered. He'd loved using the crop to tease her clitoris, but nothing compared to spanking that ass, to feeling her skin against the flat of his palm. Warm flesh filled the palms of his hands as he cupped her cheeks. He rolled them, spreading her wide so he could see the plug resting deep in her asshole, a mark of his possession. No one had ever claimed her ass. It would be his and his alone for now.

But she was small. If he had more time he would properly prepare her, spending night after night opening her up, making her ready to take his cock. But their time was almost over, so he needed to give her something to distract her, pleasure to make the shock of his cock splitting her open more savory.

Stefan Talbot had thought of everything. Bishop reached onto the nightstand, where he'd placed the items he'd prepared earlier. He grabbed the nicely sized rabbit vibrator and lubed it up.

"What are you doing?" Nell tried to look behind her.

They were going to have to talk about trust, but he didn't mind because it gave him the perfect excuse to smack her lovely ass and hear that whimper that always went straight to his cock. She was so fucking perfect for him.

He slapped at the fleshiest part of her cheek, loving the way it pinkened. "Keep your eyes to the front. You don't need to look back. I'm going to fuck your ass, baby. Do you have a problem with that?"

Her head nodded, but her eyes stayed to the front. "I have several concerns, actually."

He smacked her again, forcing down a laugh. There wasn't an ounce of fear in her voice, the brat. He could practically hear the smile on her face. She loved this. She loved the push and pull of play.

She would need this again.

He forced that thought out of his head. If there was one thing he'd learned about this town, it was that they took care of their own. Their sheriff might be lackadaisical, but Rye Harper was going to take over, and he would watch out for Nell. Stef cared about her, too, and he understood what a woman like Nell would need. She would need a strong partner who would make sure she was taken care of while she tried to change the whole damn world, a man who would love her for everything she was. Stef could find her a Dom, a husband.

And Bishop would love her from afar. Always.

"Are you telling me no?" He knew the answer to that, but they were playing.

"I'd never tell you no. Yes. Yes. I want to experience it all with you. But you could spank me again." She wiggled her ass his way.

She was going to kill him. He slapped her ass, giving her the erotic punishment she'd requested. He spanked her over and over until she was moaning and submissive. Until her head had dropped and she was on her elbows, her backside high in the air.

That was what he wanted. He lubed up the toy and started it humming.

"Henry, I won't last long." Her words sounded dreamy and a little far away.

"Come as much as you like. I want you to come a hundred times tonight." He lined the vibe up and started to work it into her pussy, pressing until the rabbit head was nestled against her clit. He pushed it in, fucking in and out of that pussy as Nell started to moan. "I'm going to fill you, baby. I'm going to make you scream for me."

Her ass moved, pressing back to take the vibe. He could see the plug peeking out of those cheeks. He couldn't stand it another minute.

"Hold the vibe, baby. I need to get inside you."

A hand came back as she held the vibrator, moving in long, slow passes into her pussy.

He watched her fuck the vibrator as he lubed up his cock, anticipation building every second. He gripped his dick hard, spreading the lube, getting himself ready.

He spread her cheeks and toyed with the plug, twisting it slightly. Her spine shook, that slow rhythm of hers interrupted as he played with her asshole. He pulled on the plug and pressed it back in again and again until he couldn't stand another second. He pulled it out, tossing it on the towel he'd placed on the nightstand. The plug had done its job, opening her up for his dick to plunder.

"Please, Henry."

Yes, this would absolutely please Henry. God, he'd thought of himself as Henry. Her Henry.

He pressed his dick to that hot hole and rimmed her with his cockhead, opening her further, forcing his way inside.

So tight. He pressed in and pulled out in tiny movements that threatened to make him lose control. Patience. He had to make it good for her. He had to make it last.

He gripped her hips and fed his cock inside, pushing past the tight ring of her anus. She gripped him hard, lighting up his dick. "Press back, baby. Open up for me. Let me in. I want to fuck you so much. I need you, Nell."

She thrust back against him, pulling him in. His cock slid home, pressure making his balls draw up in pleasure. She was squeezing his cock, her asshole pulsing around him. He resisted the driving need to come because this was fucking heaven. He wanted to stay here.

"Are you all right?"

"So full. It's almost too much," she said, moaning. Her cheek was against the bed, her whole body spread and submissive.

"Play with the vibe. Don't forget your pussy." He held himself still while she pressed the vibe up.

"Oh, my god. Oh. Henry. Henry."

Somehow it felt right to have her call out that name. He was Henry with her. He would have to go back to being that sad-sack bastard John Bishop soon enough, but being Henry Flanders had been the joy of his life.

He felt her shudder as she came and let himself off the leash. He forced his dick back, the massage of the vibe ensuring that it wouldn't last as long as he wanted it to. He pounded into her, forcing her to take every hard inch he had to give.

Nell shouted out again. His spine shivered as his balls drew up tight and gave up the fight. Arousal poured from his cock as the orgasm filled his body, his soul. This wasn't sex. He finally understood the difference. This was making love. This was pure connection.

Nell fell forward, all her energy seemingly depleted. He followed her, covering her flesh with his own. He wrapped her up in his arms, and a peace unlike anything he'd ever known came over him, settling around him more securely than any blanket. Her fingers threaded through his own, winding around and allowing her to cuddle up. He shifted and spooned her.

"Don't you go to sleep." He had plans and they didn't involve a nap.

"Not on your life," she said back with an intimate smile.

She was his life. He knew that now. She would be the last thing he thought of right before he died. He could also see now that he'd been looking for a way out for a long time—a way out of life. He'd put himself in the most dangerous situations he could and told himself that he was protecting his country or doing good, but all he was really doing was looking for that one bullet that had his name written on it.

Funny how that had worked. Now he was a little afraid of it, and that was exactly what would get him killed in the end.

One more night and then it would be over.

He rolled off the bed and picked her up.

"Henry?" Nell's eyes opened as he settled her into his arms. "I love it when you carry me."

He loved to carry her. If he had his way, it would be his only job. He could carry her around and protect her. She was everything that was pure and right and good about the world. He'd started out thinking she was a naïve idiot and ended up here realizing that she was the very thing he'd sought to protect. She wasn't the status quo. She wasn't some economic interest. She was hope for the future. She was everything.

"I'm going to take care of you, baby."

He would, if only for the rest of the night.

* * * *

She hadn't meant to fall asleep. Her eyes flew open, and the creeping light of day filled her with utter panic. Clutching the covers, she sat straight up in bed and winced as every muscle in her body ached.

What time was it? How long had he been gone?

God, she'd thought she had longer. She shouldn't have fallen asleep. She should have stayed up all night long, but Henry had utterly exhausted her. He'd put her in the shower and tenderly washed her body and her hair and then dried her off and then he'd gotten her dirty all over again. He'd been on top of her all night until she'd finally drifted off to sleep.

How was she going to survive the next sixty years without him?

"I drew you a bath. It should help with the soreness."

She turned and he was standing there, dressed as he had been when he'd first come to Bliss. He was buttoned up, and every piece of his wardrobe looked like it had been pressed to perfection. She liked him casual, naked even. This was the Henry Flanders the rest of the world knew, not the private lover that was only for her.

"I love you." She was glad she got to say those words to him. His suitcase was packed and sitting at the door. He was leaving, but she could say it. "I love you so much."

His eyes closed behind those intellectual-looking glasses he wore. "I wish I could stay."

It was right there on the tip of her tongue to beg him, but he had to make that decision himself or he would resent her one day. If he stayed because of guilt or out of pity, then nothing between them could last. She couldn't stand the thought of that. "I know. It's okay, Henry."

He looked down at her, his jaw tightening. "Don't do this. Fight me. Yell at me."

Make it easy on him. She wasn't going to do that. If he was going to leave, then she wanted this moment to be perfect, too. The last few days had been the most beautiful of her life. She wasn't going to end them with a fight that had nothing to do with how they felt. "I love you."

She let the blanket drop as she got up. She wasn't going to hide from him.

"I have to go. My flight is at three. I have to get all the way to

Colorado Springs." But he wasn't moving. He stood there by the door, but he didn't go to open it.

"I love you." She couldn't say it enough. She wanted to make sure he knew so he would always know, no matter where he went, that she would be here loving him, wishing the very best for him.

A long moment passed before he answered. "I love you, too, but it doesn't fix all the problems. It actually makes them worse. Baby, if I could stay I would. I want nothing more than to be here with you, to be the man you need me to be."

"Tell me why. Tell me what these problems are, and we can fix them together."

He shook his head. "No. That's one thing I won't do. I love you. I won't drag you into my world." He cupped her face and dropped his forehead to hers. "God, I love you so much."

Tears started. She'd promised herself she wouldn't cry. "I can handle it. If you can't stay here, then I'll go with you."

She wasn't sure how it would work, but she was willing to try. She would leave Bliss for him. He was the important thing. Home was where Henry was.

He took a big step back as though that was the most horrifying thing he'd ever heard. "Never. I would never take you with me. God, I should have left before you woke up. This is too hard. I stayed because I wanted to say good-bye and wanted to explain the plans I've made for you."

"Plans? When did you make plans?"

"I started calling to make some arrangements a few days ago. I knew I would have to leave, but I had to do a few things first. Your cabin is being fixed up as we speak. It's my gift to you, and I won't take no for an answer."

She opened her mouth to protest, but he stopped her, his hands on her shoulders.

"I can't stay. This is all I can give you. I'm begging you to take it. I'm already going to be miserable. Please don't make it harder." The words came out tortured.

"I wish I understood." What was so terrible that he couldn't take her with him?

"I can't talk about it. I know it's wrong, and that's why you should hate me. You should tell me to go to hell. You deserve better than me."

He was trying so hard. It was obvious that he was trying to keep it together. He needed that calm, that coolness. He needed it to feel in control. She didn't want to take that from him, but she also wasn't going to lie. "I can't hate you."

"I took your virginity."

"I wasn't doing anything interesting with it anyway."

His eyes hardened as he stared down at her. "Damn it. This isn't a joke."

Her heart twisted in her chest. "I know. Trust me, I know. There is nothing funny about this, but you can't feel guilty. I'm not some starry-eyed teen. I knew you would leave, and I still said yes. I would do it all over again. I didn't sleep with you to make you stay. I slept with you because I love you, and that won't change because you do what you said you would do all along. You never lied to me."

He turned and picked up his bag. "I've taken care of the cleanup at your cabin, and I've taken care of your mother's medical bills."

Her jaw dropped open. Her mother's bills were so expensive. "Henry, you can't do that."

"I can and I did. I need to know you're safe. I need to know I did something to make your life better."

She knew what the medical bills were like. She often worried she would be paying them forever. "But, that's so much money."

A sad grin tugged his mouth up. "Yeah, it's about everything I had. I wish I had more. I wish I could make your life easy. I know the writing thing takes time to pay off."

She shook her head. "The writing thing is a bust. No one wants to read about sharecroppers and protests and how man is killing the earth."

"People like to read love stories. They like happily ever afters because so often they don't get one. Seth sent over a top-of-the-line computer. It's got everything you can need on it. You shouldn't have to find work for a while. You could give the romance thing a try. Happy endings. I think you should give us one." He turned and there was no hiding the tears in his eyes.

"I won't leave Bliss," Nell vowed. "I know I said I would, but I won't ever leave here. I won't leave because this is the last place I saw you. If you ever want to come home, I'll be right here. There will be a place at the table for you and a place in my bed. I'll be here waiting."

"I can't come back." The words sounded strangled out of his throat.

"Then I'll wait until the next lifetime." She would wait forever if she had to.

He kissed her forehead. "I love you. You have a good life."

He walked away. The door closed with a shudder of finality.

He was gone. She was alone again.

Nell sat down on the bed, pulling the covers around her. She'd been warm before, but now she felt the chill. The shades were closed, but she knew if she looked outside the world would be a snowy, frozen white.

Tears started to fall. Winter wouldn't last forever. Spring would come, and she would likely still be alone and Henry would be somewhere else. She would look for pictures of him, and one day she might find he'd moved on and had a family. And she would be here, alone, because she couldn't love anyone else.

She cried, ignoring the knocks on her door. Callie came first and then her mother. They stood outside and finally the knocking stopped. She cried for the longest time, letting everything out.

The morning turned to afternoon, and when long shadows fell across the room, Nell got up. She washed her face and dried her eyes and sat down at the new computer.

Nell Finn believed. She believed in so many things, but most of all she believed in the power of love and kindness and positivity. She believed that if she put good and beautiful things into the universe, perhaps whoever was at the center, whoever looked down from that Nirvana or Heaven or whatever a person called it, perhaps that being would send it all back.

She was still a child, clapping her hands so that Tinker Bell could live.

She couldn't have Henry, but she could hope. She could believe. She started to type. She had a whole world around her that needed something good. Max and Rye. Callie. Stef.

Maybe she should start there. She couldn't write about Henry. Not yet. But she could give her friends a happily ever after even if it was only on paper.

Nell began to write, her hopes and dreams for all of them flowing like a comforting wave.

Chapter Fourteen

Six months later
Bolivia, South America

Bishop took a long breath and wondered why he was fucking bothering. He followed the sergeant into what had to be the shittiest bar he'd ever seen and wondered why he hadn't stayed in the jungle. Taggart and Tennessee had been relocated. They were working together in the Middle East and his other charge, a young former Chinese operative, had a new handler. Whoever Levi Green was, Bishop wished him well with the young woman because Jiang Kun wasn't her twin. There was something dark about the woman. Of course, he'd sent her twin back to Chinese intelligence in her place and without letting the woman know her sister was alive, so he had that sin on his soul.

He'd been reassigned. Again. Oddly his new assignment felt a whole lot like all the rest.

So why the sergeant was walking into a tiny village watering hole. "Uhm, is there a problem? We need to get back to La Paz."

The Delta Force operative simply walked up to the bar and ordered a beer in perfect Spanish. Sergeant Mark Dawson wasn't someone he'd worked with before, though he remembered the dude's brother from another mission. He'd worked with Dare Dawson in Chechnya the year before.

"You're an odd duck, Bishop." Dawson wiped off the top of the bottle of beer and took a long drink. For the last two days he'd been almost perfectly silent, simply playing the part of escort as Bishop did his recon on a suspected arms dealer who might have ties to a certain terrorist everyone was looking for. Bishop and Dawson had spent days in the jungle setting up surveillance on the group's compound. Jihadist groups were popping up all over South America and Mexico. Everyone was worried about the Middle East, but terrorist cells were closer than most people in the States could imagine.

Nell probably understood. She kept up with the news.

"How am I odd?" Bishop asked, not honestly caring about the answer. He leaned against the bar. Talking to Dawson would take his mind off Nell. He thought about calling her a thousand times a day. There wasn't a minute that went by that something didn't remind him of her. And at night, he always dreamed of her.

He was becoming utterly useless.

Dawson studied him with careful eyes. He was dressed casually, no uniforms for them this time around, but Bishop knew the guy was armed to the teeth. "I'm talking about the way you work. I've been working with guys like you for three years now, and if there's one thing I've figured out, it's that my life doesn't mean shit to someone like you. Or it shouldn't. You Agency guys are all about the op. The rest of us are pawns in your game, and you don't mind losing a couple of chess pieces, if you know what I mean."

Unfortunately, he did know what the sergeant was talking about. "The operation is everything. If you know these things are more important than one soldier's life, then you know it's sure as fuck more important than mine. The Agency isn't going to come in on a white horse to save me if everything goes wrong. They will leave me high and dry and expect me to take care of the situation."

But he was questioning the status quo more and more these days. How did this op serve the long-term good? How long was he supposed to simply follow orders? Who was he really saving?

The sergeant kept talking, his voice low. "Then why did you save that operative's life last year? You know what I'm talking about. I'm talking about Chechnya. Don't freak out. Dare didn't tell me shit. I'm sure you were going by another name then, but I think it was you. I have another brother who's pretty good with a computer. I read the reports on the mission. Yeah, yeah, I could get shoved into Leavenworth, but I had to know what happened. It would have been easier for you to leave him behind. It's not the Agency's job to save our asses. It's pretty much your job to dump our asses at the first sign of trouble."

Bishop sighed. He hadn't been able to leave the young soldier behind.

He'd ended up losing the man he was following because he couldn't leave Dare Dawson to bleed out and he was still paying for his humanity. Yes, he'd gotten his ass chewed out for that. It was the exact op that had gotten him shipped to South America. Saving Dare Dawson had gotten him demoted. Of course at the time he hadn't realized Dare had a brother and liked to talk too much. "It was nothing, and we shouldn't talk about it."

It was supposed to be classified.

"That's not how I heard it. You see, that was my brother and the way I see it he's alive and walking the earth and being a pain in my ass today because of you. So when I got word that I might be able to pay you back, that was a mission I was interested in."

Bishop felt his eyebrows crease. "What the hell are you talking about?"

What was going on?

"We guys in the service talk. Bill Hartman is good friends with my CO."

Suspicion crept up his spine. "I don't know who you're talking about."

Dawson nodded shortly, an arrogant smile on his face. "Sure you don't. Look, I know how this works. You left the Army when the Agency recruited you and now you have to pretend like that time didn't exist. The Agency can cook the books any way they like, but a soldier never forgets. A soldier never forgets who his family is even when they walk away. Bill Hartman sent you a message, and I am here to see that you listen."

Bill was playing fast and loose with his identity. "What's the message?"

"He says choose again. He says you'll know what that means."

Bishop hated the way his eyes misted over. He shook his head, trying to banish the emotions that welled up. *Choose again*. If only he could. The Agency wouldn't give him a do-over. "I can't do that."

Sergeant Dawson nodded and took another long swig of his beer. "Well, I guess that's all I can do. Let's head back to the meet point."

Even though it was perverse, he found himself arguing. "Really? That's all I get?"

Dawson shrugged. "I delivered the message. What you do with the message is all on you, man. The way I see it, you must really like your life. I mean, what could be better than living completely alone and never being able to talk about anything you do? Man, there's a whole lot of freedom in that. Talking about shit is overrated. And you don't have to worry about women. One starts to give you trouble and the Agency moves you and gives you a whole new identity. I don't see why you would have to choose again when you chose so well the first time."

Oh, the fucker thought he knew everything? "Yeah, it's awesome. I love being alone all the time. I love the places I get sent to. They expect me to die, you know. If I get taken in, I'm supposed to kill myself, if I can. It's a great fucking life, buddy. You might not be able to talk about the ops you work, but you're respected because you're a soldier. I can never talk about what I do, so don't start telling me what I should love about my life. I adore the fact that I will never see her face again."

He hadn't meant to say that.

Dawson turned. "So this is about a woman?"

He should have kept his fucking mouth shut. They both should have. They were gossiping like two teenagers and that shit didn't fly. Even though they seemed to be alone, there were always ears listening in. "Stay out of it, man."

"I would fucking love to, but then we come to the whole 'I owe you' thing. I don't like to owe people." He stared for a moment. "You're in love with a woman and you think you can't be with her because you can't get away from all this shit."

"Lots of people want me dead." If he walked, the Agency would likely want him dead, too. They didn't tend to like for their operatives to go rogue.

"So, maybe you give them what they want," Dawson said.

"What?"

Dawson rolled his eyes. "For a top agent, you're slow on the uptake, brother."

He pulled out a small device and pressed the button. A massive explosion shook the dingy bar.

The elderly bartender didn't even look up from his magazine.

Bishop ran to the door. Sure enough, the jeep they had been using was now in pieces all up and down the street and blown into the jungle. It was completely destroyed. He turned back and walked to Dawson, who was now working on his second beer.

"What the fuck was that?"

"Your untimely demise." Dawson gave him hearty thumbs-up. "I've been setting that shit up for days. Antonio here made sure no one was around to see anything."

"Antonio doesn't care enough to see anything," the elderly man said in perfect, heavily accented English.

"Antonio likes cash and a lot of it," Dawson assured him. "He's going to disappear after assuring the local authorities that one man matching your description got into that car."

"A couple of men from the cartel came and hauled the body away," Antonio said, never looking up. "That's all I know. I need to get to La Paz." He finally brought his head up, a light in his eyes. "My granddaughter is having her surgery. We thought she would die, but I came into a little cash."

Holy shit. He was dead. He could be dead. If he was dead, the world opened up to him.

Bliss opened up to him.

"Choose again, Bishop," Sergeant Dawson said. "Bill is waiting for you. He said something about the kid keeping your cover up for you all these months."

Seth. Seth had kept his identity up. He could be Henry Flanders. All he had to do was choose.

He would always choose Nell. Oh, god, he could choose again. He could choose for all the right reasons. He could choose who he wanted to be.

He shook his head, the enormity sinking in. Dawson would tell his CO about the explosion. The Agency would investigate, but they wouldn't find a body. According to sources, the cartel took it.

He was free.

"Thank you." Henry Flanders shook Dawson's hand and staggered out into the bright light of the day. He had two cell phones. One for the Agency, and a backup. He always had a backup that no one knew about.

He clicked a button, and within seconds, a voice came on the line.

"Henry? Holy shitballs. Is this really you?" Seth Stark asked.

The little fucker had his private phone number. Oh, if he had a lick of sense, he would kill the kid, but Henry Flanders was nonviolent. He felt a brilliant smile cross his face as he walked down the dirt road. The jungle was lush and green overhead, but he could already smell the clean pine of Colorado. "Hey, Seth. I'm going to need a favor from you."

He was trusting a twentysomething kid. It was stupid. It was ridiculous. It was right. Seth was family now. "Anything, man."

"I want to come home."

"That's awesome. I can totally make that happen. I can make it look like anything you need." Because Seth was a wizard. Or a nerdy faery godmother.

"I'm going to need a plane ticket, and you're going to have to find me the best burger joint in La Paz because I get the feeling it's going to be a while until I have another one."

Henry walked, his boots turning up dirt. It would be a long walk home, but he didn't mind. He was following his bliss.

* * * *

Nell turned her head up to the sun. The fairgrounds were filled with sunshine and friends and family.

"What a beautiful day," her mother said.

Nell reached for her hand. Six months and still going. Her mother was in decline, but these months had been a blessing. She felt closer to her mother, closer to everyone.

The day after Henry had left, she'd gone home and found her cabin filled. Holly and Stella and Callie had baked and stuffed the freezer with vegan delights. Max and Rye had fixed her porch. Seth and Logan had installed a better router for her computer. There had been so many people who showed up to let the Finn women know that they were not alone.

Bliss had ceased being a way station. Bliss had become her home.

"It's gorgeous." She looked around. The whole town had turned out for the picnic. Even the Glens had shown up despite the fact that Noah had recently left town with his new wife. James was still bitter, but he'd brought his dad out.

"Do you have room for a couple more?" Callie smiled at her. Bill and Pamela had come. They were clothed, in deference to the new sheriff's ordinances. Nell was sure Rye Harper was simply trying to raise money for a new chair. Logan had recently been named deputy, and he was busy handing out tickets right and left.

She fully planned to protest at the next town meeting. "Sure. There's always room."

She got up and helped Callie spread her blanket out. Pam and Bill started talking to Moira, and Nell sat down with Callie. They had been leaning on each other, holding each other's hands when the loneliness seemed too much.

"I invited Holly to join us," Callie said. "She's bringing the new girl with her. I think her name is Laura. She started working at the Stop 'n' Shop. It's weird. She's been in town for half a year and I think she's been holed up in her cabin until now. Something's up with her."

Maybe she just needed a friend. Nell vowed to be Laura's friend. She'd seen the pretty blonde. She looked haunted and so very alone. Nell had tried talking to her, but she'd been rebuffed.

Patience. Sometimes that was all it took. She wasn't going to let the blonde's obvious gruffness scare her away. Everyone needed a friend. Sometimes all it took was one person to not give up to turn someone's whole life around.

Nell never gave up.

She let the sun warm her. It was the same sun that would shine down on Henry's face. They were still connected. She could feel it. Distance didn't mean a thing. She sent out a silent prayer for him.

To be safe. To know he was loved.

"Nell." Callie grabbed her arm.

"Give me a minute." It was a dumb ritual, but it was hers. She reminded herself of all the ways she and Henry were still connected. The sun and the moon and the stars. They were the same. The land they stood on was connected. Oceans might lie between them, but the earth was the same. The very air she breathed would someday find its way to him.

"Nell," Callie insisted.

"Nell, dear, you really should open your eyes," her mother's voice said.

No one would let her dream, it seemed. She opened her eyes. "Fine. What do you need?"

Callie was smiling, tears in her eyes as she pointed toward the parking lot. "Look. Oh, I'm so happy for you."

Nell turned, following Callie's hand. Max was parking his Ford truck and another man was with him, his arm going to the bed of the truck and picking up a backpack and a suitcase.

"Is that who I think it is?" her mother asked.

"I always said he was a smart boy," Bill replied with a grin on his face. "He makes good choices, that one."

Henry. He turned, and there was no question who it was. She would know that square jaw anywhere. She dreamed about him every night.

Henry had come back.

"Hey, Nell!" Max screamed across the yard. "I found something you lost. You might want to put a leash on him this time."

Tears pooled and a cry came out of her mouth. Henry had come back, and that could only mean one thing. He was here for keeps. He was here for her.

She'd prayed for happy endings for her friends. She'd written two books in the time that Henry was gone, each a hopeful dream for the people she loved, a prayer that the universe would bless them.

But the first real happy ending was hers.

Nell got up, tears clouding her vision, but she didn't need to see. She only needed him. She took off, not caring who saw.

Henry was here.

He dropped his bags and ran to her, catching her in his arms. "Hello, baby. Do you think there's room for one more?"

Always. "I can make that happen."

"I love you." He squeezed her so tight she was sure she would break, but she just held on that much tighter.

"I love you. I love you so much."

Henry looked down at her, a grim expression in his eyes. "Nell, I want to tell you…"

She interrupted him, putting her hand over his mouth. She didn't need explanations. She didn't need anything at all now that he was here. "Don't. You're here. That's all that matters."

Relief was plain on his face. He kissed her, pressing his mouth to hers. "I'm here and I'm all yours. I won't ever leave you again."

All around her spontaneous applause cracked through the air. She looked and everyone was watching them, but it wasn't awkward. This was her family, her home, and now it was complete.

"Way to go, Nell," Callie yelled, giving her a thumbs-up.

Henry picked her up, cradling her to his chest. "Let's take this reunion someplace private."

"You do that, Flanders," Rye shouted out with a grin. "I'm the new sheriff around here, and we have laws about public sex. I need a new desk after all."

Nell put her head on his chest and let him carry her away.

Epilogue

Present Day
New York City

Seth Stark took a long gulp of his fifty-year-old Macallan and wondered how much longer he would have to wait.

Georgia had kissed him. She'd put her arms around him and placed those big soft lips on his, and it had taken everything he had not to take her right there in the limo, to peel back those designer knockoffs she insisted on wearing and lay her out.

She was making him crazy. Holding out on that blonde goddess was going to kill him.

She was the fucking *one*. He'd waited his whole goddamn life for Georgia Dawson and he'd been forced to push her away.

He groaned as he looked out at his spectacular view of Manhattan.

Nothing was going the way he'd planned.

He'd turned her down because despite the fact that he loved Georgia with all his heart, it wouldn't work without Logan. He had no intention of getting married without his best friend by his side. He'd known the type of relationship he'd wanted since he was nine and he'd sat at Jamie and Noah's kitchen table and listened to their mom and dads flirt and argue and live their lives.

He'd known then and there that he wanted to share a wife with his best friend.

If only his best friend hadn't turned out to be such a fucking nut bag.

Logan loved Georgia, too. He was being idiotic and stubborn and posttraumatically stressed. It was time for him to get over it, but Seth couldn't figure out how. Nor could he find a decent reason to haul them all where they needed to be.

They needed to go to Bliss.

The hum of his computer changed and Seth turned. His computer was almost always on. He knew its every sound. He'd made a billion dollars off his software, and he'd programmed his personal system with a hundred distinct sounds that alerted him to what was going on.

Sometimes it chimed because it was uploading new data or installing new versions of software. It pinged him when Georgia sent him an e-mail. He handled those first. He told her it was because she was his assistant, but he'd utterly ignored his previous assistant because he'd been a Harvard-trained douchebag. Georgia always came first.

But there was one sound he hadn't heard since he'd programmed it. A low thud that sounded like doom.

Fuck. Fuck. Fuck.

Someone was searching for Henry Flanders.

Someone was going deep. Someone knew something they shouldn't.

He stared at the computer screen for a moment, panic setting in. After all these years, Henry's past was catching up to him.

And Seth could use that to his advantage. He picked up his cell and dialed an all-too-familiar number. A gruff voice answered almost immediately, and Seth replied. "Hello, Momma Marie. It's Seth. I'm going to need your help."

It was time to bring Logan back to Bliss.

Logan, Georgia, Seth, and the whole Bliss family will return in *Back in Bliss*, now available.

Author's Note

I'm often asked by generous readers how they can help get the word out about a book they enjoyed. There are so many ways to help an author you like. Leave a review. If your e-reader allows you to lend a book to a friend, please share it. Go to Goodreads and connect with others. Recommend the books you love because stories are meant to be shared. Thank you so much for reading this book and for supporting all the authors you love!

Sign up for Lexi Blake's newsletter
and be entered to win a $25 gift certificate
to the bookseller of your choice.

Join us for news, fun, and exclusive content
including free short stories.

There's a new contest every month!

Go to www.LexiBlake.net to subscribe.

Back in Bliss
Nights in Bliss, Colorado 9
By Lexi Blake writing as Sophie Oak

Logan Green is back in Bliss, but only for a few weeks to help out at the sheriff's office. Everything changes when Seth Stark strolls into town with Georgia Dawson on his arm.

Seth's arrival is anything but a happy accident. He always dreamed of a big house on the river and a wife he could share with his best friend, Logan. After building a software empire, his only goal has been to make that dream come true. He just needed the perfect woman.

Georgia is still haunted by the dark, troubled man who saved her life. She can't get Logan out of her head. Her boss brought her to Bliss to help him decorate his new summer home, but when Logan Green walks through the door she discovers Seth has something different in mind.

Seth has a plan for their mutual happily ever after, but he never dreamed that coming home would put all their lives in danger.

Lost in You

Masters and Mercenaries: The Forgotten, Book 3
By Lexi Blake

Robert McClellan was forced to serve as a soldier in a war he didn't understand. Liberated by McKay-Taggart, he struggles every day to reclaim the life he lost and do right by the men he calls his brothers, The Lost Boys. Only one thing is more important – Ariel Adisa. The gorgeous psychologist has plagued his dreams since the day they met. Even as their mission pushes him to his limits, he can't stop thinking about taking his shot at finding a life beyond all this with her.

Ariel Adisa is a force to be reckoned with. Her performance in Toronto proved she's more than just a brilliant mind, but Robert still acts as if she is a wilting flower who needs his protection. Joining him on the mission to Munich should be the perfect opportunity to test their skills and cement their relationship. She and Robert are an excellent match. But when a stunning secret from Robert's past is revealed, their world is turned upside down and nothing will ever be the same again.

While they chase dark secrets across Europe, Robert and Ariel realize that the only thing worse than not knowing who you are could be discovering who you used to be...

* * * *

There was a knock on her door. Ariel glanced to the clock. It was getting late. The pizza had likely arrived. She didn't want pizza. She wanted to start the day again and not have any of this hanging over them. When she'd gotten on that plane, she'd been filled with anticipation, and all of it was gone now. She'd expected dinner to be a quiet affair with only her and Robert. Now she would have to referee between Owen and Dante. She needed to get the whole group together for a session to get at the underlying problem.

"I've got to go, Damon."

"Be safe."

She hung up her mobile and slipped it into her pocket before answering the door. She'd expected Rebecca or Owen, but it was Robert who stood in her doorway.

And he looked delicious. He'd changed out of his traveling clothes into a set of perfectly pressed black slacks, a snowy white dress shirt, and blue tie. It should have looked staid. It would have on most men, but on Robert it made her wonder what she would see when she peeled off all those clothes.

She had a damn degree in psychology and it didn't mean anything when her hormones got involved.

"Hey, I know I acted like a massive asshole earlier today." He had a grim look on his face that changed to charming when he brought his hand around from his back and showed her the perfect white rose he offered her. "Would you please let me make up for it?"

There were a thousand reasons to say no. She could do it gently. She could remind him that the first chance they'd had to prove they could manage a relationship and still work together they'd blown. She could point out that there was still the hope of a cure out there.

Or you could live in the moment, my love. You could stop being so in that head of yours and let yourself feel.

Sometimes she could still hear her father's wise voice in her head. He'd done so much, taken so many chances to bring his family to a better place.

"Ariel, please. I'm sorry I treated you like that. I took out my bad day on you and it wasn't fair. I wanted our night together. I planned it all out, but I forgot that the only really important part of the night wasn't the restaurant or the hotel. It was that we got to be together. Be with me for a while."

She took the rose from his hand, all thoughts of why this was a bad idea flying out of her head. "Yes."

But she wasn't nearly as dressed as he was. "Give me a minute to change."

He shook his head. "You look beautiful and we're only going to the kitchen."

"You dressed for the occasion."

"I was also the asshole who challenged the authority of my commander in the field. Trust me, I like this far better than dropping to the floor and giving you a hundred like I..." He shook his head. "Not going there."

She stepped in, putting a hand on his face. "It's okay. Let the visual piece go and tell me what you felt."

He pressed his cheek against her hand. "No therapist stuff tonight. I promise I'll write it down later and talk to Kai about it, but I want you to stop thinking about me as a patient. This can't work if you don't. Please come to the kitchen with me. I managed to shove everyone else in the media room. They're watching a football match. Well, Rebecca is reading on her e-reader and rolling her eyes when the guys yell at the screen, but the kitchen is on the opposite end of the floor. I promise it's quiet there."

She was still in the slacks and blouse she'd worn this afternoon. They were casual and comfortable. Certainly not something she would wear on a date. Robert was far better dressed for the occasion.

A vision of a private dinner where he was in a suit and she was wearing absolutely nothing floated across her brain. Sir wouldn't want her in clothes. Sir would want to see nothing but her own skin so he could touch her everywhere, whenever he pleased. They could spend long hours like that. She wouldn't worry about anything at all but pleasing her dominant partner.

"Come on." He used that deep voice on her she'd heard him use at The Garden. Like her, Robert spent at least one night each weekend playing. She'd seen him paired up with some of her friends, but never had he taken one to a privacy room or up to his flat.

She hadn't indulged herself in sex in a long time.

She followed him down the hallway and sure enough, heard someone yelling from the far end about a ref's call. Poor Rebecca.

Robert led her away from it, his loafers making no sound over the carpet. This part of the club was comfortable, much more like a home than downstairs, and it made her wonder if Peter often had guests he put up here. She'd talked briefly to the man and he appeared to be very interested in teaching and training new D/s couples.

Were she and Robert going to be a D/s couple?

She stopped that line of thinking. This was nothing more than a pleasant way to spend an evening with a man she liked enormously.

With a man she might be falling in love with.

About Lexi Blake

Lexi Blake is the author of contemporary and urban fantasy romance. She started publishing in 2011 and has gone on to sell over two million copies of her books. Her books have appeared twenty-six times on the *USA Today*, *New York Times*, and *Wall Street Journal* bestseller lists. She lives in North Texas with her husband, kids, and two rescue dogs.

Connect with Lexi online:

Facebook: Lexi Blake
Twitter: authorlexiblake
Website: www.LexiBlake.net
Instagram: www.instagram.com/lexi4714

Sign up for Lexi's newsletter!

Made in the USA
Coppell, TX
26 July 2020